Marked For The Hunt

A Diana Warren Novel

Leah Chiasson

CHAPTER ONE

Outside the plane window was a home that had become foreign and distant to me. The dawn sky was shades of navy blue and teal rising over the black silhouettes of evergreens. Below us was a small city that was just awakening. Watertown, Maine.

The wilderness was dense and rife with wildlife in this part of the world. Nature pressed in on cities that had died nearly a century ago. It seemed fitting that there was a clan of Faoladh, Irish werewolves, hiding in its hills.

The plane shuddered as it made its descent. I grimaced as the small cabin made the pressure in my ears bulge to a painful degree. The woman beside me reached out and laid a compassionate hand on my arm. I gave her a queasy smile, not thinking as my lips split to show teeth. Her hand jerked back and she stared at me for a long moment.

Sometimes I forgot what I looked like. My canines were sharper than they had once been. My eyes were an inhuman blend of yellowish gold and black. I hadn't always been this way. I sighed and looked back towards the window. I'm coming home, Wolf's Head. A heavy weight settled in my stomach.

I grabbed the duffel bag that sat between my feet, the only luggage that I brought for this trip. I didn't plan on staying in town for very long. There was nothing that could make me stay in Wolf's Head, I thought as I trudged single file off the small plane. The airport was a small, single room building. It was a place to pick up your luggage and huddle against the harsh cold of November as you waited for your taxi.

The hairs on the back of my neck prickled. I spun my head, staring at the woods as if something would jump out. There was nothing in these woods, I told myself. Nothing to be afraid of. I shook my head, trying to fight off the feeling.

Across the parking lot, I spied a familiar body leaning against a green sedan. Aunt Magda pushed away from her car, wearing a gray jacket over her bright hoodie. I let her pull me into a hug. She smelled of coffee, herbs, and wood smoke. I melted into her, feeling safe for a glorious moment. I told myself that it had only been Aunt Magda watching me, but the hair still stood up on the back of my neck.

"I missed you so much!" Aunt Magda whispered into my hair.

I pulled back, taking her in. She was the younger sister of my late father. There was a new streak of gray running from her temple down the length of her dark hair that hadn't been there seven years ago. Soft lines had begun to set in her face, lines that betrayed her age. She didn't have the werewolf gene. Her years weren't being reset, they were finite.

I gave her a half smile, genuinely happy to see her. "Can we get in the car?"

The feeling of being watched wouldn't leave me and the wolf inside me was beginning to panic. My human body kept her caged while her instincts told her to run and she was inches away from fight or flight. We needed to leave. Now.

Aunt Magda's smile faltered but she nodded and punched a button on her key fob. The car doors made a clicking noise and I slid myself into the passenger seat. The inside of the car smelled like baked goods and steaming coffee. There were two thermoses in the console cup-holders and a small paper bag. Aunt Magda slid into the driver's seat and caught me eyeing the paper bag.

"Can I?"

I remembered my Aunt's cooking. I knew that it could only be pure satisfaction, bliss, and euphoria in a paper bag. I was excited to figure out what was hidden behind this brown paper.

"The blue thermos is for you too," she said. "I thought you could use a treat after flying all night from San Francisco."

Hidden inside the bag was a pile of mini-muffins, each topped with cinnamon crumb. I stuck my nose into the bag and inhaled.

Pumpkin. Mini Pumpkin Muffins. It made me ecstatic that everything came up pumpkin in the fall months.

"I'm so happy that you're home," my Aunt went on.

"I'm not staying." I protested through a mouthful of muffin.

No way in hell was I staying here. Home was in California. Not here.

Aunt Magda's lips twisted and her shoulders slumped just a little bit. I didn't mean to be a buzz kill, but I had my reasons for staying away from Wolf's Head. The only reason that I returned was to attend my Grandfather's funeral after my mother's stern insistence. I jammed another mini muffin into my mouth, slouching in my seat.

"A lot has changed since you left," she continued. "There's no official Alpha right now."

My grandfather had been the Clan's Alpha, the head of the household so to speak. For a short while my father had carried that torch. My grandfather had been forced to pick it back up when his son died. I shoved those memories to the back of my mind.

It's not my problem, I wanted to tell her. The Clan hasn't been my problem for a long time. I swallowed down another muffin and took a swig of the chocolate laden coffee. Everything was better with chocolate. It eased the panic that I had felt earlier and I felt my wolf ease away from the surface.

CHAPTER TWO

Silence began to permeate the car. I could hear the squeal of the fan belts in the heater and the hum of the old engine. Soon enough, we passed an oval wooden sign, painted in tones of brown and green, that read:

Welcome to Wolf's Head.

The dawn light was just settling over the town, glowing golden. That bright light made it seem like a ghost town. Lichen, grayish green, had settled over the wolf statues that flanked the entrance to town hall. It covered their faces and dulled their teeth. My lips twisted as I realized they looked more like gargoyles than wolves.

All that was left of the flowers that had surrounded the building were skeletal husks. It was dreary and seemed bereft of hope. I remembered my Grandmother telling me that those same flowers had once bloomed all year round. They braved the cold winters of Maine, yielding fluffy blossoms in white and deep violet. They had been a gift from the Goddess that was thought to have created us. Turning my head, I caught a glimpse of the old standing stone that used to serve as an altar to that goddess. There were no flowers or other offerings on it anymore. It was just a stone, a pagan symbol out of place in the tourist town full of cafes and antique shops.

We passed the old playground, a wooden castle that circled a towering maple tree. There were no fiery leaves scattered about and the wood looked damp and black. November had settled in and taken a hold onto Wolf's Head.

Every bit of magic was gone, I thought. There was no Goddess for these wolves, only the horrible human in all of us. I sank into my seat and closed my eyes against the world outside of the car. I wanted nothing more to do with this sad sight.

The story was told to all of us as children, the story of a mother who wished to protect her family and her home. Weak and feeble in the minds of those that would hurt her, she stumbled out beneath the moon and pleaded with the wild gods to give her the strength. She became the first of us, the first Faoladh. She could slip between the skin of a woman and the skin of a wolf because of the Goddess's admiration and love.

But it felt like a tall tale told to children. Had there ever been a Goddess for the horrible creatures that we were?

The next thing I knew, someone was shaking me, calling my name. I cracked open my eyes, fighting against the sleep that held them shut. Panic gripped me. Where was I? Something smelled wrong. My hand clawed at the car door. Distantly I could hear someone shouting. I needed to get out. I needed to escape.

"Diana! Calm down!" Fingers touched me and I leapt into action.

With my other hand, I lashed out. My fingers curled into claws and a growl was on my lips. Through the blood thundering in my ears, I heard someone scream in pain.

The smell of pumpkin and coffee brought me back to my senses. I was in Magda's car. I was in Wolf's Head for my grandfather's funeral. The rush of adrenaline made the food in my stomach turn as it receded.

Aunt Magda clutched her arm to her chest, blood seeping between her fingers. There was a look of mistrust in her eyes that cut me to the core. I opened my mouth to apologize, but shame trapped the words in my throat. She just turned away, throwing her door open and leaving. I had to give her props for not slamming it.

Left alone in the car, I had a moment to get a hold of myself and my surroundings. The car sat in front of an old white farm house, squares of colored glass lining the windows of the porch and the door sitting wide open. A wind chime made from bent forks and spoons swayed in the wind as Aunt Magda marched up the steps. There were other cars in the driveway. There was a clunky, black, two door Hyundai and a sleek, white Lexus. I grabbed my bag and reluctantly scooted out of the car. The green Ford was a pop of color amongst the other cars.

I took in a deep breath, scenting the air. Wet bark and rotting leaves came on the strongest, comforting my wolf with the idea of home. Beneath those smells I could catch the sweet scent of baked goods, cookies I hoped. This isn't home, I reminded her. We couldn't stay here, at least not alive.

No. He will hunt us. He will kill us.

Then another smell hit me hard. It was sweet and coppery, potent enough to make my head spin. It suddenly smelled as if I was covered in blood. I grabbed for my arms and wiped at my legs, trying to brush off something that wasn't there. My breath came fast and hard to keep up with. My wolf raised her head to scent it, a new gleam in her eye. She growled and it rumbled in my ribcage. I could feel my teeth pressing against my lips as they grew long and sharp. I turned away from my Aunt as the fear rode me. I was bound to lose control.

My bag fell from my hand. I spun and took off before it could hit the ground. Behind me I could hear my Aunt yelling, calling my name. I didn't think twice about it. I didn't question where my feet were leading me. I simply ran. I ran from the smell of fresh blood, towards control.

Not safe, she agreed with me. We aren't safe here.

My chest burned with the cold November air. Caffeine raced through my system and my stomach churned the coffee. It was a long time before I felt safe enough to slow down. I found myself standing under a giant maple tree that was dripping scarlet leaves into the air. They fell all around me. I dropped myself to the base of its trunk, my heart trying to beat its way out of my chest.

"No!" I screamed into the dark woods. "I won't let you!"

Inside of me, I felt her lower her head. The smell was gone and the fear was ebbing. The terror that raced through me made her lash out like a feral animal. She was beyond reason, only an animal ready to

8

defend herself. I didn't want to be that monster. I didn't want to senselessly lash out at anyone.

I slammed my fist into the ground. It left a deep little half-moon in the dirt. They wouldn't make me into a victim once more and I definitely would not become a monster. I could feel my wolf raise her head again. She was scared. She felt cornered, tricked. We had been safe back in Monterey. Other wolves knew not to bother us anymore. Here the Clan could hurt us again. The Clan always hurt us.

She pushed forth and I felt my human body begin to slip away. It never hurt. Yet, it was an odd sensation to feel your spine bed and pop, to feel your ribcage realign, and your legs reshape. I pressed my cheek into the dirt as my tail stretched and my fingers curled into paws. We melded together, reason and instinct.

It felt natural.

As a wolf, I lifted my nose to the air. I could smell the exhaust of cars on a nearby highway. I could smell the slow burn of someone's charcoal grill. I could smell the possum rotting amongst the piles of leaves. I tested my wolf feet, stretching and digging my claws into the earth. With my clothes hanging from my muzzle, I ran once more.

Claws. Teeth. Running. We are safer.

No longer was I in California, I thought as I picked my way through the path of fallen leaves and dirt. All around me were thick trunked trees, even a few with tin buckets still attached to draw sap for maple syrup in the springtime.

Red leaves clung to the trees above me, only found on maple trees like the ones so plentiful here in the east. The setting sunlight dappled the forest floor with golden shapes that danced across stones and dirt.

This had been my home once. This was the home of the Faoladh. Like the werewolf of popular culture, we could take the form of a wolf whenever we pleased. When the full moon rose, we fell to our knees and let the change take us, our supposed Goddess's forced offering. But, unlike the werewolf of popular culture, we were supposed to be protectors.

9

Sure, we hunted. Small game like rabbits and gophers when running on your own was nice and even hunting deer in a pack had a kind of satisfaction to it. We always ate our kill, never hunting simply for blood lust. We hunted to learn how to fight, how to keep our loved ones safe.

Or, at least that's what we had been once upon a time. I found myself at the edge of Magda's yard, feet rooted to the ground for a moment.

There was no blood in the air this time. My wolf stirred only a little, just enough to peek. There had been enough blood to kill a Faoladh earlier, I thought. My wolf growled at the thought, sitting up straighter. There should have been a residual smell in the air, no matter how well it could have been cleaned up. You can't hide something like that from a wolf.

I pushed the thought aside, trying not to worry about whatever had been going on here. This wasn't my problem. I was going to leave again in a few days.

The back door of the farmhouse was left open for me. Barefoot, I padded into the kitchen in the dark. All the cars had left and the only person in the house was my Aunt. The air was full of lingering smells, familiar and not all at once. I'd been gone too long to recognize anyone by their smell. But, there no smell of blood in the living room or the kitchen. There wasn't even a trace of cleanser.

Quietly climbing the stairs, I found my bag sitting outside a spare bedroom. I was thinking that this must be my room when I heard the floor creak. I froze halfway to my bag.

A shape appeared in the darkness of the hallway. It was feminine and there was the smell of shower products in the air.

"What happened to you earlier?" Aunt Magda's voice asked. There was white gauze wrapped around her arm. How badly had I hurt her? Had that been what I smelled? How could a scratch have set me off like that?

I swallowed hard, unsure how to answer her. I had panicked. No one in Wolf's Head, not even my Aunt, needed to know how broken I was. She didn't need to know that I ran away to keep from losing control.

"Not talking to me now?" a new bitterness tainted her voice.

I opened my mouth to toss a quick lie, but she spun around. She disappeared into her bedroom and guilt sat heavy in my chest. I glanced at the red numbers of the alarm clock in my spare room. It was almost four in the morning. She would be getting ready to head to Balefire, her restaurant. Shuffling forward, I snagged my bag and shut the door behind me.

Four days. That's all I had to make it though. Four days in Wolf's Head. Could I survive that if my father's killer was still here?

I crashed into the twin mattress and let sleep claim me.

CHAPTER THREE

Two gold eyes peered over piles of sheets. She could still feel her legs humming from running in her dreams. The wolf stretched her limbs and yawned wide. Tongue lolling out of the side of her mouth, she caught her reflection in the full-length mirror.

Goddamn it. Let me out.

Claws and teeth, we are safe. She growled low as she settled back into the piles of sheets. She could fight. She could run. Claws and teeth were much safer than fists and words.

Damn it. I pushed my way through the wolf's protests, eager to reclaim my own body. Gathering every ounce of my will, I pushed from the inside out. My legs stretched into long limbs as my spine realigned itself and my skull shrunk back.

Our consciousnesses switched places, the last whimper my wolf made fading from reality and into my own mind. I ran a hand through my hair, pulling it in my fist as tears began to well in my eyes. This was going to be a hard four days if this is how every morning would begin.

I had to take several deep breaths before I could put my feet on the floor. I had no real desire to get out of bed, to go out into the world of Wolf's Head, but if I didn't prove strong then my wolf would keep pulling stunts like that. I had to show her that I was capable of surviving and that began with day to day functioning.

Instead of cowering in bed like I really wanted to, I pulled a pair of running pants and a sports bra from my bag. I grabbed the Avenged Sevenfold t-shirt from the day before off the floor and threw it on as I left the room.

Outside was chill, but not so cold that my breath was caught in the air. Give it a couple of weeks, I thought. Then again, I wouldn't have to. My sneakers crunched on the gravel of the driveway as I began. Heading in no particular direction, I ran. The pounding of my feet against the earth was rhythmic; the burn in my chest was masochistic pleasure.

Lost in a blur of my own thoughts, it was quite a while before I realized that my feet had led me back into town. I ran past old shops that I had once known and the playground that I had conquered as a child. I ran until I came to the doors of Balefire.

The doors were heavy, dark wood, decorated with two stained glass windows that held warm reds and oranges. The building itself was a towering and ancient brick building that had vines climbing its facade, slowly tearing it apart. On the sidewalk was a chalkboard sign advertising handmade French toast donuts and granola cakes with fresh fruit. My stomach growled in protest at me, willing me inside.

I pulled on the curved wrought iron handle, throwing my weight into it. A burst of warm air greeted me, as did a soft glow that I had long ago forgotten about. Inside the restaurant, there was a kind of warmth that would wrap around you much like a hug. It sat down with you at your table and encouraged you to drink a little more wine, to smile a little wider. I liked to believe that warmth came from the glow of the quartz veins that ran through the bricks of the pizza oven. It seemed completely illogical, the bricks of natural and rough stone yet fitting together as if they had been created for this very purpose. The fire inside the oven sent light through the thick veins of quartz that dance with shades of jade and amethyst. We called it the Balefire, never dying and the heart of our town. The heart of our Clan and my Aunt's child, her only true love.

Mesmerized, I was pulled in. How could I have forgotten about something as great as this?

I walked past the empty hostess podium, heading for the bar that sat on the far wall, close to the Balefire oven. My legs thrummed with the run as I pulled myself atop a barstool. The available space on the back counter held an espresso machine and numerous glass bottles of alcohol. The Balefire was open twenty-four hours a day, always open, always a place of peace and sanctuary to the Clan. Of course, they served breakfast and happy hour.

I couldn't help but smile at the absurdity of this place, my Aunt's one and only child. Through the long windows that flanked the glowing oven, Aunt Magda caught sight of me at the bar. She gave me a tight-lipped smile and said that she would bring me something.

"Can I help you?" a heavy set auburn haired waitress asked from behind the counter. The neck of her Balefire t-shirt had been cut open to show off the colorful tattoos that sprawled across her chest. More danced down her right arm, flowers that looked vibrant and alive.

I shook my head. "I think I may have already ordered. But could I get a coffee in the meantime?"

She nodded and went about her job. She had the kind of hourglass figure that was heavy bottomed but she still worked skinny jeans. Auburn curls were trying to escape the sloppy bun they had been wrangled into and there were flour hand prints smeared across her jeans.

She set the coffee before me, adding a small milk carton shaped glass of creamer beside it. She gave me a friendly smile that said she had no clue who I was. I beamed back at her.

"My name is Diana," I offered.

"Sabrina," she motioned to her name tag before returning to her job.

As I waited for whatever Aunt Magda was going to bring me, I sipped my coffee and looked out into the restaurant. Wooden support beams towered over the patrons, slanting into the peak of the ceiling. Small and narrow stained glass windows glowed from the morning light. As I lowered my eyes into the crowd, I realized that people were sneaking glances at me, whispers humming in the restaurant.

A few friendly smiles were offered, telling me who still trusted me. Many others just cast quick glances in my direction, lips twisted or quickly spewing some tale I couldn't hear. I wondered how they could be such harsh with their judgment. Had they heard the true story?

"Just for you," Aunt Magda pulled my attention away from the crowd. She set a plate before me. Eggs scrambled with chorizo and cream cheese was flanked by long points of toast that, from the shape of them, came from homemade bread. My stomach growled as the smell tickled my nose.

"Thank you," I dug into it just as I heard the door open.

Aunt Magda glanced up, her face turning somber. Forehead crinkled in confusion and a mouthful of food, I turned to see whatever had changed Aunt Magda's mood. I should have swallowed first, because what I saw almost made me choke. Standing beside my ethereal Grandmother was another ghost from my past.

CHAPTER FOUR

Darren Blackford was a good foot taller than when I had seen him last. His dark mahogany hair flopped over his eyes, as if it had once been styled and after running his hands through it a few too many times it had given up. His shoulders were wide and his lean waist led into an ass that filled his dark jeans well.

This was one person I had hoped I wouldn't see.

I turned back to my food, eager to finish it and run. Why was he with my grandmother? Was this the man that my family wanted to follow in my Grandfather's footsteps? I couldn't tell if he made my heart race in fear or lust. He had grown up well, grown into a man while I'd been gone. No, I couldn't be attracted to Darren Blackford. The entire notion was simply ridiculous. I shoved the yellow egg scramble around my plate, picking out the chunks of meat smeared with cream cheese.

Memories that had been long locked away were breaking free. I gripped my fork in my hand, knuckles turning white as I tried to breathe. Darren had helped the man who killed my father. He had also been my best friend at the time. Son of a killer, friend of the victim. That day was coming back, vivid as when it had happened. Darren held me back while I listened to my father die.

I shoved the memory down deep and followed it up with a bite of homemade bread.

Yet, now my Grandmother was accompanying him. She stood tall and proud, wearing nothing but white. Her salt and pepper curls were neatly pinned back and she smoothed the lapels of her white jacket as she sat across from Darren. She looked as if life were a business meeting. Maybe it was, I thought as I watched her converse with the spawn of the man who had killed her only son.

Feeling my breakfast form a heavy lump in my stomach, I pushed myself off the barstool. I swallowed down some water before turning to leave. His head shot up, hazel eyes immediately finding me. I looked forward, unable to acknowledge him. I couldn't deal with Darren Blackford just yet.

Outside I pushed myself into a jog, feeling my stomach churn. I forced myself past the nausea. It was only nerves, I told myself. That's all it was.

"Don't let her out of your sight again," Chris jabbed a finger at me before leaving the store.

I had escaped, run as far I could. The boys had caught up with me though. Christopher had tackled me to the ground, wrangling my flailing limbs. Together they had dragged me into the general store.

Darren and I sat at the general store's ice-cream counter. There was a throbbing in the side of my head. Mrs. Kapinski looked between us with suspicion clear on her face. We lied and told her that the blossoming bruise was a result of too much rough housing. No, his father hadn't beaten me. He hadn't killed my dad.

She set a tall stainless steel cup before me, frost already crawling up its surface. Inside was creamy chocolate malt milkshake. It tasted bland in my mouth so it sat on the counter, slowly melting. Darren tried to move closer, grabbing the spoon floating in the milkshake. I spun my stool away from him.

I could smell the fear and blood that clung to my clothes. I remembered my father's body lying on the floor of his own home, of my home. Jonathan had caught me; he had hit me. Everything after that was missing. I laid my head down on the cool counter top to ease the throb. His blow had meant to kill me. I knew that his every intention had been to kill me.

Why was I still alive? I knew I shouldn't be in one piece either.

"Are you alright, sweetie?" Mrs. Kapinski asked when she saw my untouched milkshake. "This isn't like you."

17

I turned to look at Darren. He reached out to me, but his hand fell when I flinched.

"I'm going to call your mother," Mrs. Kapinski disappeared.

The bell over the door rang. I turned to find Christopher hot on the heels of his father. Jonathan. My body tensed. I didn't know how much fight I had left in me.

He turned on me. There was a wild gleam in his eyes. The only evidence of what he'd done was a spray of blood across his left cheek. Darren shot out of his seat, coming around me. He turned his face up to his father in challenge.

You held me down, chased me, and now you want to defend me? No way.

I stood up, shoving Darren as hard as I could. He tumbled forward into his father. I could hear the roar of an engine coming up the road outside and Mrs. Kapinski returned from the storeroom. Her eyes were wide with fear and worry. Even as a human, she could feel the tension that was building in the room.

Suddenly, the general store doors burst open. My mother came in, her own storm of anger and human dominance. She was a slight figure, but she commanded obedience. How she had arrived so quickly, I would never know. She seemed to know exactly what had happened, a sadness already weighing down her eyes.

"Time to leave, Diana."

I ran into her arms, pushing both of us out of the doors and towards her car before anyone could react.

Sirens pulled me back to the present, my feet still beating the ground. White cars with blue and red lights spinning raced past me. My breath coming fast, I picked up my pace. The cars slowed down as they rounded the corner. A white Lexus brought up the rear of the entourage. I knew what was just past that bend and a shot of adrenaline rocketed through me.

The General Store was up ahead, stationed at the intersection that connected the main road to the one that led to the family Manor: the Kapinski's General Store. I pushed myself hard, my lungs burning with the effort. By the time I arrived in the dusty parking lot, the sirens had been shut off, but the lights still spun in dizzying patterns. They bounced off the windows of the little shop, is weathered wood facade lovingly painted while I had been gone. But something was obviously wrong.

I could smell dust and blood in the air. My heart skipped a beat. One day back in town and someone had died. The smell was far too strong for someone to just be hurt. There was so much blood in the air. I waited for the panic to wash over me like it had yesterday, but nothing happened. Filing it away to question later, I raced over to the storefront, past black garbed policemen that called out for me to stop. I wanted to be wrong. I wanted it to be deer blood that I was smelling, but I knew that it wasn't.

"Diana?" someone called out.

I slowed down, trying to pinpoint the voice. The scent on the wind sent a flare of panic through my mind. My wolf moved inside of me, the same thoughts flowing through our mind. I shut her out as tight as I could. I couldn't lose it now. I clenched my jaw and found Christopher Blackford leaving the general store. Two Blackfords in one day?

He was taller and leaner than his younger brother. The years had stolen his air of control and dark circles were blooming under his eyes. He had always been under his father's thumb, and the toll was starting to show.

Before I could even open my mouth, he growled at me.

"What is the point of you even being here after all we did?" He said through clenched teeth. "Get the fuck out of Wolf's Head. You don't belong here anymore."

Fuck you, Blackford asshole.

I turned away from him, the heat of anger burning across my skin. My feet hit the pavement in a steady rhythm that sent jolts up my spine. I smelled blood again. Closer and closer I ran; it got stronger and stronger. It was everywhere. I pushed past the uniformed cops, rushing into the general store.

I came to a grinding halt when I saw what lay before me. Rusty red was smeared throughout the store. It covered the black and white

19

checkered floor in a mess of hand prints and footprints. There was too much blood for someone to still be alive.

A hunt is over, my wolf said. She sat back on her haunches, alert but not yet afraid. I trusted her. I let myself relax a little as I pressed forward.

My grandmother and Darren stood at the other end of the store. They looked up when the door slammed behind me. The aisle shelves gave me a choppy view of the body that lay on the floor before them. Threads of a knit sweater were glued to the floor in blood. There was a thick brown arm, fingers pointing to the aspirin. It lay too far away from the old work boot that I could see past the potato chips.

My stomach churned, again threatening to throw up what little I did eat.

"Out, Diana."

My grandmother stood; her spine as straight as ever. There wasn't a speck of blood on her white pant legs. I shook my head at her, unable to speak yet.

"Listen to Petra," Darren added.

A cop grabbed my upper arm, but I jerked it away from him.

"You think I can't handle this?" Even as I said it, my wolf snapped forward and my stomach rolled.

My grandmother sighed. "We know you can handle this. I don't want you seeing it. So, get out." She pointed a long finger at the door behind me.

Darren watched me, his eyes shadowed and a sad twist to his lips. Who would want to see this, they seemed to say. I took in a deep breath, trying to get beyond all the blood. I could smell spoiled milk products, pine-sol, and something naggingly familiar.

I crept forward, careful to keep my sneakers from the blood stains on the floor. The messy black curls and threads of sweater yarn that splayed over the floor let me know just who was lying there. I knew exactly who was lying there in pieces.

Mrs. Kapinski. My feet pedaled backwards. They pulled me away.

It isn't safe here. It never was. Turn away. Run. I could see her white canines gleaming in my head as she growled.

CHAPTER FIVE

I didn't lock the door when I left for my run this morning. It hadn't even occurred to me. Now, as I climbed the steps, smelling of blood and fear, I saw that the door was slightly ajar and realized that I had truly misjudged the gravity of Wolf Head's situation. With a death grip on the door knob, I took scent of the air inside. I caught onion skins, coffee grinds, and a smell that had haunted my nightmares for eight years.

My blood froze, but my feet kept pushing me forward.

Was I insane?

Maybe I was. My sneakers squeaked on the hardwood floor and I cursed under my breath. There was no sneaking up on him anyway and if it came to a tussle, I wanted traction on this floor. I would not get caught off guard by this man. If I did, then it would surely mean the end of my days.

"Stop wandering and come join me in the kitchen for a cup of tea, Diana," Jonathan's voice called into the house.

Three Blackfords in one day. I guess I was just lucky like that.

Curse words hung on my lips, but I kept them to myself. Reluctantly, I stepped into the kitchen, arms crossed over my chest and a false defiance put on my face. Inside, I was dying to turn and run. My wolf was growling and scratching to escape. I couldn't let her control me like she did the day before. My head began to throb.

On the small table were Aunt Magda's blue kettle and two mugs. In the kitchen sink was a mess of rags smeared with streaks of rusty red. Blood. I couldn't smell it over the scents that clung to me from the General Store.

Jonathan sat with one knee over the other as he toyed with the string on his teabag. He turned his face up to mine, a big smile on his face. I wasn't fooled at all. His eyes were as cold as they always had been.

"Just thought that I would come to welcome you back to Wolf's Head," Jonathan said.

He nodded to the chair across from him at the table, but I stayed standing. He shrugged and sipped his tea.

"It is so nice of you to take time out of your life on the west coast to visit your family, Diana. How long will this visit last?"

"If you're worried that I'm staying here then let me take a big load off your shoulders. I have a return ticket to Sacramento in two days."

He nodded his approval, serene smile never quavering. I watched his hand wrap around his mug, manicured nails hiding a line of dark grime. He'd missed a little bit. I took an involuntary step back, my hips hitting the counter. Taking in another deep breath I could smell his joy and ebbing excitement beneath all the blood.

"Helen," I whispered, raising my eyes to meet his.

His eyes narrowed but he didn't say anything. He had killed Helen Kapinski. But why?

Empty air hung between us. He turned pale blue eyes upon me, his charismatic smile just a tad too wide. Seeing him there, that air of confidence just barely hiding the fact that he was insane. He was just another person, another werewolf.

It had been a long time since I had last seen Jonathan. I had run into Clan-less wolves before, creatures determined to mate or kill. And I had survived. Jonathan wasn't much different. I smiled, letting myself lean against the counter and cross my ankles. Something dark flitted through Jonathan's eyes.

"You're just another person."

His smile disappeared. Launching himself from the chair, he was suddenly in front of me. I gripped the counter behind me, hard.

"Maybe you're just another monster," he growled, baring his teeth inches from my face.

23

"Get out," I growled at him. My wolf's hackles were rising and I could feel her rage beginning to burn beneath my cold fear.

He raised his hands in surrender and the smile slipped back onto his face. My heart was pounding in my chest. Was he going to try finishing what he started eight years ago? I would fight back this time, but I was sure that I wouldn't survive. Images of the General Store flashed through my mind. I would become chunks scattered around Aunt's Magda's farmhouse? I looked into that smiling face and saw the spark of something crazed in his eyes.

"Just remember where you kept that return ticket," Jonathan said, throwing in a wink, before he spun on his heel. His jaunty step took him out of the kitchen as if we'd had a friendly conversation over tea.

I didn't relax until I heard the click of the front door closing behind him. My knees began to shake and I let myself fall to the linoleum. Bile rose in the back of my throat and I struggled to keep it down. I never should have come back.

CHAPTER SIX

Finally alone in farmhouse, I picked up the nearest object and chucked it across the room. A small candle holder hit the sheetrock and left a dent in it. Still pissed, I threw myself into the shower. My grandfather's funeral was only a day away. Once that was over, I could leave. I could do exactly as Christopher and Jonathan had asked.

There was no staying in Wolf's Head for me. I'd be a dead wolf.

I thought I would have felt better after the shower, but my chest was still tight with worry and fear. I pulled on a pair of skinny jeans and I had just gotten my bra on when I heard the door downstairs open again. My heart thumped in my chest and I raced to grab a t-shirt out of my duffel bag. As I bent, I could scent the rising air.

My Grandmother was here. The thumping in my chest subsided and I had the presence of mind to realize that I had pulled out an old concert t-shirt. I wondered what my Grandmother would think of Five Finger Death Punch as I clomped down the stairs, wet hair trailing over my shoulders. It made me smile just a little.

"So many visitors today," I half joked, trying to bury my anxiety beneath humor.

My Grandmother stood in the living room, not a speck of blood on her. I wondered how she went about life, perpetually wearing white as if she were the innocent of the world. She was far from innocent. The woman had been the first female Faoladh in a century and single handedly raised that to first female Guardian ever. She half turned at my comment, her smile not truly real. This wasn't the pleasant kind of reunion, I realized.

Taking a defensive stance, I crossed my arms over my chest as my feet slid apart. The rush of adrenaline from this morning made my skin ache and I could feel my scars rubbing against denim. Today was just full of unpleasant feelings.

"The police took Henry Kapinski in for questioning," my Grandmother finally said.

My heart sunk. My arms fell away from my chest and I stumbled towards my Grandmother.

"How could they do that?"

Her lips pursed. "How else are they supposed to explain what happened to Helen? Some of them know what we are and Henry is a very old wolf." She looked down at her own hands, palms up. "The older we get the easier it is to slip."

Slip. She meant to let the wolf take full control, to give up on a more human life.

"That doesn't automatically mean that he's a monster. Our wolves aren't senseless killers and Henry loved Helen! They were mates."

"There were rumors that their marriage was becoming strained," my Grandmother offered. Her eyes rose to meet mine. "We both know that he never could have done it, but how are we going to change their minds? My pull with the police department has diminished over the years."

I regained my defensive stance, letting anger ride over the sorrow to keep from crying. "I told you I had another visitor earlier. I know who killed Helen."

The look on my Grandmother's face was pure skepticism. Yeah, I had been back in Wolf's Head about all of five minutes, but there were people you didn't forget. You fell right back into your old patterns with them. Jonathan was like that for me. He was my boogey-man and always would be until one of us was dead.

"You and I both know the truth, but that isn't going to get either of us anywhere," She said. There was a shadow in her eyes, a little piece of the past that she was carrying with her. I only knew because I had that same shadow.

"But we could..."

"No, Diana. Not this time. He's a prominent figure in the community. No one would believe you."

"So, we let him get away with murder again? You and the whole Clan knew what he was and you let him become a *prominent member of the community*?" I felt hot with indignation. Someone would have to believe me.

She shook her head, her fingers tightening on her handbag. "I'm going to handle this like a Faoladh. We won't..."

In the short time that her words had faltered a knock came at the door behind her. I looked up sharply. Who else could be here? When I looked back to my Grandmother I saw that all the blood had drained from her face. I felt my stomach flip as I descended the last few steps.

The knocking came again, harder this time. Out of the corner of my eye I saw something. It took my brain a moment to figure out what it was. Lights. Pale red and blue flashed across the wall of the living room.

"No," the word fell out of my mouth as nothing more than a whisper.

My wolf thrashed inside my head. I know she wasn't physical, but it still felt like she hit the inside of my skull. It made my head throb. She wanted to run. There was a door in the kitchen that I could use. She gave me visions of running through the woods.

We didn't do it, she whined.

No, we didn't. But running won't make it any easier for us.

She growled at me, low and ominous. Rolling my shoulders to ease the knot that had wound itself in my upper back, I moved to open the door. Running would only make me look guilty and I wasn't guilty. They had to see that. My hand trembled on the door knob.

An officer stood on the other side, like I had expected. His blond hair was cut short to the sides of his head, left long on the top like I'd seen on a few military men in Monterey. His feet were set apart and there was a cold look in his blue eyes that said he had detached himself from the job a long time ago.

"Diana Warren," he said as he reached for the cuffs on his hip. I didn't move even though I could feel my heart sinking. "You are under arrest for the murder of Helen Kapinski."

I could have attempted to break the cuffs. I could have run before he could have even gotten them on. Being a Faoladh made me hard to catch, but I didn't struggle. I let the officer spin me around to cuff my hands behind my back. My wolf howled inside my skull while he read me my rights. I let him lead me through Aunt Magda's front yard as more officers piled in around me, funneling into the farmhouse.

"I'll have an attorney at the station before you can even get there!" My Grandmother called as he placed his hand over my head and pushed me into the car.

I was cuffed to the table in the interrogation room. The same officer that had arrested me sat across from me. He wasn't happy with any of the answers that I had given him. Yes, I arrived yesterday. Yes, I went to the Kapinski's General Store today. No, it wasn't until I saw the police outside the store.

I didn't belong here. It was making my wolf pace, her panic at being captured rising. To distract her, I pondered whether or not I could lift this table. I probably could, even chained to it. It wouldn't be very comfortable. The cuffs would cut into my wrists.

I was just thankful that no one on the force had any mind to dip them in silver. I knew from my father that there had been a few officers that knew about the Faoladh. He always talked to them himself,

28

treating them like family. Were there also Faoladh on the force? Was that why they hadn't slipped any silver into their work tools?

"Miss Warren? Are you even listening to me?" The officer nearly growled. Well, as well as a human could anyway.

I shook my head. "Not really, no."

"Do you understand the gravity of your situation?" He met my eyes and held them.

My wolf's hackles rose and I could feel the force of my dominance slipping out. She didn't like him. She didn't like his attitude. She was sure that she could put him back in his place. I bit the inside of my cheek. The taste of blood flooded my mouth, but the pain cleared my own mind.

"More than you do, I think."

"Oh, yeah? Care to enlighten me then?"

"No. It's not my place if you don't already know."

"Oh, I know. I know what you really are," he said. There was disgust in his voice that he didn't even try hiding. Great. "I know that you're a monster. I know that everyone expects us to just put up with you living right beside us. We're supposed to just stand back and watch while you kill us."

I laughed. His disgust faltered for a moment as confusion crossed his face.

"Sweetie," I said. "We're too busy killing each other to bother killing you."

"But there's still a dead woman just after you arrived in town. Is that suspicious or am I just crazy?"

"I'm just a poor sap that got caught up in a power play once more. Someone wanted to make a show of power so they took a fragile human mate and made her into something we can barely recognize."

There was a paleness to his face that hadn't been there before, but he pressed on. "Someone. So, detached from the word. Your father was found, murdered in a similar fashion. You and your mother thought it'd be a good idea to flee the state not long after. Do you enjoy killing your own, Miss Warren, or can you not control the monster inside of you?"

My skin burned with the rage that I was feeling. Had he just accused me of killing my own father? I wanted to throw the table across the room. I wanted to scream my pain to him. Instead, I closed my eyes and drew in a long, shuddering breath.

He sighed.

"Helen Kapinski saved my life once, you know?" I began. It just kind of came out of me. "*Someone* killed my father and was working his way to me when I escaped. Another of those power plays, of course. I was the daughter of our Alpha so I had was the heir to the bloodline. I escaped and found myself hiding in Helen's general store. She stood up to him until there were too many witnesses. Had he killed me then, perhaps he'd would have been in this seat."

"We'll process you, Miss Warren, and set up a cell for you." The officer stood and gathered the file folders that he had splayed out on the table. He refused to meet my eyes as if he were hiding something in them.

He shoved the door open and two officers filed in to take his place. They unhooked me from the table and led me towards the holding cells. Officers filled the halls, hands on their weapon as they watched me trudge toward my cell. There weren't many in this station. It was a small building, meant to police just Wolf's Head.

30

They led me to a small cell that couldn't have been more than eight foot by eight foot. There was a cot in one corner and what appeared to be a toilet behind a plastic curtain. I sighed and fell onto the cot. How long would I be here? Despite what my Grandmother had said, no lawyer showed up.

Was she on my side? Or, did she think that I had lost control? Or that I'd become like Jonathan. I shuddered. It made me roll over and curl into myself. I wouldn't be like him.

Run back. Go home. We can't stay here. He is here and he will kill us.

The wolf paced the floor of the cell. She had tried to open the door, thrown her body at it. She turned her attention to the window, seeing the wooded land beyond it. She could escape. She could run back. But the window was barred. She could fit through the window, break the glass, if only she could break the bars.

You can't break steel bars. Let me back out.

The wolf dropped to the floor. No, she said over and over again. You will not let us leave. No one will let us leave Why can't we leave?

Our Grandfather, our Alpha, passed away. We brave the dangers to show our respect. We are strong, the child of an Alpha and the grandchild of an Alpha. Then someone else we loved died. When this is through, when our name is cleared and our respects paid, then we can return home.

Leave now. Run fast.

What happened to being strong and brave? What happened to the wolf that wanted to prove them wrong?

We are going to die here.

I won't let us.

As I told my wolf, I began to believe it. I wouldn't let myself die here in Wolf's Head. Not this week. My wolf started to give into my will. She believed my word and I began to push back into human form. Despite the magic that flowed around me, aching joints popped from wolf into human and my muscles burned with the effort. It hurt more and more each time I woke as my wolf. She fought me every inch and I was afraid that one day she would stop believing me.

I must have fallen asleep curled into myself again because I woke with a knot in my back and a pain in my neck. My wolf and I hadn't disagreed this much since we left Wolf's Head for Texas. Slowly, I stretched out, wondering what had woken me. The room was dim, the sun not yet over the horizon.

A figure lingered on the other side of the cell bars. I jolted upright. The smell of the officer from yesterday came to me through the scent of bleach and urine. Another, unfamiliar smell greeted my nose.

"Looks like you have an alibi, Miss Warren." The officer unhooked a set of keys from his hip and moved into view.

"Thank you for releasing my client, sir," a new voice said. As I stood, I could make out the lines of a man's face. He was tall, but not altogether lean. When his green eyes met mine, I could see the wolf in them. "I'm glad this could be cleared up easily."

I was, too. I was curious as to what my alibi was. Had someone seen me running or, more likely, had the Clan lied for me.

"It seems that we are back to square zero on this one," the officer scratched the back of his head. "We just released Mr. Kapinski not too long ago, as well. His attorney put us up against a wall."

"Might I inquire as to who is representing Mr. Kapinski?" My lawyer asked with a truly perplexed look on his face.

"Blackford and Sons. You know who I'm talking about. It's not like his sons actually take part in the firm."

Shit, I thought. Why was Jonathan pulling strings for Henry? If he murdered his wife, he wouldn't be the one bailing the guy out of prison on the charges. It didn't make sense. Did Jonathan ever make sense?

I thanked my lawyer. He said it was no problem, he represented the whole clan when times like these came about. Money from the Clan coffers lined his account and money from his account cushioned the coffers. It was a vicious cycle.

He left me on the steps to the station building. His car, a sleek Porche, was parked directly out front. He paused after opening the door.

"I usually represent Henry. There was no need for Jonathan to step in."

"I agree," I said. "Something smells of rotten eggs."

He chuckled. "Rotten eggs?"

"Have you ever smelled forgotten eggs a month after Easter? I swear it's worse than rotten fish."

And with a hearty laugh, he folded his bulky frame into the sports car. He was a big wolf, I thought. A man his size is usually found chopping wood or something else just as testosterone laden. That he was a good lawyer surprised me.

CHAPTER SEVEN

I was bounding down the steps when something caught my eye. My wolf told me to stop, but my brain couldn't figure out why. The hell? I studied the scenery around me. Beside the station stood the white brick town hall. Circling the huge building were skeletons of flowering bushes that had breathed their last breath months ago.

Finally, I stared at the bushes. It took a lot of self-control to keep from scratching my head as I searched for what was screaming wrong. I crept forward, focusing on a single gray branch when it dawned on me.

There were leaves budding on these bushes. With small green leaves budding throughout the entire mass of bushes, there was a soft, green haze taking over. Kneeling, I gingerly reached out and ran a fingertip over the edge of a leaf. Face to face with the plant, I saw a single flower bud hiding in its cage like depths. Impulsively, I reached out for it. It radiated warmth across my palm and I couldn't help but gasp.

As if I were a catalyst, the bud suddenly started to unfurl. Delicate and graceful, each petal peeled away to reveal a soft white flower. The bloom opened into a pillowy peony blossom in my hand. It was beautiful, I thought as I watched. Then, the petals began to take on a pink tinge until it opened into a deep crimson center. It was the color of blood. I jerked my hand back, heart pounding in my ears. A bad feeling came over me, settling in my stomach like stones. I wanted to vomit, but was almost certain that I wouldn't be able to.

Standing up, I looked around. There was no one else on the square with me. I swallowed down my uneasy feeling and shut my eyes, straining my ears for anything. Sure enough, I heard the faint rumble of voices not far away. Opening my eyes, I followed the sound between the town hall and the old Thurwell building. Against my better judgment, I crept forward.

I could still feel the warmth of the blossom in my palm and I closed my hand around it. I pressed my shoulders against the brick of the Thurwell building as the bushes scraped against my running hoodie. The parking lot on the other side came into view and I crouched low. Branches tangling in my hair and leaves tickling my ear, I looked out into the parking lot. Three people stood in a triangle, only one of them faced me. Inside my mind, my wolf growled. Something wasn't right.

Even from the distance I could tell that the man facing me was Henry Kapinksi. He wore a button-down shirt and slacks as if he had just left court at the town hall. Images of the general store flashed through my mind. I had to close my eyes tight to fight away the memories. I needed to get closer, to hear what they were saying, so I crawled between brush and bumpers. Peering around the bumper of a Toyota Corolla, I could see the profile of at least one of the men talking to Henry.

Even seven years later, I could recognize the large nose of Todd Jackson. It had a bump in the bridge that hadn't been there in middle school, but it was the same thin lips and thick, furrowed brows that I remembered. He had been one of Christopher's friends, spending a large amount of time at the Blackford's manor. The man on the other side of him was bulkier with wider shoulders and a barrel chest. I couldn't see his face, but they both smelled of wolf.

"Your cooperation was found to be a little lacking, Sir," Todd said as if he were counting missing eggs, so matter of fact. "Mr. Blackford was nice enough to post bail for you today in return for nothing more than your respect."

"And you think you have successfully scared me into submission?" Henry growled back.

"Our Alpha thought it pertinent that he punish you for not submitting to him. This is on your own shoulders. All you had to do was take a knee, so to speak. Since you didn't, he took two."

"And a bit more," the other hulking figure laughed to himself.

Mr. Blackford? Christopher didn't have to balls to operate on his own like this. Darren wasn't the greatest guy, but I knew deep down that this was a level that he would never stoop to. Jonathan had practically admitted to killing Helen Kapinski during his visit. These had to be his errand boys, making sure that his blatant message had been received. And he thought posting bail would win Henry Kapinski?

"All you succeeded in doing was taking away the one thing I had to live for."

The sad sound of Henry's voice made my heart break. His age was catching up to him now that Helen was gone. There were lines in his face and a slump in his shoulders. His body language said he didn't care if they killed him right then and there. I couldn't let him throw his life away, not yet. When the barrel-chested wolf stepped forward, I darted from my hiding spot.

I was faster than I thought.

My shoulder collided with his spine. The impact reverberated through me. He stumbled before turning around with a rabid snarl. I had just hit Marcus Cumberland. My blood ran cold as I fumbled to find my footing. He let loose a growl that rumbled into a loud roar as I turned to run away. I darted between houses, jumping short fences while his footsteps thundered behind me.

Marcus would kill me. Wrong. Marcus wouldn't just kill me if he caught me, he would enjoy it over a very long time. He was a few years older than me, with a reputation for killing small animals well before his first change. I burst out onto the street, hoping that it would shake him, that he wouldn't risk a public fight. But the houses became fewer and the odds of someone seeing Marcus catch me became slim. The tightly knit neighborhoods gave way to manicured lawns. I leapt over an empty kiddie pool and fumbled over a low fence into farm lands.

My wolf howled inside of me. I told her that I had a plan. I begged her to trust me.

Not sure if my plan would work, I veered back into the woods. I was smaller than Marcus, easily ducking under low branches and fitting between closely nestled trees. Behind me, he wasn't faring well but he was keeping up by crashing through the underbrush.

I cursed under my breath. My chest was on fire, but it was a burn that I had become accustomed to. I saw the rough stone edge of a cliff. Another jolt of adrenaline shot through me. Cutting to the left, I ran for it. Marcus was storming through the brush behind me. This was my only option. I shed my hoodie and my t-shirt as I ran, stumbling and losing ground. The ledge was only feet away. My foot left the stone, the ground looming below. Weightless, I let my wolf come forward.

She pushed into reality, bending my limbs and bones midair. My shoes and pants slid off in the fall, four feet hitting the ground running. My bra was still on, but I didn't care if I looked silly as I ran. Fight of flight. Four feet were faster than two, lower to the ground. I heard Marcus jump the ledge, landing with a thud and groans. Yet, he kept coming. He seemed tireless and inescapable.

Asphalt appeared when I broke through the woods again. The light was bright, but I could hear the low rumble of an engine coming. I shot across the road. Marcus huffed and puffed behind me. Suddenly, I heard a loud thud behind me. The sound of Marcus's footfalls stopped. Casting a glance over my shoulder as I ran, my pace slowed. Marcus rolled off the hood of a gray Chevrolet truck. The driver motioned me over.

Henry Kapinski impatiently revved the engine of his truck. Avoiding the unconscious Marcus, I ran for his open door. The truck started rolling forward as I threw myself inside.

"What in hell made you think that it was a clever idea to throw yourself at Marcus?" Henry glared at me. I couldn't answer in this form, but my wolf growled. "That boy has just gotten worse over the years and I'm an old man who doesn't have anything to live for anymore. That was just plain stupid of you."

My wolf barked at him, a reprimand. In the mirror, I saw the corners of his mouth twitch, trying not to smirk. I settled into the seat. The feeling of safety chased away the rush of adrenaline. My wolf wasn't very happy with my actions, but she was happy that Henry was safe because of us. She was happier that Henry had run Marcus over. The ridiculousness of the situation made even me laugh.

Maybe I did have a death wish, but someone was safe because of me. The relief let me pass out in the back of his rumbling truck.

CHAPTER EIGHT

I was woken by the sounds of clinking plates and smell of coffee. Voices blended into a soft murmur. Outside the window closest to me, the sky was dark and the stars shone like bright pinpoints. I wondered what time it was as I unfolded myself from an uncomfortable position.

Beside me was a stack of clothes that I recognized. I yanked on a pair of black and purple floral pajamas pants and my Batgirl tee. Following the smells and sounds that woke me up, I stumbled right into an informal meeting. I stopped dead in my tracks, face to face with not only Aunt Magda, but my Grandmother, Darren, and two other men whom I didn't recognize gathered around the massive table. Limbs splayed everywhere and a skateboard leaning against his chair, the wolf with the floppy blond hair looked like he'd rather be skating, but there was a hardness in his dark brown eyes once his bangs fell away from his face that I didn't expect. The other wolf stood, feet spread apart and tattooed arms crossed. He looked ready for a fight, the close cut of his red hair screaming military.

I fumbled for words, but my sleep addled brain came up with nothing. It had been a long couple of days. Aunt Magda laughed at me and handed me a mug of coffee. The smell of coffee and vanilla rose to greet my nose. It was so strong that it masked the smell of a kitchen full of wolves.

"You're going to need this if you want to keep up," she explained.

"Keep up with what?" Reflexively, I wrapped my fingers around the warm mug.

Everyone looked amongst themselves. Everyone except for Darren. He watched me as you would watch an animal in study. He took me in from head to toe, evaluating who I had become. When our eyes met, there was something in them that I couldn't quite read. It burned, making me uncomfortable. Whatever it meant, I didn't want to know. I tried to ignore him and leaned against the far wall, keeping my eyes on my mug.

"We want to help Darren become the next Alpha," my Grandmother answered finally.

"Then why don't you just appoint him?" I said over the mug I held. I bristled at her tone, knowing that just hours ago she had confessed that no one would trust me, that they knew my dirty little secret. A good man was being questioned for the murder of his wife because no one would believe my word.

She shook her head. "It's not that simple. That would have to come from Alpha to Alpha and Arthur is..."

"Sorry," I muttered, having the grace to feel ashamed of myself. My grandfather, her mate, was dead.

Taking my mug with me, I retreated. This meeting was no place for me and that was obvious. Upstairs, I set the coffee mug on the nightstand before reaching for my phone. There were a couple of checking in texts from my mother and step-father. I quickly replied with non-informational texts just to let them know I was still alive. Mom had stayed behind with her new runts, my tiny human siblings that I loved so much. She had sent her respects with a card buried deep inside my duffle bag. Even the runts had signed it, sharing their love with a man they had never met only because Mom and I had loved him.

A knock on my door made me jump. Dropping my phone, I found Darren in the doorway. He stood in there, awkwardly stuck between moving forward and giving in to retreat. Lips twisted with words unspoken, I thought that he wanted to apologize for something but he gave up. Instead, he came inside and shut the door behind him.

"Do you know who I'm running against?" he asked.

I shrugged, not caring which young male wolf thought that he had what it took to reign over a Clan. Whoever he was, he was crazy. I gave Darren a look that said as much.

He shook his head, running his hand through his hair as he sunk to the floor. Toying with the strap of the duffel bag near him, he wouldn't look at me as he spoke.

"I'm running against my father," he said.

I shot up straight, "No one will let that happen, will they?"

Darren looked up to meet my eyes. In his grassy green and brown eyes, I could see an apology, fear, and an iron core. That grim expression said that it was his job to stop Jonathan. Yet, I wondered who would back Jonathan in anything, giving Darren the popular vote in the very least. I let myself fall back onto the bed, staring up at the ceiling as my mind worked. Jonathan had just killed a human woman. Other than the fact that he enjoyed it, why would he have bothered if he was working to become Alpha? It could ruin his chances.

"He's using scare tactics, isn't he?" I said to the ceiling.

"What else did you expect?" Darren's voice answered. "He's blinding the dumb with charisma and more than willing to subdue the rest with force. The visions he has for us take a few evolutionary steps back, getting very dark and gruesome."

I swallowed hard, thinking only of the wolves that I met outside of Maine. That was what Jonathan wanted all of us to become. The point of the Clan had been to create community and to foster the need to protect one another. He was systematically destroying that very foundation.

Jonathan was playing a very bloody version of King of the Mountain.

"And you want to be the hero? Run in and save the day?"

He looked away, the muscles in his jaw tightening. That was only the surface of the truth, I guessed. Darren wanted to be the hero, the opposite of his father, but there was a lot more depth to his desire to be Alpha than I thought.

I shrugged, pretending not to care. But on the inside, I knew what kind of a monster Jonathan was and I would happily take the

41

lesser of two evils any day. Downstairs was a group of people committed to making sure that any monster like that never gained any more power.

"I can't wait to leave."

"After all of this," Darren's voice almost cracked. "After everything you are willing to go back to California with not an ounce of guilt on your conscience?"

I thought of my half siblings. Karli was only five and Peter had just turned three this past August. I had family in California that I loved and wanted to protect. I wanted to watch them grow older, be the protective sister. It didn't matter that I was two decades older than them. The plane that left in three days' time would have me on it. That was for sure.

"There's nothing here for me if I stay," I said softly. "Nothing but misery and possibly an ugly, premature death."

"I wouldn't let that happen," he murmured. I don't think he realized I heard him.

"You and I both know that Jonathan is a murderer, if no one else around here can see that or wants to see that then why stay?" I had to work hard to keep my voice from rising as I spoke. Fear gripped my chest and I had to take a deep breath to calm my wolf.

"I missed you," he said suddenly.

I turned away from him, not wanting to see his sad hazel eyes or his messy mahogany hair. My wolf pushed me to go to him, wanting to soothe him by rubbing her cheek against his, her fear forgotten. I told her no repeatedly. Getting involved with Darren the way that she wanted was a path that I didn't want to go down. I hadn't since I was fourteen.

"Get out," I said as I rolled over.

Fighting the urge to turn and peek at him, I heard the creak of the door close behind him. There was hesitation in his footsteps before new footsteps joined him.

"I can understand that you trust her and all," I heard a new voice say. "But how can you be sure doll face won't just get herself killed. Or worse, someone else killed."

Silence hung in the air for a long moment. In my head, I imagined Darren leveling those dark hazel eyes at the man.

"Doll face?" Darren's voice held no hint of humor. "She's pretty despite what she's done to herself, but I'm not sure if she can keep up with me or the other wolves."

"You don't know how strong she really is. I don't think anyone but Petra can really understand how strong Diana is. Don't you dare underestimate that woman."

I heard something hit the wall. "You told me that it was your father that killed Michael, her father. Now you're expecting her to stand up against him? I think I'd piss my pants if I ever saw Freya O'Dair again."

"Who?"

"It doesn't matter. All you need to know is that she scares me as much as I think Jonathan scares Diana."

"You're saying a woman is the big baddie in your life and you're doubting Diana?"

The man's sigh was heavy. Neither of them knew that I wasn't quite asleep yet. Something rose inside of me, a desire to prove the other voice wrong. My wolf growled her approval and it rumbled through my bones. She could be strong. She could be fierce.

As their footsteps faded down the staircase, the world began to grow dark. Emotional exhaustion claimed me and I gave in willingly. I dreamed of white blossoms that turned red in pools of blood. It was a fitful and restless kind of sleep.

I arrived outside of Henry's small house, not far from the general store, in the early morning. I hadn't slept well after the impromptu meeting that I'd stumbled into. The idea of Jonathan running the Clan terrified me. This wasn't my home anymore, but to see it fall into the worst hands possible was...

What? What was it? Sure, it was horrible, but was I going to do anything about it? I couldn't. It just wasn't in me. At least, I didn't think so. Still, I'd selflessly stood up against Todd and Marcus yesterday when I was no match for Marcus.

The door opened as I slowed to a jog. Henry stood in the doorway, his face clean shaven and his hair brushed. He seemed to have pulled himself together somehow.

"How did you know I was here?" I asked, guarded.

"The kitchen window looks out over the hill. Saw you jogging down it and thought I might intercept you. Didn't think you were headed my way, actually."

"This is the tail end of my run. I couldn't sleep so I ran. Thought that I would visit you and thank you for dropping me off at Aunt Magda's."

"No problem," he said before turning back to the house and motioning for me to follow. "I don't have much to eat because...well I never learned to cook. Helen did all of that."

Henry turned around with a round loaf of bread in one hand and a Tupperware tub in the other hand. My stomach rumbled when I caught the yeasty smell of fresh bread from Magda's restaurant.

We tore the loaf apart by hand, dipping the pieces in herbed butter straight out of the tub. Neither of us cared about double dipping.

"Yesterday morning, I was ready to give in."

Henry's voice made me look at him. He stared at the chunk of bread in his hand, the gears in his head working. His brown eyes looked sad, but they had lost their defeated look.

"You won't now," I finished for him, making it almost a question.

He shook his head. "I wanted them to end my life this morning, but what you did opened my eyes."

"What I did was stupid," I crammed a piece of bread into my mouth.

"Yes, but selfless. Jonathan is going to keep trying to scare the Clan into submission and I was content with letting him do it if I didn't have my mate." He tried to look me in the eye, but ended up staring at my shoulder. I didn't realize that in my panic I had gathered my dominance around myself like a shield. I let it go with a sigh and felt my shoulders relax.

Dominance wasn't just a battle of wills with the Faoladh. It was a kind of psychic force that many of us had. The strength of dominance varied from one Faoladh to another, with some wolves being so submissive that they didn't have it at all. They were the ones that rolled and showed their bellies to the stronger wolves, the ones we protected. Even rarer were the Omegas, wolves born blind to dominance.

"It's time for me to be selfless, too. I can't let Jonathan do to others what he did to me, to... Helen."

His last words were choked. Did I just inspire someone to work against Jonathan? I opened my mouth to argue, but my heart wasn't in it. Darren needed all the help that he could get. Henry watched me as if he expected me to cheer him on, but I only shrugged.

"Jonathan boasts of dreams to create a Clan that is stronger than ever. He wants to revive us, or at least, those are his words."

"That sounds...almost noble of him," the skepticism was clear in my voice.

Henry shook his head. "It's not half as noble as it sounds. His plans include culling the weakest from the Clan, killing anyone too submissive. Less the Faoladh that we are and more of the Berserker of Norse origin,"

My heart leapt into my throat. There was something atrocious about killing a submissive wolf. Naturally, dominant wolves wanted to look out for their weaker counterpart. Clan was family and every wolf should feel safe. That was the point, but he seemed to be determined to undermine that with his every breath.

I couldn't say that I was surprised, though. Everything about Jonathan left a bad taste in my mouth, one that usually tasted of blood.

CHAPTER NINE

The wolf whimpered, burying her nose in the sheets. She didn't want to see the world today. The world was against her. The human girl inside of her screamed to get out. She fought, but it was never enough. Evil Marcus wanted to kill them now. They had confronted him, embarrassed him. He had the look of the crazier wolves that had hunted her. They fought hard. They scared her. The wolf wasn't going to give in this time. She was in control.

"Diana?" Someone called in the house.

She heard two voices in the hallway. The door eased open and a face appeared. The wolf recognized it. It was family, Magda. She came into the room and the wolf gave a low growl. Magda stopped. She put her hands on her hips and frowned. Another face appeared behind her. Petra, her grandmother.

She came closer and closer to the bed. The wolf growled, but she wasn't going to hurt family. The two women approached the bed. The growls began to turn into whimpers.

"Oh, Diana," Magda said.

"Don't do this to yourself," Petra's voice sounded pained.

The wolf turned to her, nudging Petra's hand with her nose. As Petra ran her hand over the muzzle of the wolf, Magda climbed into bed. The women curled around the wolf. They felt like Clan, a feeling the wolf had forgotten. Had she ever known the feeling to begin with? She snuggled into Petra, the older woman's fingers clutching her fur.

"Don't do this to yourself. I know how bad it hurts," Petra whispered.

We can't stay here. Our life is on the line.

Our life is on the line anywhere we go. Clan-less wolves want to keep us or kill us. Hunters sought us out, wanting to control us or eradicate us. They hunt, for weeks, months. They make us run or fight for our lives. We have the scars to remember. What makes you think we will ever be safe? This is no different than what we have faced before, I lied wanting to believe it myself.

I pushed, remembering the strength that it took to return from my very first change. My wolf's will was strong, strong enough to match my own will. Yet, in the end, we were one person and she gave in to me with the hopes that together we could survive.

My body expanded, limbs rearranging to human form. I found myself pressed between my Aunt and Grandmother, their warmth comforting and reassuring. Aunt Magda pulled the comforter over the three of us and we laid in a heap for a while.

This was family, I thought. Clan. Hot tears began to roll down my cheeks. I hid my face in the pillows and they just held me tighter as my sobs became louder. I was just a girl, but I'd already lived through so much on my own. Here were people ready and willing to stand by me through the worst of it.

I busied myself by getting dressed for my Grandfather's funeral. I threw on a black button down shirt with my black skinny jeans. When I realized I didn't have a pair of shoes to match, I migrated into my aunt's room to rifle through her closet. In typical female fashion, the bottom of her closet was littered with lightly worn shoes. There were sneakers, boots, and a few pairs of heels in the back. I reached for the pair of dark plum pumps in the far corner.

She wouldn't miss them, I thought as I slipped them on. Carefully stepping over to the full-length mirror on the wall, I realized that my grandfather had no clue what I had grown into. He probably had remembered the gawky fourteen-year-old girl all his life. Yet, here stood a woman with long and lean legs that came from wide hips. I was a woman with gold and black wolf eyes hidden behind long brown bangs.

My father never even had the chance. His little wolf girl had grown into a woman in his absence. I was a broken and disturbed woman, but a woman nonetheless.

Would they have been proud of what this little wolf girl had grown into? Or would they take one look into my inhuman eyes and know how weak I had been? Perhaps that was why there were so few female werewolves. It was something you had to be born with, a trait that many men inherited from their fathers, others through a strange kind of magical infection. My grandmother and I were the only female werewolves that I had ever known. Could women handle the monstrosity that came with the condition?

Downstairs, Aunt Magda was busy prepping for the reception that was to happen here at the farmhouse later in the day. The funeral was to be short and sweet, but the reception would be full of food, memories, and my Aunt hoped it would last all night. It was to remember her father after all. Born human from two Faoladh parents, she should have been weak. Magda was obstinate and determined to hold her own amongst her family and it must have instilled a sense of pride in my grandfather. She rose above her humanity to thrive amongst monsters.

She appeared in the doorway, bringing with her the smell of bacon and cheddar. She took in everything from my distant eyes to my lanky legs that ended in her shoes. To that, she gave a small laugh.

"They look good on you. I can barely walk in them as it is." She came over to sit by me. There were smudges and hand prints on the thighs of her jeans, the spoils of kitchen work.

We were silent for a long moment. I leaned my head on her shoulder, taking comfort in the subtle smell of herbs that hung closer to my aunt. Just this morning I had panicked at the thought of being in the room that my father had died in, like I was transported back to that day. It haunted my every movement. More so now that I was here in Wolf's Head.

"It seems as if everything around here reminds me of how dad died," I confessed. "I can't remember how he lived."

Aunt Magda wrapped me in her arms. At first, I stiffened, but then forced myself to relax into her hold. This was family that I could trust, no matter what my body said.

"We will remember how our fathers lived tonight."

We will honor them. Was I making him proud, from wherever he was now? This couldn't have been the daughter that he had once imagined that I would be. No, my father's daughter would not have been a scared wolf that couldn't claim her full humanity ever again.

Could I still make him proud? I wasn't sure how I could go about doing that.

"I have a picture of Michael on the mantle downstairs," Aunt Magda began. "I will put it with Dad's tonight."

Michael Warren, beloved Husband and Father. Clan Alpha.

"That would be nice," I snuggled into my aunt.

She laughed and told me that it was her turn to get ready for the funeral. I was commanded to head downstairs and to turn off the oven and take care of a number of other preparations. I allowed myself to wonder what a Clan would be like if it were headed by a woman, someone like Magda who was warm and in control all at the same time.

It wouldn't last. Men always wanted the power, I thought as I snuck a slice of apple. We were all basically human. We fought through greed and desire. I learned a long time ago that it wasn't the animal in us that made the Clan act the way they did. The animal in us only allowed us to do the terrible things we did.

"Are you ready?" Magda appeared wearing a slim fitting black dress and low heeled ankle boots. Her hair was swept back into a messy bun and a black fishnet veil attempted to cover part of her face.

I nodded, taking her hand. This wasn't going to be an easy day.

The funeral was held outside. Our breaths hung in the air as white clouds, a small amount of white amongst so much black. Much of the town had come to the funeral. The streets were lined with cars and those who couldn't find parking had walked. Aunt Magda and I stood at the head of the procession. She gripped my hand in hers, trying to keep her sorrow under control.

My Grandmother joined us, wearing her customary white as a skirt suit with a black blouse. There was a black and white anemone in her salt and pepper curls. She brought another Faoladh with her. Darren stood awkwardly, glancing out at the rest of his family.

"I know how you feel," my grandmother said to Darren as he stood beside her. "Arthur practically raised you."

She seemed to make it a point to those listening. To me, perhaps? I turned away from them.

Across the way, I could see Christopher's body stiffen. In the simple act of moving seats, a message had been sent. A family was now split. After the funeral and the reception, the Alpha seat was up for grabs. The dominance battle was about to begin.

Once everyone paid their respects, we claimed our seats. Darren leaned back in his seat, throwing glances at me. Our eyes caught for a second and I could see the weight that today had set on his shoulders. He had lost a lot recently. Jonathan glared at us with dark eyes. Somehow, I had been drawn into a display against him. I shifted my feet, plum heels trying to find even ground. Easing back, I moved out of Jonathan's line of sight.

CHAPTER TEN

The reception for the funeral wasn't held at the Manor. It wasn't even held at Balefire. No, instead, Aunt Magda hosted it out of her very own home. The entire farm house smelled of home and love. There were tubs of macaroni and cheese baking alongside apple crisps. Loaves of fresh bread were lined up on the counter, a thick bladed bread knife waiting beside them.

Little by little, people filtered into the house. It was loud and busy, which apparently made my Aunt very happy. Despite this being the reception to her father's funeral, she was grinning from ear to ear.

"What are you smiling about?" I said between slicing bread.

"The Clan came together," she said with a big grin.

We were situated by the front door, welcoming people inside and accepting hugs. My grandmother had disappeared somewhere along the line. We weren't quite sure where she had gotten to, but we were sure she was mourning in her own way.

Henry Kapinski came through the door. He wasted no time in throwing his arms around me and squeezing as tightly as he could. It took everything I had to return the favor. His mate was gone, I had to. When he pulled away, I could see a fire burning in his eyes. We said nothing to each other; he just moved on to Aunt Magda.

Behind him came Marnie and Norman Trudeau, another wolf and human couple. He grasped my hand tightly, a little too tightly. I turned my eyes up to him, pulling at my own dominance. I shoved it at him and it met with the solid resistance of his own aura of dominance. Was he trying to have a power play with me at my grandfather's funeral reception? I stifled a growl and gave a hard push with my dominance.

He stumbled back, letting go of my hand. Inside my wolf gave a low growl; she made a mental note not to trust him.

His wife gave me a distant nod before she ushered Norman on. Aunt Magda glanced at me, taking in what had just happened. I turned my attention to the crowd forming within the house. People were glancing at me and leaning in close to whisper amongst themselves. Some glances were warm and held pleasant surprise. Many of them, many Clan wolves, eyed me suspiciously as if I were about to start screaming or grow two heads.

"Assjacks, all of them are assjacks," Christian Waterson said as he came through the door. He had been in the same grade in school as me back when I lived here. He was cleaned up, his hair cut and tamed and skater style traded for a button down and jeans. It dawned on me that he was the skater that had been in Magda's kitchen the other night. He turned his wide smile and sparkling blue eyes to Aunt Magda and me before sweeping both of us into a hug at the same time. "We have our eyes on him."

A couple of other boys filtered in behind him, shaking our hands and sharing their condolences. They joined Darren who was sitting on the couch with a distant look on his face. It looked like the beginning of his own Clan Guard was already building.

"It's nice to finally see you," a familiar voice said.

I whipped my head back to the line coming in through the door. Danny Carston smiled wide. The floppy black hair he'd had at fifteen was gone. It had been cut short and styled up with gel. He'd grown tall and reedy while I'd been gone, but when he hugged me I could feel the strength in his wiry arms.

"Are you done hiding from me?" He asked warily, as if he truly believed I'd been hiding from him.

"I've...been busy since I got back," I couldn't just say that I'd been either losing my mind or being arrested. "But, I missed you."

And I had. Danny had been the third person in our small gang. Whatever harebrained adventure Darren had thought of, I had made bigger, and poor Danny had been dragged along for all of it. There was still a scar on his chin from the time we jumped off Grover Cliff into the lake. Danny had hesitated and I'd taken the initiative to push him just as he'd spun around to leave. His feet had slipped out from beneath him and his chin had cracked off the stone cliff. I had felt so bad that I dove in after him to make sure I hadn't knocked him out.

"I missed you, too. Come find me when you're done." He gave me another hug before disappearing into the house.

My stomach rumbled fiercely. The people coming through the door, touching and hugging me, were setting my wolf on edge. I couldn't handle it anymore. I ducked behind Aunt Magda and disappeared into the empty kitchen. Taking a seat at the scarred wooden table, I pulled a meat and cheese tray close. I rolled together a slice of honey baked ham with Swiss cheese and dunked it into the pale Dijon mustard.

Someone set a can of diet soda next to me and I jumped in surprise. I cursed myself for letting my guard down as I watched my Grandmother fall into a seat opposite me. Her jacket was gone as well as her pantyhose.

"You were out running, weren't you?" I challenged.

She leveled her eyes with mine and a smirk touched her lips. I took that as a yes and rolled her a slice of turkey and provolone. Because of the wolf inside of us we required a lot of food to keep us not only running, but tame as well. Shifting recently only amplified that need. Can you imagine how many calories it would require changing from human to wolf, even with magical help? It did mean that I never had to think twice about the extra slice of peanut butter pie.

"Yes, I was," She reached for the roll of meat that I held out. "I was a Guard wolf once upon a time. It is hard to escape the person that you become when you do that for so long."

I remembered the story that my father used to tell me. Petra had been the lonely female wolf of the entire Clan in the late sixties. She had been coddled and protected by everyone around her. She fought tooth and nail to escape that, she trained hard so that she could challenge the Guard wolves. She didn't know that when she went to her knees before the Alpha to ask to enter his Guard that she would someday leave it behind to marry him.

I studied my grandmother's face. It didn't look a day past forty-five, another perk of shape-shifting. Yet, her hair was now more white than black and the tired look still hung in her eyes. Had that look been there since my father had died, I wondered? Still, she sat in the kitchen chair with her back straight and her shoulders rolled back. She looked as if she were still ready for a fight.

She finished the roll of turkey and leaned back in her chair, reaching across the counter for the tray of cookies. Her long fingers came back with at least four cookies. She set two palm sized rounds before me. They were triple chocolate and smothered with more dark chocolate. I gladly bit into one, feeling the chocolate ganache coat my mouth and a white chocolate chip bite beneath my teeth.

"When are you leaving us again?" my grandmother asked.

"Tomorrow morning, first thing."

She nodded. "Running away from us?"

I shrugged. Why shouldn't I run away? I come back and someone that I had cared about here has been murdered within days. That shouldn't have been my first hint that this town wasn't safe. I shouldn't have come back at all. I cracked open the diet cola and chugged at least half of it.

"You're a Warren wolf, Diana. Never forget that you're a Clan wolf."

I bristled at that comment. "What does being a Clan wolf get me? We are all just a bunch of animals cloistered in a small town too busy with killing each other."

"All of us are animals?" she raised an eyebrow.

"I wouldn't say animals. I have more respect for animals. What else could you call a creature as destructive as we are?"

Yes, I said we. I'm to blame too. I know what I have done.

People began to filter into the kitchen. First it was Darren, pulling out a chair and sitting between my grandmother and me, and then Christian and the cloud of boys came in. Christian, the red-haired wolf, and even Danny milled around the kitchen island, grabbing at the numerous trays lining the counters. Aunt Magda appeared in the doorway, glancing over her shoulder to make sure no one was behind her.

I sat up in my chair. Somehow, I had involuntarily been pulled into another informal meeting. I cursed myself and shoved the rest of my cookie into my mouth before crossing my arms over my chest. I did not want to be here, but there was no getting past Aunt Magda now.

"It was customary to wait a month after the death of an Alpha before challenges were made," my grandmother said over her cookie. "While we know he doesn't play fair, we don't know how long it will take Jonathan to strike, but in that time, you can build your guard and your support base."

Darren nodded. The boys behind him had settled down, a tall and muscled red haired guy leaning over the counter and listening intently set his gaze on them. He'd been at the other informal meeting, too. I studied him more closely this time. His hair was cut short on the sides, careful not to touch his ears. When he rolled up his sleeves, tattoos graced his fair skin. His brows were set in a hard line over green eyes that could have been sweet, but were now dark.

"Jason is going to be the head of my Guard," Darren said and the red haired wolf nodded. "Christian and Danny have volunteered as well. I know it isn't much, yet."

"You have my loyalty," Aunt Magda said quietly.

Loyalty? I pushed my chair away from the table. The side of my head was beginning to throb.

"You have mine as well," my grandmother added.

They were pledging their loyalty to someone who had helped kill their son and brother? I couldn't believe it. There had to be a better choice, someone else to choose. I glared at Darren. He wasn't the hero he desperately wanted to be.

"You have Henry Kapinski's loyalty. Someone pulled him from the brink of letting his wolf take over," my Grandmother said.

"Understandable, I know what it feels like to lose someone you care about," Darren's eyes fell on me.

"Watch out for the Trudeau family. Norman's agenda isn't all that bad, but his mate keeps pushing him to be more than he is," Christian added.

I finally shoved my chair back and stood. There was no way that I could sit through this. I pushed past my aunt and made my way towards the living room. Someone came running after me. Beneath the smell of Clan and food, I caught Darren's warm scent. He grabbed my arm and spun me around to face him.

His dominance quickly surrounded him like a thick cloud. It pressed in on my chest so fast and hard that it made me short of breath. I winced, trying to pull away. His eyes widened when he realized what he had done. My arm slipped from his grip.

"Will you ever be able to forgive me?" He said between gritted teeth.

I brought my gaze up to his. My dominance nearly matched his. Nearly. I opened my mouth to speak, but a crash suddenly came from the living room. There was a new smell in the air, that of chocolate malt balls, rum, and Christopher.

"Shit," Darren muttered under his breath. He shoved past me, rushing to the source of the sound. Instinctively, I followed hot on his heels.

One of Aunt Magda's bookcases had fallen to the floor, books were lying everywhere like soldiers after a blast. Christopher was leaning against the wall where it had been, laughing like a maniac. The curvy waitress from the diner stood beside him. I could see now that she was clearly pregnant as she reached to steady Christopher, lines of worry creasing her face.

"What the hell do you think you're doing?" Darren's voice boomed.

Christopher's insane laughing stopped and he leveled empty eyes on his brother. Shoving himself from the wall, he staggered forward. The auburn-haired woman reached out to pull him back, but he threw a hand out at her. The smack echoed through the now quiet room. Sabrina, that was her name. She stumbled back, her eyes beginning to glisten. The brothers stood eye to eye, spilling dominance in every direction.

"Why can't I come to my own Alpha's funeral reception?"

"The invitation was there, Christopher, but we never asked for you to come drunk."

He shrugged. "I'm not the beloved child. Why should I act like you?"

"Let's go," Sabrina reached out again. He spun and snarled at her. She jerked her hand back as if he had snapped wolf teeth.

"Please leave," Darren's voice was calm and level.

"We can't have you wrecking more of Aunt Magda's house," I found myself saying.

Christopher spun his head to glare at me.

"Stupid little bitch wolf," he spat. "Everyone's little prodigy that ran with her tail between her legs after my brother and I saved you. You can't even change your eyes back to human! Do you remember what color they used to be?"

Before I knew what I was doing, I had stepped forward. My hand tightened around his throat and my foot hooked behind his. With a smooth jerk of my foot, he fell with a loud thud to the floor. I tightened my fingers around his throat and pressed my knee into his chest.

"Watch how you speak to me," I shoved my dominance onto him. His could barely put up a fight. He whimpered and snarled within my grip.

"Diana! That's enough." I head Aunt Magda say.

I didn't want to let go. I wanted to tighten my grip, to feel all of the air leave his lungs and watch his eyes roll back into his head for good. It took all of my self control to pull back.

"Dad tried to break you, he knew you for the monster that you are even then."

I lunged forward, but someone grabbed a hold of me. It took two werewolves to drag me back from Christopher. No one could break me. I wasn't a monster, I told myself. Not like his father was. The rage was still there, though. It sat like a hot fire in my stomach and burned its way through my body. There was a part of me that still wanted to kill Christopher.

Sabrina glared at me as she collected the drunken Christopher from the floor. They both glared at me. Do you know what Christopher did? Do you know what his father is? How could you have his child? I wanted to scream these things to her, but Christopher's words finally penetrated my thick skull.

After my brother and I saved you.

I was herded back into the kitchen while Sabrina apologized over and over again to Aunt Magda. Instead of staying put, once the boys turned to peek into the living room, I slipped out the back door. I crunched through the gravel of the driveway towards her green Ford. Inside her glove compartment was a crumpled pack of menthol cigarettes and a cheap lighter.

It seemed that we had the same vices, not that they were great for us. But that was why they were called vices, right? I lit up, but barely inhaled. Mostly, I watched the red tip of the cigarette burn in the growing darkness. I couldn't believe that Christopher had crashed through our reception. My hackles rose, thinking about how he was his father's gopher. But then again, I wouldn't be here much longer. It wasn't my problem.

It wasn't.

After my brother and I saved you.

Tomorrow morning I would be gone. I flicked the un-smoked cigarette to the ground and used the platform of the pump to put it out. It was as simple as that. I knew that I was good at making enemies. My life in Monterey hadn't been peaceful or without its own share of bloodshed either. But I wouldn't stay here and be lied to. I wouldn't stay here and wait for my death, not by Jonathan's hands or Marcus's hands.

"Who the hell do you think you are?"

My head shot up to find Sabrina standing on the porch. She stood over me with her hands on her hips and a hot glare in her eyes. I couldn't take her bearing over me so I climbed the steps to stand in front of her. She backed up almost reflexively.

"Chris was just drunk, you didn't have to treat him like that," she went on.

"You don't know my history with Christopher so don't even begin with me."

"Your history?" her voice cracked a little.

"Not that kind of history," I shook my head fervently.

"Chris's father played a part in her father's death," Danny said, appearing beside me.

"So what if his father caused some sort of accident? You don't blame his son!"

I shook my head, refusing to play into this conversation anymore. "Go back inside. Grab your drunk boyfriend. Take him home and let him sober up there. Just get him the fuck out of here."

She opened her mouth to argue, but was cut off.

"Do I have to constantly keep an eye on you?" Aunt Magda said from the doorway. "Stop insulting my guests!"

Sabrina turned back to my Aunt. Magda placed a tender hand on the girl's cheek. She just shook her head and mumbled something about how he had never acted like that. Not until I came back into town. This girl seemed to have a better relationship with my aunt than I did.

I wrapped my arms around myself, feeling lost and alone. Danny wrapped his arm around my shoulder. He pulled me into his body and I let him.

CHAPTER ELEVEN

The funeral this morning seemed ages ago as I slunk through the doors of Balefire. I trailed behind Darren and his entourage of makeshift Guardians, feeling as though I didn't belong. I didn't, but I had nowhere else to go. Magda hadn't asked me to leave, but I knew when to retreat, leaving her to pick up the mess that Christopher had made of her home. I had only been defending her, I told myself even though it was a lie. I didn't think that I would lose it like that. I wanted to taste Christopher's blood, at the very least. I shuddered to think of how far I would have gone if Aunt Magda hadn't been there.

I glanced at the boy, no he was a man, beside me. Danny had invited me along and I'd said yes. I would have said yes to anything that would have gotten me out of there. He gave me a soft smile and I attempted to give one back even though I know it couldn't reach my eyes.

I let my head fall against the table, feigning defeat to those that surrounded me. My stomach rumbled. I was in no condition to argue on an empty stomach, the fight with Christopher draining me physically and emotionally, and I knew if I spoke Darren and I would argue. Hunger only made matters worse. Hangry I think they called it these days.

Plates of food arrived, served family style. I pulled the massive bowl of mashed potatoes close and wrapped my arm around it. Several of the makeshift Guardians gave me odd looks as they picked at the french fries that were smeared with gravy and cheese curds. Then a thin crust pizza arrived. There was always so much food among wolves.

I looked at the possible future Alpha and his ragtag group posing as his guard. The red haired wolf kept a stoic and guarded face even though I caught him sneaking inquisitive glances at me. Danny and Christian were throwing food at each other, hitting casualties at other tables. I couldn't help but laugh when a man swatted his head as if a bug had landed on him only to find a french fry.

It was Darren's burning hot gaze that made my skin itch. I wanted to put on another layer of clothing because I felt as if I might get sunburn from that stare. That stare made me feel like the only other person at the table. The way that it made my skin hot troubled me.

"Don't you dare," I growled before he could speak.

I shoveled mashed potatoes into my mouth. It tasted as if I had bitten into a garden, fresh herbs bursting at every bite. It was so creamy and rich that I suspected it was spiked with cream cheese.. I missed good cooking. I had been living off burritos and salad mix for too long.

We weren't all hunters. We didn't change into wolves to hunt down people. Sometimes I wondered the truth of our creation myth or if the animal inside of us was a defense mechanism, brought about by sadistic evolution. It was a silly evolution considering it only made us meaner to each other most of the time. My fingers felt for the raised scars that ran up my thigh, just barely feeling them beneath my thick jeans.

There were legends, depicting our origins, but even with all of the magic I have seen I couldn't imagine something divine creating creatures like us. Why give a person the ability to rip another person apart with their hands? Why give them teeth and claws that they can use to murder loved ones? It wasn't right.

"So you're going to deny Clan and family? You still plan on running back to the West Coast to play human?"

My head shot up, piece of pork loin half chewed in my mouth. Was Darren freaking serious?

"I'm pretty sure you of all people remember when Clan turned its back on me first. Can you blame me for wanting to leave?"

Darren's head fell. For a moment, I thought he was going to give in. I was wrong.

"You still think you're just going to leave and let the same man that destroyed your family wreak havoc with the rest of the Clan?"

A growl rumbled through my chest. I couldn't stand up to Jonathan again. I didn't know what he was trying to ask of me, but he wouldn't get anything. I just couldn't help them. I would be of no use. I wouldn't become the person that attacked Christopher again, either. I'd felt myself become a monster for a moment.

Trying to finish my meal in silence, I shoved more food into my mouth. Yet, there was no escaping him.

"You are, aren't you?" his fork clattered to the table. "You're just going to get back on that plane tomorrow."

"Yep."

"He plays nice when people are around, smiling that big smile that sucks everyone in. They lie to themselves and say that he challenged your father fair and square. There are wolves supporting him, saying he was wronged when Arthur took back the position of Alpha. I can't let him win," his voice ended on a pleading note.

No, Jonathan couldn't win. I'd seen what that charismatic man could do if you didn't play by his rules. That's why I couldn't help them. I remembered red splatter, climbing the walls and soaking into the beige carpeting. Pieces, my father had been in pieces when I found him. The pieces of Jonathan's first wife. The pieces of Helen Kapinski. I knew that Jonathan would kill me. It was only a matter of time if I stayed here.

"I can't." I choked on my words. "I can't help you."

I pushed away from the table, grabbing my bag and running for the door. I was focusing on his death again, but how could I ignore the fact that everything here reminded me of it? Once the big wooden doors shut behind me, the warmth faded. I wrapped my arms around myself and began my trek up the street.

Run. Flee. We need to leave!

My wolf wanted to thrash and bite inside of me. It made my back and my head ache. I tried telling her that we would be leaving in the morning, but she didn't believe me. What did she know that I didn't? I crossed my arms over my chest and put one foot in front of the other as I pushed my wolf to the back of my mind.

I found myself stopping outside the Town Hall. The thick peony bushes were green and full of life when they should have been withering away in the cold November air. I stopped between the two wolf statues that flanked the steps of the building. The peony bushes pressed in against them, somewhat like a hug. Some blossoms were heavy with dark violet petals while others were a fluffy white.

"Magic is returning," a voice said. "It is returning, albeit slowly."

I spun, a chill racing up my spine. Jonathan stepped forward, his hands casually placed in his pockets. His black button down shirt hugged his slim form. The man who had killed my father was standing before me, pretending at civility. Again. I stepped back, bumping into a gray statue. A stone wolf raised its head to the moon behind me and somehow I felt safer.

A smile split Jonathan's face and a gleam crept into his eyes. It was less mischievous and more psychotic. It wasn't something he let through in public. No, I was pretty sure he saved it for me. Did he do it to scare me or had he simply stopped pretending around me? It was me that had walked in on him chewing on bits of his last wife. It was me that saw him rip my father into small pieces.

"Do you understand why I am doing what I'm doing?" Jonathan asked, his voice holding a hint of true curiosity.

I raised an eyebrow, crossing my arms over my chest, feigning bravery. He didn't wait for me to give a reply, but went on with his monologue anyway.

"We play at being human, running businesses and keeping face amongst our mundane neighbors. We were never human. We are werewolves, creatures under the moon," His pale eyes gleamed white in the dark. "I'm sick of pretending to be human when the urges are so loud. We crave blood and flesh. We desire the conquest of the hunt and we dare deny ourselves that satisfaction as if we were monks?"

Was I understanding him correctly? Did he just call us werewolves? Did he want us to give in to the blood thirst? Did he want us to hunt humans, to eat their flesh? I'm pretty sure that was cannibalism, no matter what we were.

"If we gave in to the natural urges that we feel then we will finally assume the strength that we were destined to have! It is what nature intended us to be and we are avoiding it as if it weren't the gift that it is. We'd become the army that we were always destined to be."

My stomach rolled. He was describing monsters, pure and simple. He wanted us to revel in bloodshed and savor the kill. I remembered the feeling I had when I arrived at Magda's farmhouse for the first time. The smell of blood in the air had made me wild. It cracked my control and let the wolf body slip forward, neither of us quite in our right mind. I thought of holding Christopher's throat beneath my hand, choking the life from him. Yet, I hadn't given in.

"You're wrong," I whispered. I wasn't a monster. I was better than that, better than him. Yeah, keep lying to yourself. "That feeling? That is just you and me. I am what you made me."

"If I am so wrong then why is when human blood has been spilt that magic starts to return to us?"

My jaw dropped. No. He couldn't spin it like that. The Clan magic had been thriving when my Grandfather first took the role of Alpha, when he married my grandmother. I remembered the heavy blossoms as a child. The flowers hadn't begun to fade until my father's death.

"You know that's not why it's returning," I jabbed a finger at him rather brazenly. "Fuck you and your army."

He shrugged with that crazy smile still on his face.

"How else would you explain it, Diana?"

I opened my mouth to argue, but nothing would come to me. Jonathan stepped closer to me. My back was pressed against the cold stone, but the blossoms caressed my arms. They made me feel stronger. I bared my teeth at him, pulling my spine straighter.

"You grew quite feisty while you were away," he laughed.

"Fuck you."

"Nasty, nasty language. Don't make me take you up on that." He brushed a strand of hair behind my ear.

I shuddered. Was that a threat?

"Magic is returning for a reason and I'm pretty sure that you're not it," I said.

"Yet, the Warrens have lost the position of power. How are you going to explain that one, little Warren Wolf?" His hand cupped my chin as he tilted my head up. His fingers sharpened and lengthened, biting into my skin.

He was shifting his hand.

How long had Jonathan been strong enough to concentrate the change? I looked up into his crazy eyes and felt the push of his power against mine. It was no match. I was far more dominant than Jonathan. If he could do it then so could I. I pushed every desire for fight or flight into my palms. My fingers bent, burning with the shift. The wolf inside me raised her head in defiance. She saw that we were stronger than our fear.

Suddenly, he shoved me back. My head struck the stone wolf and the air rushed from my lungs. I lost concentration. The burn receded into a cold chill that swept up my arms. Jonathan's face was suddenly very close to mine. His hot breath fell across my face. I felt my stomach turn.

"Leave tomorrow like you planned on and you won't have to worry about a thing," he said.

My heart thundered in my chest as my feet hit the ground again. He pulled his hand back, smoothing down the front of his shirt.

"Good evening, Miss Warren," he said as he begun to leave. "Just remember what I've said."

While I knew that I was a more dominant wolf than Jonathan, I also knew that I had a long way to go before I could stand against him and live. He was stronger than me, faster than me. My dominance would only get me so far if I couldn't be more. There was no way that I would live in this town. One way or another, someone would see me dead and I wasn't strong enough yet to take on everything that waited for me here.

Yet, a part of me wanted to try.

I stumbled over to a bench nestled in the overgrowing flower bushes. Letting myself fall onto it, I let out a breath that I hadn't realized I held. My heart was still thumping in my chest. My wolf was angry and wanted to pace, but the rush of adrenaline had made my knees shaky. My hand moved to the back of my skull where my skin was already knitting itself back together. It came away with a palm of blood. Head wounds bleed so much, I thought.

My eyes went to the massive stone wolf that had cut through my scalp. The smear of blood across its shoulder was mine. Pushing myself up, my wobbly legs led me back to the stone wolf. My hand covered the smear of blood. It smelled like wet earth and coppery blood where I stood. I closed my eyes to take it in.

In the distance I heard the baying of wolves. Something seemed off about it. I cracked my eyes open, looking in the direction of the sound. A long moment passed before I heard it again. It moved about like a bodiless entity. As I followed it, my mind tried to process the sound. It wasn't wolves. No, it sounded more like a pack of dogs.

I shook myself and pulled my hand from the stone. The sound dissipated and vanished. What had I just witnessed? More magic, of that I was sure. The question that remained: was I the only one that heard the ghost hounds?

CHAPTER TWELVE

"You were right after all."

Aunt Magda looked up from the comic book she held before her face, guarding her mouth with it. I was almost certain that she was smiling, but didn't want to show it. I could see it in the crinkles around her eyes.

"Glad you're happy," I muttered and kept shuffling towards the kitchen. I needed a drink.

I heard the thunk of the comic book against the coffee table and quick footsteps behind me.

"What happened?" she appeared in the doorway, alert and caution in her eyes.

I shook my head, reaching for the bottle of white Moscato that sat atop the fridge.

"I will say it one more time, Diana. What happened?"

The tone of her voice made me turn my head. With her arms crossed over her chest, she had a glare that could stop armies or make a scared young woman blurt out the truth. I watched that determined and protective face and wished that she could be the new Alpha of the Clan. But through all of her fierceness, she was still human.

"Jonathan visited me after I left Balefire," I confessed.

"At least the boys were with you," she let out a breath. I said nothing as I filled half of a stem-less wine glass. Her eyes widened. "You left without them?"

"Darren was being a dick. I didn't want to be around him.."

"Of everyone, he knows the risks of going against his father the most. He knows that if he doesn't win he's a dead man."

"You think I don't realize that either?" I snapped at her.

She pursed her lips, holding back whatever she was about to say. I turned away from her, my back to the fridge and wine in my hand. Sliding down, my butt hit the floor and a heavy sigh escaped me. I took as sip, waiting for my head begin to fuzz over.

"Magic is coming back," I began. "The flowers came back to the town hall. I have no clue as to why it chose now to return, but Jonathan is going to use your father's death as a reason."

Magda let herself fall to her knees, her jaw slightly slack. How could she be so surprised that Jonathan would play this dirty?

"But he knows why the magic is back," Magda muttered. I turned to look at her. "We all know why the magic is coming back."

I gave her the I don't know so spill the beans look, eyes wide in anticipation.

"Really, Diana?"

"What are you trying to insinuate?"

She face-palmed. Was I being stupid or was it just too far out of my reach to grasp? There was no way that she could be saying that the magic was returning because I came back. Was there? I remembered the feeling of the blossoms caressing my skin. I remembered the safety I felt beside the wolf statues and the sounds of the ghost hounds. But that didn't mean I was some special snowflake.

Did it?

"Why me?" I pulled my knees up to my chest, cradling the wine in the space between my knees and my chest. Up until an hour ago, I had no plans of staying in town. None whatsoever. Yet, some goddess saw it fit to return the magic we once knew simply because I made a trip back into town?

I chugged the rest of my wine, setting the glass in the deep sink. There was no way that all of this would be sitting on my shoulders. Jonathan destroyed my family once, and while I knew I had more potential than him there was no way that I could best him right now. By the end of this I would die.

But I thought of how Aunt Magda and my Grandmother had cradled me in the morning, when my wolf had taken over. The safety that I had felt with them was new and comforting. The playfulness of

Danny and Christian at Balefire spoke of the potential for happiness here. Even Henry Kapinski had found a new resolution after losing the love of his life. There was so much here, amongst the Clan, that I was learning to love.

I wanted to protect them all. Was there ever any other option? My phone vibrated, two quick hums, in my pocket. I pulled it out to find a new text message from someone.

Are you alright? Darren.

How did he get my phone number and did he know I ran into his father? I texted back with a simple yeah. While I wasn't okay, physically I was still in near perfect order. I still had all of my limbs and appendages.

I had just fallen down the most dangerous rabbit hole ever, is all.

I'm sorry if I pushed too hard. I know this has to be a sour subject. He must have been talking about our conversation at dinner, the one that made me up and walk out. I hadn't even left money for my portion of the meal.

 Don't worry. I'm in one piece.

I might even have to stay in town for a while. Just for a while. He didn't need to know that just yet. If I could make it through helping Darren become the next Alpha, then I would book the next flight back to California.

The smell of evergreens and wet leaves coming through the window brought back all sorts of memories and dreams. I threw open the window and hoisted myself up to sit on the sill. The moon was just a slice in the sky and I could feel her light prickle along my skin.

I turned my face up to the moon, letting her pull at my skin. What was it about her, this moon, that called us to her? I closed my eyes and felt her light fall across me. It felt like safety and comfort. Perhaps the wine was buzzing a little too strongly through my head for me to think.

Just past the edge of the roof was a ten foot drop to the ground. I laid back, heels firmly planted against the shingles to keep from slipping as I inched down. At the edge of the roof, I pushed off and landed on the soft grass, crouching to soften the blow. There was no one here but the moon and me and perhaps a few stars. Somewhere, a wolf howl echoed through the clear night. It filled the air as if it surrounded me. It sounded familiar and musical, I thought.

Once upon a time, we had worshiped the Goddess. She was a goddess of wild nature, of the hunt, and a protector of the small and weak. Somewhere along the line of time, we gave up on her. There still stands a stone altar in the center of town, often decorated with lights in the holiday season. Yet, no one left offerings there anymore or visits in their time of need.

Why had we given up on her? Had the magic faded so much that we ceased to believe? We were creatures of magic in and of ourselves. We turned away from that fact. I knew that I had during my grief, refusing to believe that a higher power would do this to me. Some of us even became monsters.

There was a tightness in my chest, one that told me that I wouldn't be able to get out this time around. I had come back and now escaping was beyond my grasp. Helen Kapinski was dead. I had to clench my jaw, fighting back memories of sitting in the general store to chat over chocolate malt milkshakes.

Who would..?

Why would someone do such a thing?

She had been human. She might have been an old woman, but she was someone' mother, someone's mate. I remembered Darren's clenched fists as we all stood over her body. He had been there every time, sharing the chocolate malt with me. Once upon a time, we had been close friends. Now I had wolf eyes and sharp teeth and he had shadows in his eyes and a heavy weight upon his shoulders.

I began walking, not knowing exactly where I was going. My feet led me at a slow pace across the lawn. My wolf was silent, her head turned down in mourning with me. Her ears strained for even the furthest sounds. Her guard was never fully down. I couldn't say I blamed her. I remembered my father's blood on my hands. I remembered Jonathan's sharp blow to my head. Just the thought of it brought back a throbbing pain in my temple. I remembered the rage that I had felt.

It was something close to what I felt now, thinking of Mrs. Kapinski's death.

I am what you made me.

A monster. He'd see just what kind of monster he made.

My feet had led me into an open field. With wide open space all around me, I threw my arms open to the sky, feeling the cold wind slice off them. My head fell back and I howled. It was filled with all the pain that I had felt since I was fourteen. I howled so loud.

"Diana Elizabeth," someone whispered.

My howl cut short. I dropped low, fingers clawed into the dirt and eyes searching the dark trees around me. A tall body stepped from the forest as if it were perfectly natural to be naked in another person's property at this time of night. Darren had been running on all fours.

"What are you doing here?" I snapped, not moving from my position.

"I needed to get out," he rolled his shoulders as if his own skin was too tight. "Do you really have to leave again?"

I turned my eyes away from him, searching the stars above us. There wasn't an answer there. At least not one that I could read.

"Of course you have to leave again," he fell to the ground beside me and I followed suit

"Why should I stay?" He didn't need to know that I was considering it.

Silence hung between us. I could hear the distant hoot of owls and the crinkling of branches from nocturnal creatures. My wolf turned to the forest, her attention caught by something that wasn't quite right.

"Stay for the Clan," Darren began, pulling my attention away from the forest. "Stay for Magda if anything. I'd ask you to stay for me, but that would be pointless."

I stared at him, my jaw threatening to drop. I clamped it shut, not daring to speak.

"I loved you back then. I thought I was helping you," he added.

"Don't even try, Blackford." But as I said it, I could feel the wine making my head spin.

"You call me by my last name as if you lump my whole family into one person. I am not my father! I'm not my brother." He growled his words in frustration.

The hackles of my wolf rose. She told me to get away as fast as possible. Run, Diana. Instead, I stood my ground, staring back into his eyes. I felt my dominance settle on my shoulders like armor. He growled and pounced. My back hit the wet grass and I tried to flail. He had my arms pinned to the ground and my legs stuck under the heavy weight of his body.   His dominance pressed in on me. It was smothering. Against my will, a small whimper escaped me. His body froze and he suddenly pulled it back. I turned angry eyes to him. A heavy sigh left him and he let his head fall into the bend of my neck.

"I never meant to..." he began.

I had challenged him. He had been too dominant to let it go. I understood. It didn't mean that I liked it.

"I don't want to lose you again." His breath was warm on my neck. It sent chills through my body.

I wanted so desperately to throw him off. My body trembled beneath him and I didn't like my own reaction. Part of me wanted to curl into him, to wrap my arms around his wide shoulders.

"Don't leave us again, Diana," his teeth gently nipped the skin of my neck.

The feeling that shot through me was like nothing I had ever felt before. It was fear and lust and a mixture of other things I tried to run from.

"Don't leave me again," his big hands grabbed my jaw and pulled my face to his. Giant lips crushed mine and my body arched into his. He growled into my mouth. His hand left my arms, grabbing at my hips with desperation.

My fingers were lost in his hair, wrapped so tightly around him. His hips ground into mine and I could feel the length of him pressing into my jeans. It made me moan. It made my head spin. His hands traveled the length of my body, fingers pulling at my clothes.

We lost ourselves.

I shouldn't stay, Darren. My jeans slid off. It's not safe here. Warm hands brushed the inside of my thighs, traveling further up. I watched his back curve as he lowered his head to my stomach. His arms wrapped tightly around me as he laid kisses along my torso.

Safe. I was safe. Right. Here.

Cold wind blew over my bare skin. I opened my eyes to see the sun rising through the naked trees. It cast an orange and red flame over the world, one that faded into a pale blue higher into the sky. The world burned cold, I thought.

There was a gentle heat pressing into my back, a weight lying over my waist. I could smell damp earth and a familiar wolf. Oh, shit, what had I done last night?

I wriggled out of Darren's embrace, careful not to wake him. Gathering my clothes, I threw one last glance back. His jeans had been tugged around his hips, but not buttoned. It led my eye up his flat stomach to the soft brown curls of hair that hung sideways across his forehead.

I gripped my clothes tight to my chest and sprinted back to the house. The only voice I heard inside my head was my own panicked regrets. The wolf was still sleeping, deeply sated. I hated her even more for it. Quickly, I threw on a pair of over-worn skinny jeans and a soft Avenged Sevenfold t-shirt.

I knocked on Aunt Magda's door before pushing it open. She was already awake and when she saw the look on my face, she knew what I was about to say. I saw her face drop, a grimace tightening her lips.

"I need to leave."

She nodded and pushed past me without another word as if she'd expected me to run away all along. She would be moving slow, not wanting to see me leave just yet and hoping that I would run downstairs to say that I changed my mind again, that I'd be staying.

While it seemed like a good idea for a short while, it had outlived its welcome. After what I had done last night, I couldn't wait to see that dinky little plane again. I would be on my way back out of the state once more. I would be back at my Mother's side. I would resume my job at the convenience store and the few hours I could get cleaning at the tattoo shop. My life would return to mundane and normal. I wouldn't have to think about ancient magic, dead gods, or stupidly fucking Darren Blackford.

I sat on the edge of the bed, glaring at myself in the closet's full length mirror. My yellow-gold eyes burned beneath thick lashes. Dark brown, almost black bangs were growing long enough to be swept aside, the rest of it trailing just beyond my shoulders. There were purple crescents along my neck and leading down past my shirt.

"Fuck," I mumbled. Standing up, I lifted the shirt to see purple bruises from his hands around my hips. They would be gone in no time, I tried to reassure myself.

Still, I buried my head in my hands and groaned. I couldn't look at myself anymore, so I pulled on my dark brown leather boots and went back outside. My feet knew where to lead me, cutting a path through the woods that sat between Aunt Magda's farmhouse and the Warren Manor.

In a patch of the woods sat a small cemetery. I pushed aside the wrought iron gate with the stylized 'W' on it. Old marble headstones were covered in lichen, cracked, or leaning in the changing earth. The tallest stood in the back, my great-great-something grandparents whose headstones were tall male and female wolves that stood growling over the rest of the cemetery. They were magnificent and nearly untouched compared to the other, old headstones. Half melted candles and wreaths of wildflowers sat on the thick base of the wolves.

I turned to one of the newest headstone, Michael Vincent Warren. Engraved on the top of the headstone were two oak leaves surrounding a wolf's paw. I leaned in, tracing my nail over the letters of his name to carve out the lichen that grew over it. There were several green votive candles in glass holders at the base of his headstone.

Someone had been here, remembering my father. Magda perhaps. Even my grandmother.

"I miss you, Dad." Only the sounds of birds in the trees answered. "I wish you could be here. I wish you could tell me what to do."

A row behind my father's grave sat the most recently engraved headstone, the dirt over the grave still freshly turned. Arthur Franklin Warren, Alpha of Wolf's Head.

My phone vibrated several times, suddenly receiving two texts. I scrolled past Darren's message, not ready to see it, to Aunt Magda's text.

We need to get going if you want to go home. Where are you? Why is Darren here looking for you?

Back tracking, I opened the other text message. Darren asked where I had disappeared to. I groaned and laid my cheek across the cold marble of Dad's headstone. My wolf woke, her fur brushing against my skin in an attempt to comfort me. I imagined her nuzzling me inside my human shell and smiled.

I always had my wolf.

Back at the farmhouse, Darren was gone and Aunt Magda was ready to leave. She had the car warmed up and a bag of cinnamon rolls waiting alongside a thermos of coffee. I threw my bag over my shoulder and clomped down the porch steps in my heavy leather boots. My stomach rumbled. There was an ache in my hips as I stomped that reminded me of what I had done. I cursed myself over and over again.

"Can we just leave now?" I threw my bag into the back seat and turned to my aunt. "Please?"

She gave a sigh and nodded. She didn't want to see me leave, that I understood. We drove through town in relative silence, only the radio between us. She didn't ask why I smelled of sex and earth. I didn't offer any explanation.

The whole Clan was in upheaval. A family fought for control of a Clan of animals. A dear friend was dead. She was torn apart and left in her own haven. I hated this place. I hated it so deeply. There wasn't anything for me here. I had to go home. I needed so desperately to go home. My body ached from what I had done the night before. My conscience told me that I was stupid. It told me I had never done anything so stupid. Had I?

Just let me out.

On the ride to the airport, I had devoured four cinnamon rolls and all of the coffee in an oversized travel mug. No amount of food could quiet the feeling in my stomach that I was making a bad decision. I had made a lot of bad decisions lately. This wasn't the first, nor would it be the last.

Thick trunked trees lined the old streets of Wolf's Head, spilling yellow and red leaves across the sidewalks. Pumpkins had been removed from the windows of the shops, replaced by gold and bronze fall decorations. We drove past Balefire and all of its glory. A chalkboard with the specials leaned against the brick of the building and it seemed brimming with people.

We passed the old wood playground that had been built in a circle around a massive maple tree and the two churches that flanked it. In some distance, between quaint houses and garages, I could see the steel gray glimmer of the lake.

If I turned around in my seat, I would see the hill that looked over the town and Warren Manor sitting on it. I was leaving Wolf's Head once again.

CHAPTER THIRTEEN

When I leaned my head against the wall of the plane cabin and closed my eyes, I was brought back to the scene in the general store. I could smell the blood that had been smeared across the floor and the sour milk from the ice-cream that had been sitting on the counter. I could see the bits and pieces of her limbs, but not her face. I wanted to remember her soft smile when I visited her as a preteen and the gentle curl to her black hair.

Helen Kapinski was dead. Ripped to shreds. I couldn't suppress the growl that vibrated through me. For a moment, I wanted to hurt whoever had done this. It wasn't my problem though. I had left the Clan for good. I decided that when I was fourteen and fatherless.

Yeah, perhaps I do focus a bit too much on my father, but I was there when he died. I was two rooms over and I had been able to hear him scream and there was nothing that I could do. A close friend had betrayed me that same day. How do you recover from that?

We were fighting over a game controller. Laughing and smiling, he had fallen over me and I was sure that he could feel my small breasts pressing against his chest. He was sixteen and I was fourteen then. The way he looked at me, before he pushed away, I said I would never forget. It's a lost memory now.

I remember the way he froze as he sniffed the air. I could smell his father entering the house too, but thought nothing of it. Jonathan had his own business with my dad. Darren had hung his head as someone else entered the room. I looked beyond him to find Christopher with the same grim look on his face.

"What is going on, guys?"

They looked to each other, saying a thousand things without words as brothers do.

"Tell me," I pleaded.

When they wouldn't answer, I shot up from my seat. I bolted for the door, but someone caught me by the hood of my sweatshirt. Chris lifted me off the floor and dropped me onto the couch face first. His knee pressed onto my back. I wriggled out from beneath him and made a break for the door.

Suddenly, leaping across the room, Darren caught me and clamped his hand over my mouth, motioning for me to be silent with one finger over his lips. I would have trusted him with my life. He grabbed my wrist softly and pulled me from my seat. My heart hammered inside my small chest. He led the way down the Manor halls, leaving me confused.

He swore softly under his breath once we reached the door to the living room. Darren pulled me back into the hall, holding me close to his chest. I could hear our fathers coming from the other hall. I shoved myself away from Darren, afraid and reaching for the doors. Chris jerked me back, his grip on me hard and bruising. He shoved me against the wall, hand clamped over my mouth and my arms pinned behind me. I wanted to cry out to them. I cried and whimpered, confused as to why my friend would do this to me.

"Whatever you do, Diana, don't say a word." He warned. "Close your eyes; I can only protect you from so much."

Protect me? What was he protecting me from?

The footsteps grew closer, as did their voices. They argued in hush tones between themselves. It was only my father and a man I had known most of my life, the father of my best friend. Darren was scaring me.

"I don't know what you could be talking about, Jonathan." My father said.

Through the thin crack in the door, I watched Dad enter the room.

"I am challenging you, Michael." Jonathan slammed the door behind him. "It is my right to be Alpha. Mine! You took that away from me!"

Dad spun around, blocking my view of Jonathan. Challenge? Was Jonathan being serious? I couldn't imagine anyone challenging my father's Alpha position.

"You cannot do that without a formal circle." My father's voice remained calm and even.

"That clearly isn't how I plan on doing things." Jonathan said, hs voice almost happy.

I tried to call out, but it was muffled. I saw my father glance back just before a fist slammed into the side of his head. I bucked and attempted to scream, but Chris held me tight. With one foot Darren nudged the door closed so I couldn't see what was about to happen. I listened to the snarls and howls, unable to help. Panic flared in me.

Memories rose to the surface. I saw the face of a monster behind my eyelids. It had Jonathan's face, eyes wide and wild while sharp teeth protruded from its mouth. I stood in the doorway, only a child, seeing this man standing in a pool of red liquid while my head pounded. The smell was sweet and overwhelming. I wanted to taste it. But the beast growled at me, squeezing the meat it held in its hands. It was an arm, a woman's arm. I remembered the gleam of the diamond on her thin finger.

"Shush, please be quiet." Darren begged with a whisper. I could smell the sweet scent of my father's blood fill the hallway.

I turned my head away from him. This wasn't protecting me.

The noise beyond the door finally ceased. I kicked my foot back into Chris's groin. His grip loosened enough that I had the leverage to elbow him in the ribs. Chris shoved me back against the wall so hard the air fled from my lungs. Instinctively, I bared my teeth in a growl. Weaseling one arm free, my fist flew at his face. The impact was enough to make him stumble back, allowing me time to run. Darren frantically reached out to grab me, the hem of my shirt slipping through his fingers.

Jonathan stood over my father, his face smeared with blood, a crazed fire burning in his eyes. The same fire that burned when he killed his wife. I stumbled forward, falling to my knees by my father.

Warm blood soaked through the knees of my jeans. There was no rise and fall to my father's chest. The man that I loved, that had taken me to meet fae and vampires, that I loved more than anything was dead. Rage built until I couldn't contain it. I screamed until my throat ached.

Jonathan lunged forward with a growl. In what seemed like slow motion, I turned to run. Out of the corner of my eye, I watched his fist collide with my temple. My knees buckled as my vision narrowed. I dropped to the floor as the world spun, and then everything went black.

It was the smell of wolf that brought me back to reality. I hadn't expected another werewolf to be on the small plane to Chicago. It didn't feel right. Taking in a deep breath, the scent was naggingly familiar, as if I had just come across the wolf recently. That idea sent a chill up my spine.

How did I think that pissing off Jonathan and Marcus would leave me safe? I scanned the boarding passengers still searching for the source of the scent and came up with nothing. No familiar faces came out of this crowd. Yet, the smell was strong. My fingers clenched the head rest of the seat ahead of me.

Someone was following me, or worse, hunting me. That meant that I would be leading the hunter back home and Jonathan's wolves have shown no mercy for anyone. I couldn't bear the idea of my little siblings being caught up in this. I'd rather die.

My decision seemed to be made against my will, but that didn't mean I wasn't going to embrace it. I would be staying in Wolf's Head to protect my family, human and Clan. That also meant that I would find my stalker as well.

CHAPTER FOURTEEN

I squeezed my way between overweight passengers and seats, trying to reach the head of the plane. No matter how many times I said 'excuse me' or 'sorry', people still gave me dirty looks and nastier words.

"What are you doing, crazy girl?" One man grumbled.

"Get back into your seat," the big woman shrilled at me.

Someone shoved me to the side. I tumbled into an occupied seat, suddenly drowning in werewolf scent. Turning my face up, I found Marcus sitting beneath me. All evidence that he had been run over by an old truck had disappeared. Damn werewolf metabolism.

My heart thundered in my ears, but I still grabbed him by his coat and pulled him into the aisle. Using him as a shield, I barreled through the other passengers. People yelled at us, but I couldn't hear much over the sound of my own fear. What was I going to do once I got Marcus off the plane?

Unsure and running on adrenaline, I shoved forward.

"Excuse me," the steward stopped us, suspicion clear on her face. "I can't let you off the plane right now."

I peered over Marcus's shoulder with a big, apologetic smile. "I'm so sorry, sir. My cousin here is a little slow. He left some of his medication with my Aunt. He can't go without them. It would ruin his entire vacation!"

He opened his mouth to argue, but one look at Marcus's face made him snap his mouth shut. Maybe the steward didn't buy the slow cousin shtick, but he whatever he saw in Marcus's eyes kept him from arguing at all. Who would want this guy trapped on a plane anyway?

As we made our way down the flimsy steps, Marcus grumbled at me. It was probably something about missing limbs, blood, and maybe gnawing on my bones, a typical picnic for him. My knees began to tremble. As soon as I stepped off the metal staircase, I shoved Marcus in one direction. I took off running in the other. It was a replay of the other morning and Henry wasn't here to hit him with a truck again.

He followed, slowly at first. Once clear of the crowd, I glanced back to see him set into a full run. There was a smile on his face, not the rage that I had expected. Someone had given him a free pass, one that had my name written all over it. I cursed myself, he had been on the plane with me for a reason. I just led myself right where he wanted me, secluded and alone.

There were almost no cars there on this cold November morning. Aunt Magda's green sedan was empty. I thought my heart had stopped beating for a moment. Closer to the car, I saw her dark head over the hood of the car. What was she doing?

"Magda!" I shouted.

She shot up from her seat on the ground. Confusion flashed across her face for a brief second. It was followed by fear when she saw what was following me. I slid over the hood of her sedan, tumbling onto the other side. I was faster than Marcus, but he would catch up if we didn't do something.

Aunt Magda used shaking hands to pull her phone out. She quick dialed someone and I turned away, trying to steady myself. Clothes began to fall to the ground and I knew what I had to do. My wolf came forward with a snarl on her muzzle, her sights on Marcus. We let the change ride us and it came fast, leaving a bomb of sensations in its wake. Dazed for a moment, the angry growls of Marcus prodded me back into reality.

We heard a heavy thump and the car shook. I glanced up to see Marcus standing atop Magda's car. His eyes fell on me and a wide smile stretched over his face. It was a demented cheshire cat kind of grin that said I was in for all kinds of hurt. His ham sized fists reached down for me, but I was quicker. I darted to the tail end of the car.

Aunt Magda used the distraction to crawl away from Marcus and toward the front of her car. The ground was frozen and hard under the pads of my paws. Marcus rushed in head first, tearing after me. I prayed that he hadn't seen Magda as I tried to draw him away from the car and her.

I zig-zagged across the lot, drawing him behind me. I didn't know what to do if he caught up with me. Marcus would tear me apart.

Teeth. Claws. We will protect.

The wind carried another scent past me. It was familiar, but I couldn't place it. Had Jonathan sent more wolves just in case? My wolf might have been confident in us, but I was shaking inside. There was no way I was going to make it out of this one alive. But didn't I always think that? This time I was outnumbered.

I knew I would die here.

But not without a fight. I swerved away from the woods and the mystery wolf. I heard the crash behind me, but I didn't spare the time to look. All I knew was that the other wolf had revealed himself.

An angry howl suddenly filled the air. I skidded to a stop, spinning to see what had happened. The other wolf's sharp teeth had bitten through Marcus's calf. The other wolf worried his leg, but Marcus threw the wolf to the side. His muzzle came away with strings of muscle fibers and he slid across the hard ground. Marcus stumbled and dropped with his leg shredded. Blood seeped into the ground. With his lips drawn back, he snarled at him as he prowled closer. He tried to circle him, to get to his leg again.

I wasn't alone after all. And I wasn't outnumbered. I said a silent hurrah in my head.

His massive fist swung out and collided with the other wolf's skull. His body flew through the air and rolled across the lot. He struggled to get back to his feet, swaying as his leg gave out beneath him. Marcus growled, pushing himself to his one good leg. He dragged the other behind him as he trudged forward. There was no amount of pain that would stop him.

I raced towards them and launched myself at the distracted Marcus. My teeth sliced into the back of his knee. When he jerked away, I bit down harder and pulled. Tendons snapped with a loud pop. The leg crumpled and he fell to one knee. If we were lucky, he wouldn't be able to give chase now.

I jumped over to the other wolf, nudging him to move before Marcus could recover. We raced back to the car. The changed fluttered over me, faster and smoother than ever before. One moment I was running on four feet and the next I was on two. I snatched up my forgotten clothes and whipped the back passenger side door open. Magda revved the engine of her little sedan while the wolf and I threw ourselves into the back seat. We sped out of the parking lot with a naked woman and a werewolf in the backseat.

I wish I could say odder things had happened to me, but I was pretty confident that this took the cake. I sat back in the seat while the other wolf tried to get comfortable. Every muscle must have ached from how much he had been thrown around. Finally, he settled with his head on my leg.

We sped down the interstate, Magda's shaky hands on the wheel. I fumbled with my coat. My head was thrumming with an adrenaline hangover and my knees were still shaking. I glanced over Magda's shoulder to see that our speed was fluctuating, rising to eighty five at times. I tapped her shoulder and motioned to the nearest exit. There was no way we could afford to get pulled over right now.

How would you explain a naked woman and massive dog to a cop?

With only a jacket haphazardly thrown on and a shirt tucked around my legs, we went to the drive through of the closest burger joint. Aunt Magda mumbled something about the sub-par standards of a place like this, but it would have to do. We desperately needed something to eat and I prayed that it would chase away the shaky feeling of exhaustion.

I ordered five of the largest burgers, large sodas, and a two small vanilla ice-cream cups with chocolate sauce for myself. It wasn't prime meat, but it would do until we could ingest some real food somewhere safer. The ice-cream was more for comfort value than anything else. Who didn't want ice-cream after facing down a sociopath werewolf?

The kid at the drive through window gave us funny looks as Magda passed him a debit card. He handed over our food and asked if I needed help. He followed it with directions to the nearest women's shelter. I politely declined as the wolf beside me raised is head with a low growl. Fast food kid's eyes popped open, mouth suddenly out of order. With a quick thank you, we gunned it out of the drive through and found the parking lot of the sketchiest outlet store.

I scarfed down my flame broiled goodness in record time in the parking lot. As I savored my ice-cream, the other wolf quickly ate two of the five burgers. I set the other ice-cream cup on the floor board so that the wolf could eat it out of the cup. The chocolate would be good for him right now. My hand moved over the wolf's shoulders, memorizing the markings while I wondered who had come to my rescue.

"You could have taken the time to put some clothing on before eating," Aunt Magda said before she drew a sip from her soda.

I shrugged, I was decently covered for now. It wasn't until the last gurgle of my soda that I pulled on a pair of pants. Checking the parking lot for lurkers, I pulled the jacket off and felt around for my missing bra. Maybe I was odd, but I hated being braless in human form. I didn't bother with shoes, just tucked my feet beneath me while Magda directed the car back to the interstate.

I knew where we were headed, whether I liked it or not.

We didn't say much to each other on the drive back to Wolf's Head. We didn't have to. We were both alive and safe. I made a mental note to dip into my savings; I owed Magda, at the very least, artisan chocolates. Maybe some coffee too. She did just help save my life and prevent Marcus from following me back to California.

I owed the wolf beside me a whole lot more.

CHAPTER FIFTEEN

I woke up in the spare bedroom of Aunt Magda's farmhouse with human limbs for the first time. It was strange considering I had finally resolved to give up any sense of normalcy and self preservation by staying in Wolf's Head. Had my own, human fear been causing the chasm between my wolf and I? Turning my attention inward, I felt her curled up inside of me, complacent and happy.

"Fighting for your Clan, with love and fierceness." A bodiless voice said. "A true Faoladh."

Oh, good goddess, we were insane. Perhaps it didn't help that I thought of myself as two personalities. As I rolled out of the bed, I silently thanked my step-father for never sending me to a therapist. I wouldn't be here today if he had. I'd be locked up behind white walls and only visited by doctors with sedatives.

Yet, as my feet touched the floor, I thought I might still need that therapist. I stood in front of the full length mirror like a deer caught in the headlights. The voice still swam in my head like an echo in a deep, dark cave. As the echo faded, I watched the color blossom across my skin, appearing almost like an sudden bruise. Shades of purple, white, and green began to spread across my ribcage and down my thigh. Slowly, it took shape. My jaw dropped as I realized what it was.

What looked like a bruise at first became a realistic tattoo. Images of flowers were appearing in my skin. These were peonies, like the ones that were suddenly growing like weeds downtown. The deep green leaves wove themselves into an intricate Celtic knot behind the blossoms. The closer I looked, I found hounds and horses and even armed knights in the leaf knots.

I fell back onto the bed, still naked and watching the tattoos grow in the mirror. I couldn't look down at my skin yet, somehow saved from shock by watching through the mirror. What was happening to me?

"You feel my love and you share my love."

Her voice filled my head again. My wolf pulled back and I had an image of her rolling to bare her belly. There was a ringing laughter in my head that filled me with warmth and joy, like sunlight. The goddess was returning to us. My fingers traced the darkening outlines of the peonies on my thigh, thinking about her words while the sunlight still warmed me.

Love wasn't something that I had considered in a long time. Much of what I did throughout life was for survival, but now that I chose to stay in Wolf's Head something had changed. Here I was, risking my life for the animals that I thought had betrayed me. No. I was risking my life to protect the animals from the monster that betrayed me. Was that what she meant?

Beneath my fingers, just above my hip, the peony I traced began to turn white. The cream color flooded the fluffy petals, followed by shadows of violet and purple. Her sunlight warmth emanated from the white flower. Our lost Goddess was on my side, I thought to myself.

Almost reluctantly, I pulled on a pair of skinny jeans and a t-shirt over my flowers. On the way down the staircase, I raised the hem of my shirt, just to make sure that they were still there.

I shuffled about the kitchen on my own, still basking in the warmth that was blossoming across my side. My stomach rumbled and I followed my nose to whatever sounded good. Two slices of handmade bread made their way to the counter, as well as a bunch of vegetables and cheese. Tomatoes, onions, roasted red peppers, and baby spinach filled my sandwich. I cushioned it with a slice of gooey Monterey jack and a smear of Dijon mustard.

Grabbing my plate and a bag of white cheddar puffs, I migrated to the living room. Now that I was staying in Wolf's head, I wanted a place to live on my own and a way to make money that didn't involve family. I doubted that Aunt Magda wanted me on as a waitress anyway. While my jaunt on the web began as a job search, my mind wandered.

I couldn't stop thinking about the voice that I had heard this morning. The flowers decorating my body enthralled me. I should have been freaking out. I should be scared, but I wasn't any of those things. I wanted to tell someone, but I wasn't sure who I should turn to first. That seemed to be answered for me when I heard the front door open. Carefully, I leaned forward and set the laptop on the coffee table preparing for anything. But, the new draft from the open door only brought Darren's scent in with it.

I turned to sit with my arm on the back of the couch, watching the arch that Darren would soon appear in. The smell of him filled the room. It made my wolf giddy. In my head she barked and yipped as if she were trying to play.

"You're still here," His voice said.

"Yep," my hand unconsciously went to where Darren's love bite marks had been on my neck. They disappeared after the change to run from Marcus. I found that I was disappointed they were gone and frowned.

He came around the corner, studying my face.

"You don't look happy about it."

Skirting around the truth, I quickly said: "I never wanted to come back here in the first place."

He lingered in the doorway awkwardly. His feet kept shifting and his eyes moved about the hallway. I couldn't say that I blamed him. My hips still had a slight ache from what we had done two nights before. It hadn't been planned, but it had happened.

I stood and took a step forward, not entirely sure what I was about to do when someone appeared beside him. Excitement drained and left me with a feeling of anxiety that rolled in my stomach.

She was tall and thin like someone you might see on television. Her eyes had an almond slant to them that cast an exotic feel to her Scandinavian blonde looks. She looked to Darren, placing a loving hand on his shoulder. He turned to her and took her hand in his. That was when I saw the diamond on her hand.

"I have to head out soon, baby," she said.

I thought my stomach might roll again, but I forced myself to stand up straight and bite my tongue. The pain forced the anxiety to turn hot and bitter. It turned to anger.

Darren had lied to me.

"Is this your cousin?" she asked, looking to me.

A feeling of déjà vu crawled across my skin, but I couldn't place it. All I could see was the beautiful woman clinging to the man who had begged me not to leave the other night. He had told me I was gorgeous. He had told me he was afraid to lose me.

Was it a game? Had he played me?

"I'm Diana," I said, holding my hand out. "Our fathers go way back"

Darren's eyes shot open. I saw him swallow hard and look away. The woman seemed to miss the bitterness in my statement. She smiled wide and reached for my hand.

"Fionna," she said. Her cool hand grasped mine. I heard the jangle of bracelets and a sudden searing sensation washed over my wrist. I jerked my hand back, hissing in pain.

A look of soft confusion crossed her face. My eyes fell to the silver bracelets on her wrist. She was engaged to a Faoladh, but still wore silver jewelry?

Darren touched her shoulder, gently pulling her back to get her attention. He reminded her that she had to get to work. She threw me an honest apology and a sweet smile before ducking back out. Distantly, I heard her car come to life, rumbling softly as it backed out of Magda's driveway.

Our eyes met again and the fire of my anger returned.

"Come with me?" he asked.

No, not again. I looked away, nostrils flaring as I remembered the night outside.

"That's not what I'm asking." His face grew red and he looked away. "I want you to come with me to the Manor. My Guard is waiting for me and I thought you might like to add something to the meeting. If you're still here I'm assuming you wanted to help."

A long moment of silence passed between us. All I could feel was the hot rage building inside my core. How could I have been so damn stupid?

"The very least that you could do is come and thank Jason for helping save your ass yesterday."

I sighed, feeling a low growl vibrate through my throat.

Grudgingly, I pulled on my running sneakers and followed him up the hill trail to my old home. There were several of cars packed in the driveway, any number of werewolves now filling the Manor. I bit my lip and followed Darren into the house.

Wolves were crowding in the large kitchen, milling around the island or stuffing their faces at the table. I recognized Danny and Christian, fighting over a bottle of mustard. Gravitating towards those that I knew, I pushed my way in between them and snatched the bottle away. They both froze, simultaneously looking down at me.

Darren called the meeting. The room quieted as everyone turned their attention to him. He stood at the head of this little Clan as if he belonged there. The teen that I had crushed on once upon a time was gone, in his place stood a werewolf with the ability to lead a Clan of monsters. He pushed his dark hair out of his eyes with big hands, muscles working beneath his button up shirt. My breath came fast and I couldn't tell if I was turned on or slightly afraid. A twisted part of me suspected that maybe it was a little bit of both and I hated myself for it.

He opened by welcoming me back into the Clan and announcing that I had chosen to stay in Wolf's Head. A round of hard claps on the back came my way as well as a big bear hug from Frank, a member of my father's old Guard. His hug was crushing and I thought I heard a choked sob, but he only gave me a nod before moving back to the table.

The meeting went on, discussing Jonathan's resort to fear tactics. Many of them acknowledged Jonathan's hand in Helen's death. My eyes met Darren's, gaze unwavering. We both felt the cut of her death, but where was it bringing us? I looked away, unable to hold his gaze without feeling hot anger.

"I found Todd Jackson and Marcus Cumberland trying to intimidate Henry Kapinski behind the town hall the other day," I announced.

Everyone turned to look at me. Whispers started to buzz, but I kept going.

"Henry wants to help whatever way he can now. I also think that I may have pissed Marcus off a few times now."

"Are you fucking kidding me?" Danny's voice cracked.

Jason shot him a questioning sideways glance. Darren sighed, his fist in his hair.

"Marcus is the most twisted of all of us, enjoying the hunt for more than just food if you get what I'm saying," Danny explained to Jason before turning to me. "And you managed to get on his bad side?"

"Twice. I will admit that I had a little help in both cases," I said, catching Jason's eye. He gave me a stiff nod.

"Just great."

I shrugged. I had survived a number of Clan-less wolves over the years. While I admit to being afraid, I was starting to believe that I wasn't alone any more. Darren scowled at me, but finally turned his attention back to the meeting when I refused to say anything more.

"Now that we know who he is using for some of his intimidation tactics," he went on.

I glanced around at the wolves filling the space in the Manor. I looked at Christian and Frank and other wolves that had once tried to just live a normal life. Most of them had shied away from these animal politics when I was a kid but now they rallied behind Darren, the lesser of two evils.

Danny was following Darren like he always had. He had followed us everywhere when we were kids. But that was back when we had been kids. Now, we had grown up into monsters, or at least it looked like Darren and I had. Danny seemed to be his same old self. He gave me a lopsided smile as I looked up at him and I pushed back the urge to hug him. Jason smacked his shoulder and pointed towards Darren as if to say Listen!

Not wanting to hear more about Jonathan's ruse, I ducked out of the kitchen. My decision had been made. If I was to stay, I wanted to know everything I had missed out on. I locked the door to the Manor's office behind me. Thankfully, there was a Keurig coffee machine sitting atop a small black refrigerator. I had a hot porcelain Wonder Woman mug of coffee at hand as I poured over stacks of files and log books.

Once upon a time, this had been my Grandfather's office, then my Father's office. Now I sat behind the desk as if I ruled it. I pinched the bridge of my nose, not wanting to think about it more. Instead, I rolled the chair across the floor towards the filing cabinets. They could probably hear the chair over the hardwood downstairs, but I didn't care. The door was locked and I was on a mission.

What were they going to do? Break it down?

There were so many businesses owned by members of the Clan that supported the Clan. They gave a small pledge to the Clan's funds, available to any member of the Clan that presented a dire need. It was like someone keeping an emergency bail fund. There was Aunt Magda's restaurant, Granger and Katherine's winery, Norman and Marne's farm, and even the real estate that my Grandmother owned across Wolf's Head. We even had a doctor's practice on the books.

There were years of history that I had to catch up on and members of the whole Clan that I had to re-acquaint myself with. According to the records there were around fifty werewolves residing in Wolf's Head. All except for two, if I counted myself, were male.

Possibly more than forty eight male werewolves in a twenty mile range? Many of the werewolves were old. We could live for a very long time, but it became lonely and sometimes an old wolf would pick a young mate. That is how my generation came around. Young and bullheaded, we were on the other end of the spectrum. How did we survive so long without a civil war before now?

Then I came across something else that made me pause. It wasn't another business, but another name. Everything else fell away, unimportant now as I stared down at the trembling paper. I set it on the desk and shoved my shaking hands under my legs.

There had once been another female werewolf in the Wolf's Head Clan. The name on the file was Bianca Hale. I racked my brain for the name, but nothing came to me. Why hadn't I known about her? Faoladh like myself were so rare.

All I had was a woman's name on a Clan roster from 1992. I shoved away from the desk, gliding in the chair towards the filing cabinet. I grabbed a fistful of old Clan rosters, searching through them for her name. There was no Bianca Hale in the roster after 1993. I had been born in 1990, but there was no way that I would have remembered her if she left in '93. There was no expulsion form, a figurative boot from the Clan.

Why had she defected? Memories of my life as a Clan-less wolf came rushing back to me. I had my first change shortly after we moved from Wolf's Head. I had been unable to control it, unable to return to human for form a very long time. Other Clan-less wolves had hunted me, sought to mate me. Bianca would have gone through that if she left the Clan. What had been so great as to make her voluntarily leave?

"What are you doing in there?" Someone knocked at the heavy door. The voice was unfamiliar even though it rang in my memory somewhere.

I didn't bother to answer, instead I rolled back to the filing cabinet and continued to look through the old files. Moving a decade back, I pulled another roster file and scanned it for her name. There was a Bianca on the list, but the last name was different. The name in this list was Bianca Blackford.

The file slipped between my knees and clattered to the floor. There came another set of knocks on the door again. It was hit so hard that it shuddered on the hinges, threatening to give any moment. I quickly gathered up all of the files and laid them on the desk before moving to unlock the door. Jason stood on the other side, a questioning look on his face.

The smell of male wolf wafted into the room, it was spicy and carried the bright scent of green apples. I looked up from the files to see Jason still standing in the doorway. A deep green and blue flannel shirt hung open from his wide shoulders, a gray tee underneath, and his hands were shoved in his pockets. He took in the mess that I had made of the office from the scattered files to the empty coffee mug. This was the man that Darren had appointed to become the head of his guard. I watched him, wondering what there was about this formerly Clan-less wolf that made Darren trust him.

"What do you think you're doing sneaking around in the Warren Manor?" He asked, on the offensive.

I was taken aback. "I'm not sneaking around. I used to live here."

"You slipped out of the meeting without warning. I call that sneaking."

My lip twitched, barely holding back a snarl. I recognized his voice now as the man who'd stood outside my door the other night, calling me Doll Face and questioning my strength.

"I'm not fooled by you; I've dealt with your kind before."

"My kind?" He stalked into the room, slamming the door shut behind him.

It took all of my will not to flinch at the boom. I turned my eyes up to him, challenging him with my own glare, gathering the psychic presence of my dominance.

"What do you know of my kind?"

"I know that Clan-less wolves like you hunt anything that runs free. You try to own it or kill it," I shot out of my chair.

"You were a Clan-less wolf," he growled back at me.

Fight taken out of me, I slumped in the chair with my arms crossed over my chest. He was right, but I was nothing like them. Nothing like him.

"You know," he said. "I was the one who had to help you out yesterday."

My head jerked up. I took in the man pacing the room, from his tattoos to his military hair-cut. This was the wolf that had charged out of the woods yesterday. This was the wolf that had set his head in my lap when we left. I knew it when Darren said I owed him, but it was just now registering.

94

He turned away from me, pacing across the room. After a few times around the room, he paused and glanced at the desk. Not approaching the desk, he asked:

"What were you doing?"

I sat up in my seat, fingers moving to lie over the manila folders. Looking up at Jason, I debated sharing what I had found out with Darren's right hand man. He stared me down, dominance pushing out around him as if he was trying to use it against me. I let my own dominance out and let it fill the room. His nostrils flared as it hit him. His eyes darted away and his knees wavered as his dominance pulled back.

"Now I see why Darren likes you so much," he muttered. "Feisty with the punch to back it up."

I couldn't hide the grimace that twisted my lips. Jason cocked an eyebrow, but didn't say anything more. This wasn't personal, this was work. He seemed to understand that and I respected him for not pushing.

"I was trying to catch up on what I had missed the past eight years, but I got sidetracked. I found a name that I didn't remember."

Jason shrugged, pulling up a leather chair. "And that means something? It's a big town."

I stared him down until he turned his eyes towards the desk's surface. He grabbed the file laying on the top of the pile.

"While I lived here, my father was the Clan's Alpha. He knew everyone in town," I gestured to the rosters. "Dad took me everywhere with him when he was...alive. I met everyone."

"Okay then," he nodded. "What does this mean then?"

Jason had opened the file folder. I leaned forward, scanning until I found Bianca's name. This was the roster from further back. His eyes followed my finger, face not showing anything. I wanted to leap across the desk and smack him. How could he not understand?

"As long as I have ever known there have only been two female werewolves in this Clan. My Grandmother and myself. Apparently, I was wrong."

His lips parted as he read further. "This would make her related to Jonathan, perhaps his sister. Maybe she knew best what her brother really was. Pushed her out the same way he pushed you out."

He pulled the file closer. As he leaned back, tapping his finger to his lips, I felt something fall into place. I smiled wide, enjoying myself for the first time. We tossed ideas back and forth, speculating on what had driven Bianca from the Clan. We didn't know how it would help Darren, but it was worth checking into. We needed anything we could use against Jonathan.

"You are staying to help, aren't you?" Jason changed the subject.

I looked at the mess of manila folders, forms, and photos that we had strewn about the office. I had enjoyed our work here, it gave me hope. Hope that Darren really was the right man for the Clan. Hope that everything that his father had put him through hadn't so much twisted him as shown him right from wrong and good from evil, cheating on his fiancée notwithstanding. I thought of him standing before the crowded room of wolves downstairs, including the men who had once followed my father. We could really do this if we worked at it, I thought.

"I'm here to help," I finally agreed. I suddenly looked up, knowing where he was going with this. My jaw clenched for a moment, regretting that deep down what part of me had already decided. I had the moment I stepped off the plane with Marcus.

I was going to ask to be initiated into his Guard.

Yet, it meant something else as well. It meant that there couldn't be anything between him and me if he accepted me into his Guard. My grandparents had faced the same problem, only circumventing it when she chose to leave her position in his guard. If I remained in my position, then it would only add to my power to maintain a distance between us. Yes, I needed that right now.

I raced downstairs with Jason hot on my heels. Following Darren's scent through the house was easy, my wolf led me to him like she was in heat. My will was strong and my decision was made. I dropped to my knees before Darren, while half of the Clan watched, looking up at him through my bangs.

"I ask you, Darren Blackford, to allow me to become part of your Guard," I said from my submissive position.

I heard the mumbling of the other Guard members behind me. My Grandmother sidled up behind Darren, a slight smile touching her lips. Was I playing into the plot that my grandmother had spinning in her head? I wouldn't doubt it.

"Shit, Diana."

"Answer me," I begged through clenched teeth.

My Grandmother pulled something from the pocket of her suit jacket and slipped it into Darren's hand. She closed his fingers around it, their eyes connecting for a brief moment. When he looked back to me, I saw that some sort of message had been conveyed. Oh, yeah, I was definitely playing right into my Grandmother's hands.

"Fine." His hands pushed me back so that I sat on my knees. I opened my eyes and looked up to see the pain in his. "Diana Warren, I trust my life in your hands, claws, and teeth. I accept you as my Guardian."

I held out my shaking palm under Darren's. The warmth of his hand radiated up to mine. He placed the cold pendant in my hand, his sliding out to cover mine. His eyes closed for a long moment, as if he wanted to take back the whole thing.

There was no going back now, no going back to my old life in Monterey. I was Clan whether I liked it or not. I was a Guardian. The words had sealed it; it was the disc in my hand that I didn't understand. When Darren pulled back, I saw the medallion. Two oak leaves nestled a wolf's paw print with the Warren insignia on the pad. The chain ran over the side of my hand, fluid like a snake. I pulled it over my head and felt it settle low on my breast bone.

The tattoos over my ribcage began to warm as if there were sunlight playing over my skin. It was a pleasant sensation that said perhaps I was on the right track. That warmth began to fill the room and I felt my cheeks flush. I watched the faces of the others in the room as they felt it, too. My Grandmother's eyes caught mine and a small smile truly split her lips. She knew what it was, remembered the feeling when others couldn't.

"You are the trusted Guardian of our prospective Alpha," my Grandmother said formally. "Your loyalty is to him and our Clan."

The warm feeling in the room flashed brilliantly hot. I called out, feeling it run through me. As my sight came back to me, I caught the smell of fresh wildflowers. Laughter bubbled out of me, light and not quite my own. As good as it felt, I was slightly worried that this could become a problem.

"She's returning to us," my Grandmother whispered.

I nodded. My head swam at the absence of Her as she faded. My palms touched the floor and I dropped my head. Submissive. A smile crept over my lips as I glanced up through my bangs at Darren. Submissive, but only barely.

He laughed and shook his head before falling into a kitchen chair. I remembered what it felt like to feel him inside me, his hands in my hair and his lips on mine. The remaining warmth of the Goddess sent shivers through me. My nails dug at the floor as I tried to chase the memories away. A moment of weakness was all that it was. Right?

I pushed myself up to my knees just in time to see the other Guardians look away. The way that they tried to hide their expressions, I guessed that they had smelled my sudden excitement. I was going to be the lone female in a man's world soon. Not only that, but I am the woman that slept with the boss, so to say.

Shit.

CHAPTER SIXTEEN

My alarm buzzed at an ungodly hour. I remembered falling to all fours to beg to become part of the Guard, I remembered the touch of the Goddess during my initiation, I remembered Jason grabbing my arm and telling me flat out that training began at six am. What had I gotten myself into? I rolled out of bed, grabbing for the workout clothes strewn across the floor. It consisted of black running pants and an old loose Batman shirt that Magda had lent over a purple tank top.

My phone vibrated, its little green light blinking. It read:

Warren Manor. Basement. Training.

I grabbed an apple and headed out the door with a determination set into my bones. Reaching the front door, I realized that I had no way of getting there other than running. I had done enough running, on two feet and four, lately. Reluctantly, I turned around and sought Aunt Magda to see if I could borrow the keys to her Ford. Her lips twisted as she processed my request. I was sure that she wouldn't let me behind the wheel of her precious car, but she raised a finger as if a light went off over her head.

"Come with me," she waved as she went through the back door. "She isn't road legal at the moment, but I'm sure she will do for now."

"That's a tad bit naughty," I commented, becoming curious.

She pulled on the heavy barn door and it slid aside with a loud groan. The inside of the barn was littered with junk, things that could be classified as rusty treasures or scrap metal. Dominating the center of the barn was something buried beneath a wrinkled and dusty blue tarp. Aunt Magda jerked it off with a secretive smile.

A classic muscle car appeared, beautiful in a red so dark that I thought it was black at first. Only as I circled it did I see the glitter of dark red under the dark coat.

"It is a 67' Chevrolet Chevelle," Aunt Magda said. "And, technically, she isn't mine. Thomas left her with the house when he packed up and left. He hasn't asked for her back so I'm assuming that he won't miss her."

"He left this?" I almost shouted my words. I couldn't believe that her ex-husband would simply leave behind a gorgeous car as this. It wasn't a Mustang by any means, but it was sleek and fast. I was almost crying with excitement.

"You should probably work on getting her legal, registered and insured and all that. She might need new parts, but I'm sure she will get you from point A to point B just fine for now."

I nodded with enthusiasm. I barreled my Aunt over in a massive hug before dashing back towards the house for my wallet. Excitement thrummed through my fingers down to my toes. This was mine.

I slid into the driver's seat, worried that she wouldn't start after sitting in the barn for as long as she had. Magda assured me that she had taken the car out for a ride or to and kept with the tune ups.

"Just in case," she shrugged.

Just in case a certain someone needed transportation if they ever came back? I thought it, but didn't say it. Had everyone been waiting for my return this whole time?

I turned the ignition and felt it hum to life beneath me. Not once in my life had I thought that I would be driving something so beautiful. This was truly the most exciting thing to have happened since I had returned to Wolf's Head. I made the vow, right there, that I would purchase it from Aunt Magda eventually. It wasn't her car, but it would make up for my freeloading at this time.

CHAPTER SEVENTEEN

The Manor was dark in the early morning. I let myself in with the key I had taken from Aunt Magda the day before. The dim morning light illuminated my way through the empty halls. It smelled of wolves, carrying a rich foresty scent as the Clan mingled. As if I had never left, I found the door to the basement.

Harsh florescent light burst from the entryway when I opened the door. I had to shield my eyes as they adjusted. Hesitantly, I began my trek down the staircase. Behind me was the pantry that I remembered, filled with dry goods and canning jars, but before me the long room was covered in blue sparring mats. Slices of the concrete floor peeked from between the mats.

The boys stood in a cluster at the other end of the basement, dressed in loose shorts and t-shirts. I was starting to recognize faces, catching Christian and Danny in the fray. In the center of the circle was Jason, his military stance giving away his past. It was something I had seen in my step-father plenty of times. Jason's tattoos were dark against his pale, freckled skin, a hint at the truth that lay beneath his surface. He was on our side, but he was in no way safe. His dog tags dangled over a hard chest. My heart beat frantically. This many men in a small space made my wolf raise her hackles.

Shut up, we can do this, I told her. We can show them that we aren't prey anymore.

We were never prey.

Too often we struggled against each other. This time she settled back, but didn't let her guard down. We stepped forward and the guys all raised their heads. Their nostrils flared, taking in my scent. Christian and Danny smiled widely, but Jason's face remained static.

"Let's see what you're made of today," Jason stated. The bond we had created yesterday was set aside. I could see the objective evaluation processing in his eyes. I wondered what part of the military he had been a part of. Marines? Navy? Air Force?

The boys jostled me around as I entered their circle. I swayed, my balance threatening to tip. Hands grabbed at places they shouldn't have. Instinctively, I knew that it wasn't Danny's doing. I spun around, putting my nose to Christian's. His eyes widened with surprise. I grabbed his wrist and jerked him forward, putting my foot before his as I spun out of the way. He crashed to the ground.

With a growl, he pushed himself up. His leg spun out at mine and swept me off my feet. I landed on my ass just as he pounced on me. I was pressed into the mat with another wolf on top of me. My wolf did not like that. He growled in my face, but had forgotten to hold down my arms. My elbow crashed into his cheekbone and then I pulled my knees between us to force him off me. As quickly as I could, I jumped to my feet. Someone pulled the pissed off Christian away from me.

But it wasn't over. Jason stepped forward, his feet moving apart in a battle ready stance. He knew what he was doing. I would almost bet that he knew how to kill too. That would make two of us. I rushed at him, but I found myself airborne for a split second.

What the hell-then I crashed onto my back. All of the air whooshed from my lungs.

This wasn't going to be easy. But, hadn't I already known that?

I pushed myself up, glaring up at Jason. Over and over again, I tried to hit him. No matter how I threw myself at him, he would just toss me again. This time, I leapt from my crouched position, wrapping my arms around his waist. He stumbled back, but only barely. His giant hands grabbed me by my waist and pulled me away.

Before I knew it, I was flying backwards through the air again. I heard the loud pop of my back on impact and my head kept going. It hit the concrete with a loud crack. The world was swimming in my vision, but I still pulled myself up. My wolf growled and I felt a surge of energy. Never. We would never stay down.

Jason suddenly stood over me, hand extended. I pulled back.

"You have a lot of balls, Warren."

I took the hand cautiously, waiting for something else to happen. He simply pulled me to my feet and clapped a hand on my back. The word was still spinning.

"I think it's about time that we get some food," he suggested while leading me to the staircase. "Then we can move on to training."

Training hadn't begun yet?

Still, there was a sense of accomplishment settling in as I climbed the staircase. We crowded in the kitchen while a couple of the older men began to prepare omelets. My grandmother padded in, wearing white and grey flannel pajamas with bunny slippers. The bunnies on her feet had sharp stuffed fangs and crazy eyes.

She smiled dreamily at us. It seemed that she liked having people, wolves, in the Manor again. It used to be the center of the Clan and always full of werewolves. It didn't matter what they were here for, whether they came to eat and chat or to speak with the Alpha over Clan matters, everyone had been welcome. Then Jonathan had ruined that sense of family. Everyone had been terrified to set foot in the Manor again. My grandparents ruled the Clan from their perch inside the Manor and no one questioned it.

No one wanted to get on Petra Warren's bad side. She was the one who had hoisted Jonathan Blackford up by his collar and drove him away from becoming Alpha back then. The only thing that had kept him alive was his two boys. She didn't want to leave them fatherless like I had been. Behind every good man was a badass Bitch. She sat next to me and I laid my head on her shoulder.

There was no sense of family like this in Monterey. There was my mother, the little ones, and my step-father, sure. As much as I loved them, they weren't like us though. When I had to change, I ran alone. When I ran alone, there were threats from everything: cars, coyotes, and even other wolves. Here, we ate together, we ran together, and we lived together.

The sense of safety was so convincing at times.

"Don't you worry," my grandmother said as if she could read my mind and stroked my hair.

But I did worry. I worried about my safety. I worried about who could be trusted. I worried about my urge to kill Jonathan. Was I human or animal? Which was worse?

After breakfast and a break to digest, Jason had us all run five miles and began to teach us some fundamental self defense. My grandmother ran along with us and even showed us a few things she'd learned in her days as a Guardian. There was a new life in her that I'd never seen before. Still, the day was long and despite my werewolf metabolism, I was sore and tired.

We sat around the table, food sitting between us even though it was beginning to feel more like a war council than a dinner. Aunt Magda spoke into her plate, pushing around the pieces of pot roast. My Grandmother spoke with a glass of wine in her hand, finger outstretched from the stem as she pointed to Darren.

"You need to realize that you will have a lot of duties on your plate once you win this," my Grandmother told him.

"I need to win first," he said, exasperated. "It doesn't feel like I can, right now."

"You can do it," Aunt Magda offered.

I shoved a piece of bread and roasted pepper into my mouth.

"Jonathan can only hold up this facade for so long," my Grandmother sipped her wine.

"Yes, and the moment he breaks and becomes the monster that he really is he will already have the Clan."

I choked on my bread. Aunt Magda clapped me on my back and it went down in a hard lump.

"He has half the town scared into following him, and the rest are too afraid to raise a hand against him."

"There is no breaking," I interjected.

Everyone turned to look at me.

"Your father has always been a monster. We all are monsters, but he embraced it a long time ago."

I reached out for the pot of mashed potatoes and dolloped a more than heaping portion onto my plate.

"You think we're all monsters?" Darren asked.

"Aren't we?" I shoved a spoonful into my mouth, cheese and sunny herbs blooming in my mouth.

Aunt Magda's jaw dropped. I couldn't understand why, she had seen what happens here, in a town full of monsters. I looked to my Grandmother, her wine glass pressed to her lips as the gears worked in her brain. I suspected that she understood. She had been where I am now. Only, she didn't have Jonathan gunning after her. She wasn't a threat to him anymore. She hadn't killed him back then and he thought she wouldn't now.

"What I'm saying is that we can do anything that he can, technically speaking."

Darren sighed. He seemed to do that a lot lately.

"That doesn't mean that we want to, Diana."

I threw my hands up in the air. "If that is what it takes to be safe from him, then why not? If being safe from Jonathan means killing him then that's what we have to do."

I sounded so ruthless and cold. That frightened me. It wasn't the human or the wolf in me that made me a monster. It was the need for survival and the desire to know that others would have to live in fear if we didn't win that made me this monster. If it meant that others could sleep safely in their bed, then what was a little bit of bloodshed? What was a little more of my sanity?

My wolf began to pace, anxious and worried. Hunt. Survive. Thrive. Hunt. Survive. Thrive. Survive. Survive. I tried to quiet her, but her pace became more frantic. She was trapped within me, helpless. Danger loomed outside these walls and she couldn't protect herself from inside me. She wanted to push free. I closed my eyes, trying to soothe her, reassure her that there was no danger right now. Yet, he was out there and we knew it. Safety was nowhere to be found if he was out there.

"This would be a lot easier if we could just kill him. All of these politics and policies and do-good ideas are getting in the way."

"I think you're forgetting that he's still someone's father," Aunt Magda said softly.

I grabbed my still half full plate and left the dining room. In the kitchen, with my back against the counter, I held my plate and ate standing. I needed the silence and solitude. Even if it was just for a moment. I needed people to stop looking at me as if I had grown two separate heads. What if we were all monsters? Maybe they were just better at denying it than I was.

Mashed potatoes were the god of comfort food, I thought, especially when they were made by Aunt Magda. I shoveled the creamy mixture into my mouth, feeling my wolf return to her safe corner within me. This would all be so much easier if they acknowledged what we all were.

I'm not wholly human, not in the least. Realize that you aren't either.

Outside the window, I saw glimpses and flashes of fur. In the woods there were Guards, prowling and protecting. I set aside my plate, stomach full, and began to pull at my clothing. The wolf wanted to do something. She wanted to run free and so I let her.

Just as the change finished running through me and I wobbled on four legs, Darren appeared in the kitchen doorway. I gave a little bark at him then pushed through the swinging screen door. In the woods, I found another wolf. I nipped his flank, letting him know that I would take over for now. I would watch for him. He gave a nod and bounded away.

I let my wolf take control because I'd had enough with control.

Chapter Eighteen

Aunt Magda usually wasn't home; she had her restaurant to worry about. So, I dragged my laptop down to the kitchen and set it up before I made myself a cup of coffee. I'd already gone running and sparred with the members of the Guard today and needed time to myself. I said a quiet thanks that my Aunt had wifi set up in her crooked old house and tried to figure out how her coffee maker contraption worked. It took about ten minutes to figure out, but it produced a mean cup of coffee.

I checked on my mother's Facebook page, scrolling through the photos of the kids and new paintings that she had done. After a while I moved on to browse the Facebook pages of friends that I had left in Monterey. They all seemed to be going on with their lives without me, posting pictures at local bars and family gatherings. Not a single one of them had messaged me, asking when I would be returning.

A pang of sadness shot through my chest. What kind of a life had I been living there that no one would miss me if I decided to up and leave? My fingers hovered over the keyboard, debating whether or not to message them first. Finally, they fell away.

To console myself, I began browsing shopping sites. Shoes, boots in particular, I found comfort in purchasing. My cart was full of expensive, knee high boots: some with high heels and some with no heels. In the end, I narrowed it down to one pair of boots. They were knee high and made of really light beige leather.

Feeling a bit regretful over my expensive purchase, I pulled up several news websites including one from Monterey and one from Northern Maine. I browsed the lists of DUIs and petty thefts, only semi interested. There had been a car crash outside of a small Maine city and someone had attempted to rob a convenience store in Monterey, California. What caught my eye; however, were the unsolved murders. One article had stated that a man was found along a deserted stretch of the coast. The sand had half covered his body and hidden him for a few days until a hiker stumbled over the corpse. While it had been ruled an animal attack at first, there were a few witnesses that reported seeing him harass a young woman. The witnesses remembered the tall Nordic beauty of the brutish man. One witness even vowed that they would never forget the strange beauty of the girl he'd been caught arguing with.

It was her eyes that had caught him, he said to the reporter. The witness called them gold eyes.

I cursed under my breath and closed the internet browser. Great, just great. The last thing that I needed was a reminder. The entire article was a reminder that my hands weren't exactly blood free, either. I had taken his life and hadn't felt a bit of remorse. I had left him there in the sand. His body had been in one piece, I told myself. I hadn't torn him to shreds and bits like Jonathan had enjoyed doing so much.

No, I had killed this man because he had forgotten Clan. He had forgotten compassion. Hunt and kill were his only prerogatives. Why should I have felt remorse for self defense?

I slapped my hands to my face, rubbing as I moaned in frustration. Life was never black nor white. It was built in shades of gray and red.

The Guard was always welcome at Balefire and I wasn't sure if I was eating for free because I was family or because I was now part of Darren's Guard. It brought us together in a public setting, a safe place. We dug into a bowl of melted cheese and chilies with hot tortilla chips. Christian and Danny were quickly going through their basket of chips, while the ones close to Darren, Jason, and me were going nearly untouched. I nibbled, but only half heartedly.

"Hey, Diana," Danny nudged me beneath the table. "You okay?"

I nodded, still thinking of the article I had read the day before.

"Don't worry about anything," he said to me. "Everything will work out the way that it should."

I shrugged. Worrying might have been what I did best. I worried about my moral compass. I worried about the rift between me and my wolf. I worried about the state of the Clan. I worried about everything.

I leaned back in my seat at the restaurant table, eavesdropping on my Aunt. She was leaning over the bar, close to another woman with long, golden hair and a badge at her hip. I elbowed Christian and asked him who she was talking to as I watched Magda's fingers slip over the other woman's. From what he told me, my Aunt was hitting on one of Wolf's Head Police Department's detectives. Magda was flirting with a cop?

It wasn't for information, I thought, but that didn't stop the woman from leaking little facts. She gave Magda her condolences on Helen's death, knowing she was a friend of the family apparently. But, that conversation slipped into another about a woman who had been found mauled in her own home just outside the town. The woman shuddered as she spoke of the bloodbath it had been. I closed my eyes against the images of the general store, of the Manor when I had been fourteen, and Jonathan's bedroom when his wife died.

Under the table, I pulled my smart phone from my pocket and searched the internet for recent news articles. I got a hit, clicking on an article that placed a murder in a nearby town. When I saw the name Hale my blood ran cold. I shot out of my seat, heading for the door.

I fumbled as the door was pulled open before me. A face I'd hoped to never see again appeared, a smile splitting her lips. Fionna looked as though she'd just come from a very high paying job, her pastel business suit tailored to her lithe frame and a diamond pendant hanging between her collar bones.

"Diana!" She said, happily, as she reached out to place a hand on my arm.

I jerked away reflexively, just in time to see frustration cross this woman's eyes. I eyed her arm for any trace of the silver bracelets. Why was she trying so hard to be friends with me? If only she knew the truth. If only I could tell her.

Instead, I told her I needed to go and shoved my way past her. Outside I ran towards the Chevelle, parked by the side of the building. I leaned against the brick building and texted Jason to meet me out here. I was pacing, my keys in my hands, when he caught up with me.

"What the piss is going on?" he snapped. "Darren almost followed you out here himself until he saw his fiancée."

"I think Bianca may be dead," I said, trying to even my breath to keep my hands from shaking as I passed my phone to him with the article on the screen. "I overheard that detective talking to Aunt Magda about another murder."

His face turned white. After a long moment, he nodded. "Go on ahead to check it out. I'm going back inside to talk to Darren."

I slid into the driver's seat of the Chevelle, sending the address from the article to my GPS. Fear was slowly subsiding into a sense of purpose. I had to know what happened. The car roared out of the parking lot. Ignoring the speed signs, I sped out of town. Not again, I thought.

The house that the GPS led me to was low and painted a dark green. Thinking twice about parking outside the crime scene, I kept going up the street until I found a small cemetery and parked the Chevelle in the back. It didn't take me long to walk back to the house.

It had a low stone wall that led to the garage. There was a ghost of a vegetable garden at the far edge of the house and there was limp yellow crime scene tape hanging around the front door. The juxtaposition was disheartening. I glanced over my shoulder to make sure no one was watching and made my way towards the mailbox. Fingers crossed, I pulled open the little door. Shoved in the back was a single envelope. I reached in and pulled it out, hand shaking when I read the name. Bianca Hale.

The article had said that she had been murdered a week ago, but the smell in the air was strong with blood and fur. I walked around the house to the back door, stepping in a piece of rotten zucchini from a spilled garbage container. There was a swinging hook locking the screen door in the back. I dug out my wallet and jimmied my credit card in between the door and the frame to lever the hook. The door itself just swung open at my touch.

The smell that came through was unmistakable. Blood, sweat, burnt food, and wolves. Jonathan had been here, his scent musky and woody amongst everything else. I knew that he relished in the animal that lived inside of him, claiming a strength that nature intended. I liked to think that we didn't always have to be monsters. We could push it aside, live normal lives most of the time.

I left my gloves on, knowing that a week old crime scene was probably still a fresh crime scene around here. There were no pictures on the walls or end-tables of the living room. The couch was plush and the throw blankets looked well used. The home looked well lived in, but there wasn't much evidence of who she had been.

I followed my nose to where Bianca had died; the carpet of the hallway had dried to a rusty shade of red. Nearly the whole length of the carpet, from living room to the bedroom, was smeared with the gruesome, rusty stains. It looked as if she had crawled down the hall on her stomach. Smears desperately painted the wall. I knelt down, inspecting the carpeting. The fibers of the carpet seemed slashed in places. I ran my fingers along the slashes and froze.

They lined up with my fingers, raking across the carpet like claws. I crouched lower, leaning forward to search the carpet. My right arm extended and found another raking of claws across the carpet. Curious, I leaned in close to the blood stain. After a moment of hesitation, I took a deep breath. Jonathan's scent was faint, hidden by a more feminine woody scent carried on the blood. Bianca.

Grinding my teeth together, I forced myself down the hallway and past the rusty smears across the walls. Over and over again in my mind, I pictured this woman attempting to crawl away from Jonathan. Her hands had been half changed, attempting to use claws to defend herself, to escape him. I could hear imagined screams ringing in my ears. They echoed the screams I once made, of fear and defiance. The door to her bedroom was wide open, a black comforter lying askew over blue sheets as if she had just gotten out of bed. On the night table was a picture frame.

A woman with short, dark hair smiled up at a taller man that had dark hair shaved into a mo-hawk. He wore a concert tee and she wore an open leather jacket. Behind them was a concert stage. She had the same dark brown hair as Darren, cut short around her face. Her arms were around the Mo-hawked man, squeezing so tight that you could see the fabric of his shirt bulge around her arms. She had loved this man. She had a life away from the Clan, away from her family.

Had she known about her two nephews? Would she have been able to save them from what they endured with their father if she had stayed? Or would her time have ended sooner? My gloved fingers traced the edge of the frame tenderly, as if I were able to connect with this woman who was now dead.

Suddenly feeling as if I were intruding, I set the frame aside.

I was here to learn more about her, I had to remind myself. She was gone and couldn't argue if I rifled through her past. Surely, she'd want someone to know why she had died. With a lump in my chest, I pulled open the nightstand drawer. Inside were a stack of letters and a hard bound book with no title. Flipping it open, I found handwritten pages and photos carefully hidden between the pages. Snapping it shut, I held it close to my chest. Maybe I was messing with an open homicide case, but I already knew who had killed her. I also knew that he was going to get his when I had the chance, when I had the strength.

Hearing the rumble of another engine outside, I stood up to leave the bedroom. My stomach rolled when I came into the hallway again. Bianca had clawed her way down this hallway as if she could escape her killer. He wouldn't let her too far though, toying with his own sister as if she were a small animal. How loud had she cried? Had she begged him to stop?

Would this become me?

"Diana?" Jason's voice snapped me out of my haze. His face was grim. "Darren said that we shouldn't be here."

I nodded, carefully stepping over the blood stains. How had the forensics team recovered all of her?

When the front door opened, we booth froze. No one other than Darren knew that we would be here. Jason dove into the hallway and I heard the creak of footsteps in the kitchen. The draft brought in a fresh scent. Jonathan had returned. My fingers grasped Jason's arm with a death grip. The heat of anger rolled through my head, followed by the chill of fear when my eyes fell on the smears that clawed their way towards me. I wasn't ready. I probably never would be.

"I can smell you, little huntress."

"You're a dead man walking," I mumbled. The footsteps come closer, seeming to echo on the cheap hardwood floor.

Dragging Jason back into the bedroom, I had to find a way out of the house. I ran to the window, trying to push it up. It was old and painted shut. I quickly removed my gloves to pry my nails in between the window and the sill. Paint cracked and chips splattered around me. I had to put my foot through the screen in order for us to jump out. Stupid me, I had compromised a crime scene. Big time.

We tumbled into the side yard. I prayed that Jonathan followed us into the bedroom as I ran for the cemetery. Sparing no time, Jason made a flurry of noises revving his truck's engine as I raced down the street. It would buy me some time. He sprayed gravel as he shot out of the driveway.

How would Jonathan have known that we would be at Bianca's home at that precise moment, I pondered?

I veered off the roadside and into the woods, jumping over naked brush and dodging between trees. I burst out into the graveyard, feeling victorious. Something hard hit me from the side and I crashed into the ground. I dragged my hands through the dirt, trying to push myself up when someone grabbed me by my hair. My head was jerked up so that I could see what was waiting for me. I swore under my breath as I stared down two more wolves.

CHAPTER NINETEEN

Todd stood a few feet ahead of me, smiling like he knew some big secret. I let out a breath of relief when I realized that Marcus Cumberland wasn't amongst them. Maybe I had a chance after all. But there were two other wolves here that I didn't recognize right away, one of them holding me down by my hair. The wolf standing behind Todd was short, his muscle compact against his body. He couldn't have been more than five foot four. Short for a man.

Craning my neck, I could get a glimpse of the wolf grasping my hair. His tall frame was bent over, one knee on the ground in order to hold me. His muscles were wiry and above his long nose were dead eyes. My wolf sized them up. She whispered in the back of my mind as she paced, telling me that these were truly wild wolves, Clan-less wolves. These ones enjoyed killing and we had met them before. She knew their scent.

"Can I help you boys?" I couldn't help the snarkiness that fell out of my mouth. Perhaps it was my human defense mechanism, sassing them to death.

"Mr. Blackford just thought that you would help us send a message to his son," Todd said in that friendly voice that hid the true malice of his words.

I had a pretty good idea of just how they planned on sending their message. I didn't want to play any part in it. I pulled my hands under me, readying myself to run. All I had to do was catch the tall one off guard. If I could, his grip would loosen enough so that I could make a break for it. I hated the idea of leaving the Chevelle, but I didn't know if I could make it into the car.

A shock of realization rocketed through me. I knew where I'd run into these wolves before. They were faces that I had seen during my short stay in Texas. The shorter wolf crept forward, breaking ranks with Todd. His eyes were alight with pleasure and I knew that both had been given a get out of jail free card.

I was in for a world of hurt if I couldn't escape. The short wolf to my right, with his messy reddish hair and stocky shoulders, had stalked me for a month before trying to kidnap me from a shopping mall. His face still bore the three faint scars from when I had panicked, one scar trailing over his nose and eyebrow. When I had only meant to slap him in defense, I didn't realize that my hand had half shifted. Both of us had been surprised by the amount of damage that I had done.

"I missed you," he smiled wide, a hand touching his eyebrow.

"She is all yours boys," Todd waved me off and turned around. He didn't care what happened from here on out. Climbing into his truck, he winked at me before turning the engine over and gunning it out of here.

Shit. Shit. Shit.

The hand fell away from my hair and I shot forward. I was almost vertical when he grabbed my ankle. My body crashed down into the dirt and gravel again. Gravel bit into my cheek, my jaw still vibrating from the impact. It was two on one now. The grip on my ankle pulled and dragged me through the gravel. My shirt rode up, stones scraping against my stomach. I flipped myself over and slammed my free foot into the wolf's face. He roared in pain, his hands falling away from me. I took the chance to crabwalk away.

"I cannot wait to watch you bleed out like a lonely cur," the short wolf was suddenly standing over me.

I couldn't afford to freeze now. I dropped and rolled away, but his weight crashed into me. My limbs were pinned to the ground before I knew it. My wolf thrashed inside my head. She pushed out, my fingers curling. His face hovered over mine, mouth split open to reveal sharp teeth. They looked similar to mine, only sharper.

Fuck. My heart hammered. His body pinned mine. I struggled, but his grip only grew tighter. He tensed the moment before he stuck.

Suddenly, he was jerked away. His grip pulled me along and I was flung to the side.

I knew that I was in deep shit now. My body hit the wet earth and slid down into a ravine. The tall wolf towered over me as he approached the edge of the ravine. I stared up at him, lying flat on my back. While I couldn't see the other wolf, I could hear the distinctive sounds of shifting.

I scrambled backwards in an awkward crabwalk. The one still in human form leapt down after me. His eyes swirled with colors, moving between human and wolf, as he reached for me again. I grabbed his arm and yanked him forward. He wasn't expecting it and he crashed face first into the mud as I rolled away.

I was on my stomach when something heavy crashed into my back. I clawed at the earth, trying to move. My heart leapt into my throat when I heard the low growl next to my ear. My wolf raised her head in defiance. She wasn't going to die here. She wasn't going to die in a ditch in a tiny cemetery.

A sharp pain burst in my shoulder. I saw stars as it spread. Out of the corner of my eye, I could see the wolf's head, his muzzle wrapped around my shoulder. He growled low and shook his head. I cried out in pain. It felt like my shoulder was on fire.

My heart thundered as I waited for his next move. If he decided to pull back, those long and sharp teeth would tear muscles and tendons to shreds. Over and over, inside my head, I prayed that he didn't. For once, I prayed that he wanted to play more before he began to cripple me. It would give me at least a little bit of time. All I needed was more time.

Trying to look at the other werewolf, my head swam. The throb began to set in my shoulder. I was bleeding everywhere and the wolf on top of me was lapping it up. The tall werewolf smiled, crouching to creep towards me like an animal. His lips split and I could see how sharp his teeth had become.

Like something out of a nightmare, I watched as his jaw popped and elongated. His human nose seemed to melt away as his face pushed forward. His tongue grew the fastest, the long pink thing lolling around while his bones struggled to catch up. Human skin was now stretched over the muzzle of a wolf.

He yipped and whined as he kept crawling forward. I felt the pressure on my shoulder begin to release, his teeth pulling away from my flesh. He growled, the low rumble shaking through me, at the approaching werewolf while still standing on top of me, still biting my shoulder.

"Don't fight over me, boys," I said into the dirt.

I didn't think that either of them had heard me, but it didn't matter. The werewolf's hands that were pressed into the mud beside my face began to shift. The fingers lengthened as his nails grew dark and sharp. His hand snapped out, more cat like.

It collided with the wolf on top of me. He stumbled away from his perch on top of me and I struggled to my feet in the mud. I didn't make it far. A hand circled my ankle and I was jerked off my feet. I crashed and slid into the ditch once more. I was doing a lot of that today. We were just a few slaps away from mud wrestling.

Behind me, the two Clan-less wolves growled at each other. I sat motionless, hoping that they would forget me. I was nothing more than meat and there was always a pecking order, even without a Clan. Glancing back through my screen of hair, I saw the second strike.

The one in full wolf form was dripping blood from the side of his neck, his lips pulled back over his teeth. He lunged at the hairless, half shifted wolf. The half shifted wolf jumped back, but his clumsy form couldn't escape the grace of the wolf. Teeth caught the leg of the half shifted wolf and they tumbled down into a mess of flesh and growls.

I took the chance to run for the Chevelle. Pain shot through my shoulder and I could see stars in the corners of my vision. With my heart thundering in my ears, I jerked the door open with my good arm and slammed it behind me. As I tried to turn the engine over, the commotion in the ditch began to quiet. I glanced up to see them turn their eyes on me.

The engine finally turned over and the Chevelle roared to life. I kicked it into gear and shot into motion. They seemed to think twice about jumping a moving vehicle, until the wolf lunged at the window. The glass cracked under his weight, but he rolled over the car. I slammed on the gas. In the rear view mirror, I saw the second wolf finish his shift.

They gave chase, following the Chevelle down the road like dogs chasing a car. My heart still hammered and there was mud drying on my cheek. Pressing down on the gas, I soon lost the two Clan-less wolves, but I could hear their angry howls over the rumble of my engine. I cradled my arm in my lap while cold shivers raced down my spine.

Living life without a Clan had been dangerous. The Clan-less wolves hunted each other over food and territory. And it seemed that life had followed me here.

The Chevelle rumbled to a stop in Aunt Magda's driveway. My hands were trembling as I used my good arm and my foot to kick the door open. I ran inside and locked all the doors and windows that I could find before running upstairs to lock myself in the bedroom. I fell to the floor, pain coursing through my shoulder. Peeling my shirt away from the wound, the smell of my own blood filled the air. It was a mess. Some of it had begun to heal. Flesh and skin slowly pulled itself back together, but I worried that there was more damage than I could heal. I struggled to catch my breath, to hold the wolf in.

My fingers twitched and ached. I held them back from curling, placing them flat on the floor so that they wouldn't begin to change into paws. My teeth pressed into each other, pushing on my jaw. Fear and fighting the change made my whole body tremble. I was safe now. I didn't need to change. I didn't need to run anymore. I clenched my jaw shut, willing my teeth to pull back. Tears slipped down my cheeks.

My nails scratched along the hardwood floors. I wasn't going to win this battle. I was too scared. I was alone. *Teeth and claws were safe. Hunt. Survive. Thrive.* I gripped my hair in my hands, trying to push her away from the surface. The gap between us grew the more that I fought. The more I struggled, the more that she won. The change flowed to the surface, a hot burst that ran from my core to my skin. *We are safe now. I will protect us. I will heal us.*

We need to work together, I thought. We need to stop fighting each other.

You are too scared.

I've felt your fear, too. Neither of us are alone; we are the same. Let me win just one more time. Just for today. We are safe now. There are things we have to do now.

She pulled back cautiously, not sure if she should believe me. I took in a deep breath and tried to calm my shaking body. The trembling subsided and a hunger settled in. Arguing with yourself took a lot of energy, I thought. I stood up too fast. The world spun, fast.

Still a little wobbly, I leaned on the bed to wait for my head to finish spinning. When I realized that it wasn't going to any time soon, I shakily made my way downstairs. I was completely alone. Magda was at Balefire, like always, and I had no idea where Jason or Darren had gone.

I pulled a container of cookies off of the top of the fridge with my good arm and brought it into the living room. Tossing the cookies down, I grabbed my phone and sent texts out to Darren and Jason. My shoulder was slowly healing, sucking away my energy, and I didn't want to be alone anymore. In the meantime, I had to do something to keep myself occupied.

Wiping my fingers on a paper towel, I unzipped my muddy backpack and pulled out the notebook. Bianca's handwriting was all over it, evidence of a sister wolf that I would never be able to meet. As I worked through the whole package of cookies and a foraged box of cheese crackers, I made my venture through the snapshots of her life.

I followed the curve of her handwriting, the little doodles and notes in the margins, and the smiles in her photos. She had lived the semblance of a happy life away from the Clan. There are a few times that she mentions the "Others", which I could only assume were Clan wolves that had roamed close to her territory. She never explains why she avoided us, why she left.

119

She talked about her attempts to live a normal life, balancing the wolf inside of her with the desires of her human life. She was dating a musician of a popular local band. He had dreams of making it big, but she was too happy in her small world. She couldn't leave the forest behind; it was too much of a risk. Had her boyfriend known?

I sighed, closing the notebook, and laid my palm against it. You didn't have to die, Bianca Hale. You were innocent, only trying to attempt a life of happiness like the rest of us. It had been me that had dug her out of our files and exposed her name. Only Jason and I had known about it.

Jason.

Had he been the one who told Jonathan about Bianca? He had known that I wanted to talk to her, to ask her why she left the Clan. He had known that I was going to the scene of her murder, leaving shortly after I did. That would have given him time to call Jonathan. Yet, he had helped me to run out of the house when Jonathan appeared. Yet, I ran straight into an ambush.

I slowly leaned forward to retrieve my phone. All of the texts were from Darren, asking what we had found, if we were safe, and finally informing me that Jason was locked up in the Sheriff's Department. I texted him back, asking him to come here. I would fill him in on what happened and probably have to apologize for my stupid decision.

He responded shortly that he was too busy right now. Fionna needed him. I leaned my head back, fighting away tears. There was Clan all around me, but in this moment I felt so alone and scared. I glanced at the notebook in my lap. Had I made a mistake? Had Jonathan taken her life to send me another message?

You are alone.

CHAPTER TWENTY

"How can you sit here and do nothing?" I slammed my hands on the solid desk between us.

"Sit down," Darren growled back.

I plopped my ass in a leather chair, still glaring up at him. I could feel the hot edge of tears in my eyes.

"Someone died," I whispered. "So many people were killed. Someone that I loved is dead."

He ran his hand through his hair, gripping it tight in frustration. How could he be hiding in this little office while there was so much bloodshed going on around us? How could he sit around?

"You don't care," I shot up from the seat, spinning around to leave. "Apparently you just want the power."

I was jerked back by the collar of my shirt. I tumbled into the back of the leather chair. Darren was suddenly in front of me, growling and eyes on fire. I dug my nails into the leather chair, trying to stay angry, to keep from trembling. The pressure of his dominance pushed from every direction, like he'd lost control of it.

"How dare you tell me that I don't care! You ran away from us!"

My jaw dropped. "Of course I ran away! You tried to help kill me!"

My head spun. Why was I back here if he had tried to kill me? Why had I slept with him if he did? He shook with anger before me, seeming to be on the edge of howling. I buried the urge to touch him with a snarl. Why was I back here?

"I was trying to get you out of there," his voice was low and hot. "We were trying to get you away from Jonathan. You were the one that fought us and ran right to him. He wasn't just there to challenge your father. He wanted you dead that day, too."

My blood ran cold. What was he saying? I remembered stumbling into the general store, head throbbing from my close call with Jonathan. I remembered how my father's howls echoed in my ears. I could barely hear anything else. I remembered Jonathan's livid face as he stormed through the doors of the general store. He had been after me. Darren had been trying to get me away from him.

Howls were echoing in my head again. My wolf was pacing, her footsteps quickening with fear. She pawed at my consciousness, her nails dragging like knives. She needed to run away. She needed to survive. I had to think of something else. I had to stop going back to those memories.

Darren knelt in front of me, a hand reaching out, hovering but not touching. I snarled at him. Back away. I couldn't be here. I had to be somewhere else. I couldn't be in an office, pacing and arguing. I had to get justice for Helen. She had been there to help me. That was something that I knew for sure. I had to do this for her. I had to do it for Bianca, who'd only been trying to live a normal life.

Taking one final deep breath, I steeled myself and forced the trembling to stop. Pulling myself back into a standing position, I lurched towards the door. Darren's arm shot out between me and it.

"You took an oath to this Clan," he reminded me. "You took an oath to protect me and obey me."

I hung my head, letting my dark hair fall between my eyes and his hot gaze. It moved things inside of me that I didn't want to feel ever again. Too bad he didn't take an oath to never lie to me, I thought.

"Stay in the Manor, stay with everyone else until I can figure out what to do."

"Every time I turn around, someone is trying to kill me," I said, my voice low.

"You know what that means, right?"

"That I should have never come back to this forsaken place?" Even though I said it, my hand moved to the tattoo that had instilled itself over my skin. The Goddess was here with me and I had needed her, needed Clan.

Darren gave me that look that said 'Stop That'.

"It means that they are afraid of you. They will only triumph if you are dead so I need you very much alive."

I had no intentions of staying put. I could barely sit still. No matter what he had once tried to do for me, I couldn't understand what he was trying to do now. What did he hope to gain waiting around while a killer walked free? I nodded, waiting for him to move his arm aside. Our eyes met and I think in that instant, he knew that I wouldn't listen.

He gave a heavy sigh and moved aside. As the door closed behind me, I heard something crash from within.

The house was empty and I was restless. Not entirely up to giving my wolf control, I began to pull on a pair of jogging pants and a sports bra from my grandmother's closet. I couldn't stay in the house forever, no matter who wanted me dead. Running emptied my mind and sated the wolf inside of me. Yet, reluctantly, as part of Darren's Guard, it would look awful if I disobeyed his requests to stay in the Manor.

My chances to go running had become limited. Darren wanted me to have a buddy at all times. I wasn't quite up to that, knowing that I still wasn't everyone's favorite yet. I doubted that I would ever be. Yet, I had chosen to stay with the Clan. I had chosen Darren as my Alpha and at some point I would have to start listening to his orders. Perhaps not all of them, but most of them.

I decided to take the energy that was coursing through my twitching muscles down into the makeshift gym in the basement. I wrapped my hands, weaving the fabric in and out between my fingers to keep from chafing. I'd punched the bag naked before and my knuckles had bled for a while, even with my healing abilities.

I swayed back and forth in front of the bag, trying out a rhythm before I began to jab at it. Immediately, a sharp pain shot through my left shoulder. The muscle still hadn't finished healing yet. I feared that the pain would always be there. My arm grew stiff, my thumb going numb, but I attempted to push past the pain. I wouldn't allow myself to be crippled. That was one thing that I couldn't afford here in Wolf's Head.

As I practiced quick jabs and dodges, a rage began to boil to the surface. I wasn't allowed to go outside on my own anymore. People that I had loved and trusted were dead. Jonathan was inviting Clan-less wolves into his menagerie with promises of a reign of blood. And on top of that, a long lost Goddess had decided that I would be her mouthpiece upon her return. My life had been spiraling out of control ever since I stepped foot off of that airplane.

Part of me wished that I could have just gotten back on. I wished that I could have kept on pretending to be human. But look how well that worked out for Bianca. The woman had left the Clan and lived for a few decades on her own. In time, she had friends and had even fallen in love. She had set up a life for herself and Jonathan had still managed to rip it away. I wouldn't let him have mine. I wouldn't let him take the Clan.

Lost in my own rage, I didn't smell the wolf coming up behind me. Hands grabbed my body and threw me back. I slammed into the wall, the room spinning. While I struggled to suck in another breath, I became aware of someone else in the room. My vision took a moment to clear, but when it did I recognized the face before me.

Danny.

"I'm sorry that I have to do this," he said, voice low. His eyes refused to meet mine even as I searched them, stunned.

Before I could react, his hands tightened around my throat. I clawed at his arms with human fingers. My shoulder was burning, jolts of pain running down into my fingers. My injured shoulder felt weak. The edges of my vision began to turn black. My wolf thrashed inside of me and a new, hot well of rage began to build.

"You have no idea what she is like, Diana. She is beautiful and radiant. I need her to love me."

"I...I called you my friend," I choked out. "T-t-trusted you."

I kicked out at him. My heel met the soft flesh of his groin and his knees buckled. His hands fell away and I gasped for air. Thinking that I had won, I let myself stand trembling for a moment. Growling, Danny rushed me. I hadn't accounted for his anger and the strength he drew from it. We tumbled to the ground. My right arm was pinned beneath his larger body, leaving my useless arm in his grip. He used that to his advantage, keeping me pinned with his weight as his hands found my neck again.

This was no longer the meek kid that had followed me around the Manor. He wasn't the awkward boy in school anymore. The Danny I had known was gone. In place of him was a body filled with lust and desire channeled into violence, all of that now directed at me. He needed *her* to love him, was what he'd said.

I arched and thrashed beneath him, but he rode me like a bull. I could feel the length of him begin to grow hard against me and my stomach churned. His remorse had quickly turned to excitement. I saw his dark eyes slip to wolfish gold as his animal took over. I wanted to blame Jonathan, but that wasn't who he had blamed. He couldn't possibly have been this twisted all along. His cock ground against me, the harsh fabric of his jeans burning through my cheap jogging pants.

With a loud growl, he shook me. My head bounced off of the cement floor. Ringing in my ears deafened me. Hands getting tighter and tighter, he kept shaking me. Sickened and depraved of oxygen, my limbs began to shake. My body ached, feeling as if I were about to fall apart. I had survived so much and now I was going to be taken down by a mousy brat that had posed as my friend?

The hot well inside of me finally burst. I began to slam my numb fist against the side of his head as my vision grew darker and darker. My left arm felt like lead. It throbbed with the pain that coursed through my shoulder. I let it fall to the floor, useless. As he reeled back in pain I squirmed my right arm free and continued to beat him with my good hand. I thought that I would run out of oxygen, but little by little, his hands slackened. I took the opportunity to roll us over. My knees pinned his upper arms to the floor while I cradled my useless arm. Growling low, I punched him. The hard bone of his cheek stung my knuckles but I just kept punching him. The anger burned hot across my skin. I was boiling alive with it.

"What the hell are you doing?" Someone shouted.

My body was pulled backwards, but I still reached my hooked fingers towards Danny. He curled onto his side, hands going to cover his face. I had destroyed it, his cheeks swollen over his eyes. The floor was stained with blood beneath where we had fought. I jerked my arm out of someone's grasp to touch the back of my skull. My fingers came away sticky with blood.

I was going to get brain damage at the rate I was going.

"What were you doing?" Christian asked, looking between me and Danny.

I showed him my bloody hand. "I think that's our mole."

I didn't feel anything while I said it. The thought of his hard cock as he tried to kill me made my stomach roll. I felt unclean all of a sudden. My pelvis throbbed from what he had done and my shoulder was numb, the pain too much for me to process. If I was a betting woman, I'd say that I'd undone all of the healing I'd done last night.

"Are you alright?" Jason appeared at my other side. I nodded in response to make him go away, not daring to look in Danny's direction. It didn't matter if I was physically okay. I was alive and an old friend had broken my heart. Unable to say anything, I kept my mouth shut. Christian moved to scoop him up, no doubt dragging his sorry ass out to the holding cell.

Somehow, I made my way upstairs to the bathroom. I tore my clothes off and shoved them into the bin. My grandmother could afford more. For a long while I just stood beneath the hot stream of water. Nothing would make me feel clean again. The memory of what he'd done made my stomach roll and I vomited onto the floor of the shower. Angry, I wanted to punch the wall. But my shoulder refused to move, making my arm dangle uselessly.

I heard the click of the door and felt my heart skip a beat. I jerked back the curtain to see who was there. The door was closing and a pile of fresh clothes sat on the vanity counter. I couldn't smell who had been here through the mist of body wash and steam. With a sigh, I shut off the water and jerked a decorative towel from the wall. Grandma could suck it.

In the mirror I saw the dark bruises that ringed my neck. Two, dark oval bruises stood out. They'd been his thumbs, pressing into my arteries, cutting off blood from my brain. How much longer could I have held out? How close had I come to dying in a basement by the hands of a friend?

There were yellow bruises on my face and stomach from the fight in the cemetery yesterday, the black bruising given way in the night. My shoulder was swollen and angry. My hands didn't look much better. I laid my hands out flat on the white counter, willing my knuckles to heal correctly. I couldn't feel them to know if I'd broken anything.

Exhausted and in more pain than I'd ever known, I crashed into a plush leather chair of the office with a bottle of water in one hand and a casserole pan in the others. I'd been exiled while they inspected Danny. I dug my fingers into the nutty scented blondies, pulling out a chunk as my stomach growled. The subtle taste of cashew butter coated my mouth as the soft crumb broke apart. My hand shook so much that my lap was littered with chunks of the pastry.

After half the pan had disappeared, I began to feel more normal. I sat back and looked out the big bay window and into the wilderness of Northern Maine. It was barren and grey, but I could make out the bodies of wolves moving amongst the naked tree trunks.

The door behind me opened and I could smell Darren, warm and woody.

"Well, you nearly killed him from blunt trauma alone," he began.

I shrugged, not ready to say anything. My eyes were fixated on the pelt of a particular wolf. Grey and coppery brown blended into the wintery scene so well, but I fought to keep my Grandmother in my sights. She was always out there. She wanted to protect us.

"He's not dead, but Christian said he pissed himself on the way outside."

I snorted, sounding odd coming from myself. Throwing back the last of the water, I let the bottle fall to the floor and leveled my gaze with Darren's.

"Now we know who our double agent was. He's the reason that Bianca is dead. We can't keep him anymore."

Was I in shock? I must have been. My body had become numb and emotionally, I felt empty.

"Did you have to eat all of the cashew blondies?" he gestured to the pan in my lap. I looked down to find nothing but the one corner and some crumbs left in the pan.

"I was working out," I pouted, pretending at normalcy. "My regular workouts now include assassination attempts and those really work up the appetite."

He half sighed and half laughed as he dropped into the chair beside mine. Absent mindedly, he began to play with my foot that hung over the arm of my chair. I closed my eyes and let myself relax, comforted by the warm touch. With him in the room, I felt completely safe. I couldn't decide if it was because he was to be my Alpha or if there was more to it. I wouldn't think of his fiancée right now. This wasn't about that.

Right now, I promised myself I wouldn't think about it.

"Why wasn't there anyone else with you in the basement?" Darren broke the silence.

"There was. Danny."

"That's not what I meant. Why didn't you bring a sparring partner or a spotter down with you? This wouldn't have happened had you not been alone."

I yanked my foot out of his grip and cracked open my eyes to glare at him. "I thought I was safe! This is Danny we're talking about. So scared that he couldn't jump off a diving board and he just tried to kill me inside the Manor of all freaking places. The place I thought was the safest of all."

He rubbed his hand over his face, barely suppressing a growl of frustration. I stared him in the eyes, not bothering to back down. A hot searing pain rushed through my shoulder.

"Is it not right for me to want you to be safe?"

"No, because right now you're asking me to rethink everything I do. You're asking me to give up solitude. Besides, you don't have any room to be telling me what to do." I shot up out of my seat. The sudden movement jarred my shoulder, making me flinch. "You can shove it."

I stormed out of the room before he remembered that he had every right to tell me what to do. I'd taken an oath. In the kitchen, I chucked the casserole dish into the sink. There was no one else in the room with me and I snorted at the irony. At least this time I had taken a moment to make sure that I was well and truly alone. I gripped the edge of the sink with both bruised hands and took a deep breath.

My first change had happened away from the Clan. For as long as I had been a true wolf, I had been a Clan-less wolf. Alone, I became accustomed to the solitude, to surviving on my own. It hadn't been safe by any means, but all I had to look out for was me. So much had been thrust upon my shoulders when I returned to Wolf's Head and now Darren was being overprotective.

I'm not a scared rabbit anymore. I know how to protect myself.

"Lover's quarrel again?" Someone asked behind me. I glanced over my shoulder to see Christian leaning against the counter.

"Shut your stupid face."

"No." He laughed. "Just let him say whatever he wants. We all know that you aren't going to listen to him anyway. You are probably the only one here who *could* disobey a direct order from him."

I straightened my back, trying to hold my chin up even though every small movement hurt. He was right, though. Throughout this ordeal, I had gone against nearly everything that Darren told me.

"Stop making so much sense," I said jokingly, trying to take the edge off what I felt. "What are we going to do with Danny now?"

In the past, we would have just killed Danny for treason as well as his inability to control his wolf. This was a new day and age; the circumstances were more than muddled. We had to be humane and tend more towards rehabilitation. I wanted to believe that he could become the same Danny that I remembered from my youth, not the sexual sadist that he had become. I should have wanted rehabilitation for him.

I should have wanted life for him. But I didn't. I wanted to see him hurt.

Jason appeared in the doorway, hands in his pockets and a tired look on his face. He had last night in jail at the county sheriff's office for me.

"You're cradling your arm," Jason pointed out. "What's wrong?"

I attempted to shrug, but it hurt too much. As much as I wanted to brush it off, I was scared that it would never heal right. Jason caught on and motioned for me to sit. It was a silent command if I'd ever seen one. Christian herded me toward the chair, afraid to touch me. His eyes moved to my neck, brows furrowing in concern.

Jason returned with a first aid kit and a sling. The surface wounds had healed over night so there was no reason for the first aid kit. Still, he dug out an Ace bandage and wrapped my shoulder tight before gently guiding my arm into the sling.

"If you would stop using it you might be back to normal tomorrow night," he said.

"Too bad I need it now," I grumbled. What was I going to do when I go the next surprise visit from Marcus? From Jonathan, since he liked to drop in on me so often?

"Deal with it. That's what we're here for. You can shift, but that won't heal you completely if it's as bad as I think. Magic might seem all powerful, but even it has its limits. Maybe you should sleep here tonight."

"Oh, hell to the no. You couldn't pay me enough to sleep here."

"Fine, then one of us should stay at Magda's with you."

"Fine," I growled.

I thought of what Danny said when he began to attack me. He mentioned a *her*. This mystery woman wanted me dead for some reason and he was more than happy to do it. Why had he been so eager? I figured love could make you do crazy things, but murder?

No matter how I racked my brain, I couldn't come up with any woman who might want to kill me. Hurt me, maybe. I knew I'd gotten off on the wrong foot with Christopher's girlfriend, but that didn't equate murder. And she seemed pretty monogamous. I couldn't see her seducing Danny into a murderous rage.

"Do you think we might be able to interrogate Danny?" I asked.

Jason's lips tightened. "He's in shock right now. He's so terrified of you that he can't even think straight."

My heart sank. The thought that I could instill more fear than my childhood monster broke another piece inside of me. My wolf raised her head triumphantly because we had defended our life and protected our Clan. She didn't see the evil of the situation. It was a human evil.

"That's a good thing," Christian nudged me with his elbow.

I shook my head and moved away from him. Wrapping my arm around myself, I stepped back from the conversation. This wasn't right.

"Just let him go then," I muttered as I retreated. Grabbing my things, I began the walk back to Aunt Magda's. Both Jason and Christian moved to accompany me, but I put my foot down. I shoved at them with my dominance, telling them that I needed alone time. They recoiled back from me, not particularly happy.

Once I was a good distance from the house, away from the smells of the prowling wolves, I let myself give in. I fell to the forest floor, sobs racking my body. My fingers began to curl in on themselves. The sobs were choked as my body twisted in on itself to become something new. My wolf came forward, willing to be strong for me when I was weak.

This time, I curled my fingers into fists and felt the biting pain of my nails in my palms. This time I held onto control. I laid on the forest floor for a while, soaking in the peaceful sounds of the woods around me.

I was not weak.

But I would not be a monster, either.

Chapter Twenty-One

I looked over my wide mouthed coffee mug, a smirk twisting the corners of my lips. Jason moved about the office, papers in hand as he pushed his black framed glasses up his nose. A grey knit cap covered the coppery fuzz he called hair and his flannel sleeves were rolled up to reveal the tattoos that ran down his arms, like thick black tree silhouettes beneath an empty moon.

The manor smelled like coffee and the grinding gears of werewolf brains. Okay, maybe I was just imagining the second smell. My Grandmother and Darren were hunched over the desk, discussing his possible future duties as Alpha. Darren's hand was knotted in his hair and his eyes were fixated on stacks of papers before him. The Clan was just as much a business as it was a family.

We were all anxious, waiting for Jonathan's next dirty trick. My shoulder was still sore and I was going to get brain damage if I kept getting caught off guard. Not only had Jonathan ambushed me with the Clan-less wolves, but his mole, my own friend, had revealed himself in an attempt to kill me. It was beginning to feel like this feud would go on forever.

"Earth to Diana," Jason snapped his fingers in front of my face.

I jerked upright, coffee sloshing onto my jeans. He raised an eyebrow, glancing to Darren to show that he knew who I was staring at. My face grew hot so I turned my attention to Jason's mess on the floor. Spread across the oval rug were notes and file folders, Jason's plan of attack.

"Jonathan seems to be pretty confident of whatever he has in his back pocket. It doesn't seem like he has much leverage, but I'm betting he hasn't played all of his cards yet," Jason sat back, landing on the floor. His arms resting on his knees, his thumb and forefinger pinching his lower lip as he thought.

"So, the only way we can beat him is to win a straight out challenge?" I proposed.

Darren looked up, jaw tight. It was old school traditional to fight in a challenge, contestant versus contestant, for the role of Alpha. Newer rules proposed not only the physical and dominance match, but a bout for popularity amongst the Clan. It was imposed to prevent crazed tyrants from seizing control. I snorted at the irony that it presented.

"Do you think that you could win against him?" I asked. I knew that I couldn't. Standing up to him was one thing, but if fight came to fight I would be scraps on the ground.

He let out a shaky sigh that said he wasn't truly sure. Darren's dominance was as strong as my own and I knew that despite my fear my dominance was a force to be reckoned with. It kept me alive many times. Jonathan wasn't in the habit of using his own dominance to his advantage. He relied on the monster that he had fostered inside of himself built on sheer strength and savagery. I had no idea if we could overpower him with dominance alone.

My wolf moved inside of me. She brushed her fur against my skin, an imaginary feeling that felt all too real. She was trying to comfort me.

"You could appoint someone to fight on your behalf," my Grandmother suggested.

"How could I make someone else fight him?"

Panic rising inside of me, I quickly changed the subject: "Then let's show him that we can have as much power as he does."

Everyone in the room turned to look at me. My heart hammered as my eyes met Darren's.

"How do you suppose we do that?" my Grandmother asked warily.

"I say that we look beyond the Clan. His influence would affect every supernatural in the state of Maine," I said. "Why don't we go to some of the other supernaturals and ask for their support?"

"That's a bit unprecedented," my Grandmother said. Her back straightened and her eyes met mine. She pulled on her dominance, whether consciously or not, and used it to try to push me into submission. "We cannot look weak in the face of other supernaturals."

A flash of heat swept through me. She had shot my idea down flat and I had no idea why. She hasn't treated me this way since I had first accused Jonathan of killing Helen. Even then, I wasn't sure why she had rejected me. At that time, she had said that we would handle it like wolves. Whatever she meant had gotten us nowhere but bruised and sorry.

"Why do we have to be so damn insular?" I asked, defensive. "Are we supposed to stay in our little Clan and slowly kill one another like good little monsters?"

"Stop it," Darren shot up from his seat, slapping his hand on the desk. "We protect one another. Who's is to say that they give a rats ass about us?"

I slammed my mug down onto a side table. I shot up, socked feet stomping over Jason's files and forms. Darren and I stared each other down, eye to eye. His dominance pushed at me, but my own formed a wall around my body that he couldn't breach.

"And if we don't try? Are you going to stand by and watch Jonathan destroy the rest of my family? The Clan?"

He could barely stifle the growl slipping between his lips. It was low and potent, a warning of violence if I ever did hear one. "As much as I missed you over the years, you cannot return and suddenly think that you know what is right for this Clan!"

His arms were held straight at his sides, hands balled into fists. Red spots were forming on his cheeks. A flash of gold ran through his eyes. I had never seen him this angry in my life, but I wasn't about to back down.

Jason and my Grandmother sat in shocked silence while Darren and I pushed at each other with our dominance. I was pressing hard, feeling his start to slip and give away beneath the force of my anger and betrayal.

I was the dominant.

"That is enough!" my Grandmother shouted.

Darren and I reeled back from each other in surprise, each turning to look at the woman that had just stepped into a dominance battle. We glanced at one another. I'd been about to win.

Petra Warren had always played life like a chess game, knowing her own moves several turns in advance, such as how she begged my mother to pressure me into returning for the funeral so that I would become just as much a part of this as she was. Now, as Jonathan waged a war against his own people, her game was falling apart. And, perhaps she thought that her last pawn in the game was rebelling.

Suddenly, I reached out and pulled her into me. Her arms wrapped around me in return. I whispered in her ear that we would all be okay. I told her that our Clan needed to evolve, to keep up with the times. Curls slipped from the bobby pins in her hair as she nodded, her cheek against mine.

"Daddy would have wanted this," I whispered.

When I was small, he had visited other supernaturals. We sat at the bar of a restaurant owned by a dark skinned vampire. He had told me stories of the fae that he had visited in the woods of Maine. I wanted to think that my father had wanted this all along. He would have wanted us to grow as a community, not just factions. I smiled, thinking that he had prepared me for it.

She pulled back from me, her hands gentle on my shoulders and a determined look in her eyes.

"We ask for help," she agreed.

I looked Darren in the eye over my Grandmother's shoulder. The grim look on his face said that he didn't like it. I had won this time.

But, I still didn't understand why he put up this much of a fight. What was so wrong with asking for help?

As we talked it over, I agreed to take charge of our visit to the Fae Court that resided in the forest not far from here. Visiting Thaddeus, the vampire that had staked Maine as his territory, seemed easy in comparison. He was kind of a family friend despite being a vampire. At least, a friend of my fathers.

Visiting the Court of faeries might be asking for trouble. They were tricky and selfish creatures at times. Faeries lived for a very long time, much longer than most vampires. They became removed from the real world and what went on up here. How they lived reflected that: Underhill. Their dominion below ground was becoming claustrophobic, their magic to create the once massive kingdoms vanishing. If something were to happen to us while we were down there, we might not be able to get out of the Court. That was if we could even get inside at all.

"I may know someone who could get us an invitation into the Faery Court," Darren said, his voice soft.

We all turned to look at him.

An hour later, Fionna was in the office, leaning a thin hip against my grandfather's desk. She was dressed in a tight, pastel pink sheath dress with thin gold bangles around her wrist. Her long, white blond hair had been done up in a top knot that was threaded with braids that continued across her crown. She looked elegant and refined, a big contrast to the trepidation in her eyes. She looked at us, the new keepers of her secret.

She was Fae.

A swan fae to be exact. It explained her fair hair and dark eyes. Over the course of the afternoon she explained why she left the Court of Thorns and Wine, as she called it. She and her sisters had been abused by the hands of a lord within the court. When their Queen refused to believe the accusations, Fionna abandoned the only home that she had ever known. She chose to hide amongst humanity and even managed to get a job in the nearby city.

My grandmother had taken an almost imperceptible step back from Fionna, her arms moving to cross her chest. I took it that she didn't like secrets. Not ones that she couldn't control, that is. Darren had taken a stand beside his fiancée, his rear leaning against the desk and an arm wrapped around her lower back. He beamed at her. I shit you not. It seemed that his world had dwindled down to her and her alone.

My wolf and I sulked in the corner. She held a constant low growl that reverberated through my skull, but it didn't stop my own thoughts. There was so much running through my head. Why didn't he tell us? Did he not trust his own Clan?

"I really don't want to go back there," she said, her light voice almost shaking with fear.

Darren pulled her into the protective cavern of his body. "We aren't asking you to."

"Then what are you asking of me?" She looked at us, her gaze lingering on me as if she knew what Darren and I had done.

It's all in your head.

"If you could just tell us what would get us an audience with the Queen."

I thought I saw Fionna sneer at the word queen, but it was gone as quickly as it came. She thought about Darren's words for a long while, the silence settling over the room and making me uncomfortable. She pulled herself up to sit on top of the desk and I almost growled. That was my father's desk. My grandfather's desk. I wanted her out of this room, out of my life. Jason caught my sour expression and asked me a silent question by raising an eyebrow. I couldn't just tell him that I had slept with our boss. I couldn't tell him that I was just dealing with jealousy that I didn't even want. I shut it down, trying to be professional.

"I could ask one of my sisters when they visit next. Serah should stop by tonight. If she begs an audience with Aoife, the current queen, then you will most likely get what you are after. Be sure to bring an offering. Never visit a royal without an offering of peace."

Darren nodded, his hand absently stroking her arm. She gave him a small smile.

"There are a few details of our wedding that I'd like to discuss with you later," she said, changing the subject as she toyed with the front of his shirt. "That is, if you have time. I'm sure this has you very busy."

That was it. That was about all I could stand. I lurched out of the room very conspicuously. Quickly, I formulated a lie to explain myself, but Jason was hot on my heels.

"What's your problem?" he asked.

What was my problem? That was the loaded question of the day. It started with the fact that I had feelings for a man that was about to get married to another woman. Never mind the fact that I'd already slept with him because he didn't tell me he was engaged. And to top it all off the monster that killed my father was out for my blood, too, sinking low enough to use my own friends. So what was my problem?

I shrugged. "Call me when you guys are ready to visit the Court."

"You're just going to leave right now? Darren doesn't want anyone to be alone."

"Last time I listened to him, someone I thought I trusted tried to kill me in a place that ought to have been safe. What else do I have to lose?"

"You are one bitter girl. You know that?"

I was caught off guard. It wasn't anything I had thought of before. Angry, yes. Bitter?

"You're not the only one with a jaded history or going through hell right now. We all are. All of our lives are on the line."

I didn't say anything. I hated it when someone else was right. Sucking in a deep breath, I tried to let go of the anger that I was holding on to. Jason seemed to understand that I was putting in the effort and put a hand on my shoulder. Somehow, a level of trust had grown between us. He and I had probably seen more than any of the wolves here. He understood the anger I was feeling. He also learned to not let it eat him up from the inside out.

Chapter Twenty-Two

It took everything I had in me to keep my knees from shaking beneath me. What we were about to do had been my own idea, but that didn't mean it wasn't frightening. Darren, fidgety and anxious, had already expressed how he didn't like this one bit. With paper grocery bags in our hands, we stood at the door to a Faerie Court, patiently waiting invitation inside.

I wanted to go back to Thaddeus's bar. The visit to the strongest vampire outside of Maine City had been more than pleasant. Not that there were very many vampires in Maine. It had been a reunion topped off with buffalo wings and milkshakes. While he had turned us down, he had a valid reason and we didn't walk away hungry, that was for sure. He was one man with no following, no soldiers to offer. This was something else altogether. I mean, vampires were human once upon a time. The fae never were.

The door before us was beautiful, heavy wood beams held together by silver filigree that bore rose gold flowers. It stood, defying reality, between two oak trees. There was nothing beyond the door other than more forest, but as it opened, a new world showed itself. Jason peered around the oak tree, clearly perplexed. I laughed, but it was almost forced.

Inside, my stomach was doing nervous flips. Not just any kind of flips, back 540 flips. This wasn't a good idea by any means, but it was our best bet when it came to seeking help.

We were here, at the edge of reality, to beg for help from a Faerie queen. Two fae stood in the doorway. A thin woman and a hoof footed satyr greeted us at the entrance. The woman was a foot taller than they satyr, her face long and angular and framed by white blond hair that danced in the air currents. She had black eyes that seemed blank and inattentive. I wondered briefly if she was one of Fionna's sisters, maybe the Serah she had mentioned. The satyr on the other hand, had a thick red-brown beard that gleamed with copper and sparkling green eyes that seemed out of place with the soldier's scowl. He was dressed with finely crafted leather armor and carried several blades at his hip.

"Welcome to the Court of Thorns and Wine," the woman moved back, extending her arm inside as an invitation.

"We are eager to meet your Queen," Darren said to her, careful not to thank her. "We have brought a token gift from Balefire."

"You may be wasting your time," the man said while eyeing the bags.

They held jars of preserves made from edible flowers and faery wines, the spirits distilled from grapes grown inside the Court itself and imbued with a wild kind of magic. This wasn't edible for humans or werewolves, but perfectly acceptable for the Fae. Humans would go mad with the lust for fae creations, unable to eat mortal foods again. If I were to eat one of the preserves, even Magda's food would taste like ashes. After that, if no one were to invite me into the Court, I would starve myself and fall into a depression until I faded into nothing. Just the idea of that kind of loss of self gave me chills. Aunt Magda said that a few of the fae liked to come to Balefire quite a bit and she dangerously started to cater more towards them.

"We will do anything it takes," Darren's face was hardened. "No one wants this man to head the Faoladh Clan. I hope that your Queen will see that as well."

We followed the satyr down a dirt tunnel, the swan woman following close behind us. Tree roots braided themselves, creating knots that traveled the length of the hallway and climbed the walls to craft themselves into sconces. Held tight by the knots around the sconces were jewels and flowers. The dirt of the wall moved, undulated as if something would reach out of it at any moment but couldn't quite break free. My skin crawled with a static-like feeling. The wooden door closed behind us, making Jason jump. I reached out, grabbing Jason's arm. He wasn't alone in a foreign world and I wanted him to know that. The hallway twisted and turned, leading us deep into the Court. My grip on Jason's arm tightened.

We emerged into a grand, circular room, a ballroom almost. The tree roots arched above us, lights budding over them like leaves. They cast a soft white glow over the room and everyone in it. I had been told of this room before, stories my father had told me. He said that if you didn't look right at the roots, you could see the twilight sky. There was nothing there this day.

The stone walls were carved to resemble the architecture of a cathedral, the arching windows revealing nothing but darkness. Atop columns stood statues in the shapes winged creatures. They reminded me of gargoyles, but nowhere near as grotesque. Ahead of us was only bright thing in the room, a gleaming silver throne. It appeared to be the silver stump of a tree with thin silver limbs twisting upward to create the arms and back of the throne. Soft, earth toned fabrics spilled from the the seat and three intricate rose gold flowers topped the back of the throne.

In it sat the Queen, her long and pale legs elegantly crossed at the ankle. Her coppery hair was piled at the base of her skull, ivory antlers rising out of the top of her long face. Her dress was made of silk that flowed from deep green to dusky grey and woody brown. It wrapped around her lithe body, a slit falling away from her legs atop her thighs and pooling on the floor beneath her. This was Aoife, the Queen of the Maine Court, or Court as they call it.

"To what do I owe this visit from our neighborly wolves?" She asked, her voice smooth as smoke.

Darren stepped forward, his focus on Aoife alone as he presented Aunt Magda's creations as gifts. While he addressed her, I took in the bodies filling the room. Two more satyrs flanked Aoife's throne, their woody brown hair pulled back in ties. Brown and grey fur trailed down their sides from their ribcages and dropped down into a v above their genitals. Leather holsters criss-crossed their abdomens, sheaths hanging at their hips. Women with small horns emerging from their hairlines lay around the base of Aoife's throne. Their lips were wine stained, parted to show pointed canines.

I almost felt at home, I thought sarcastically.

To either side of us were the courtesans of the Court. There were Undines with their dead-body-esque blue skin and black eyes. A few high born Sidhe huddled together, their bodies lithe like the Queen's and their long hair knotted into intricate designs. Then there were those less human. There was a woman with moth-like wings and thin arms that reminded me of an insect. A man had four, thin slitted eyes and a mouth full of sharp teeth. Smaller fae scuttled around the floor, running past like tumble weeds or fallen leaves. Birds chirped from the architecture above us, but my wolf knew them to be more than birds. They were the small fae whose bodies could change. Pixie one moment and chickadee the next, these fae were said to be harmless and loving creatures. Dad had me doing homework outside of my school work. I owed so much of what I knew to him.

Two women stood out to me. Their hair was long and floated on the air as if they were hovering, the light strands suspended in time. Their eyes were soft and rimmed with grey lashes, but the irises were dark like a bird's eye. Our female guide left our side and moved to join them. All of their eyes fell on me and some soft secret smile touched their lips as their eyes trailed down my body. Was it me or were they looking at my waist?

"The North Eastern Clan would like your support in a time of need," Darren asked.

"You aren't the head of the North Eastern Clan," Aoife's smooth voice accused him. "It has no Alpha as of now. Therefore, you are no one."

I was beginning to see how abuse happened here, why Fionna felt the need to leave her home behind.

He nodded in grim agreement, lips tight. "Yes, but I wish to claim the position of Alpha. I wish to protect the wolves of the North Eastern Clan from my challenger."

"You come to ask our help for your Clan, but you aren't the head of the Clan. You have no reason to be standing before me now because you are not representative of this Clan."

I felt a tingle of warmth run across my skin. I knew what was coming, but stayed back and watched Darren run his hand through his hair in frustration. He was fighting a losing battle with her because she wanted to speak to someone with power. This Queen couldn't see Darren gaining any ground in this battle, was what she was telling us. As much as Darren acted the part and deserved the part, he wasn't in charge of anyone but his Guard yet.

Yet.

Aoife ran a too long finger around the plastic sealed rim of the jars. "Your visit had been productive, but I would like to ask you to leave now as you, Darren Blackford, have nothing that could move me. I don't think that you would ever have anything that would move me."

The warmth was growing hot, moving across my skin, past where I thought the flowers ended. I lifted the hem of my shirt to see the tattoos moving, as if they were fluttering in a breeze that didn't exist. My breath held, I watched them in shock. This couldn't be real.

Oh, but it is.

The voice filled my head and the warmth moved across my skin. I felt it slither down my arms, tingling with power. Aoife's gaze was on me, not so much curious as it was hungry. She knew the power that was coming over me. She was old, ancient. I thought that she must miss the power, the presence of our Goddess and the joy that it could bring with it. The Goddess had once smiled upon her, shared her voice inside her head much like she was with me. How I knew that was beyond me.

I pushed my way past Darren, fingers at the hem of my shirt. Someone tried to pull me back, but I jerked my arm out of their grip. My gaze never broke Aoife's.

"This is what you want," I lifted my shirt over my head. Standing before the crowd in my lacy bra, they stared at the dancing flowers on my side. I felt something move amongst the Celtic knots, flowing through the shadows. Something alive. Warmth emanated from me, glowing white.

"Yes, that is what I want. It is what I crave." Aoife slid from her seat, her eyes wide and pleading. Gone was the aloof queen and in its place was the creature she had started life as, the forest spirit.

"She is returning to us," I began, "and not because of Jonathan Blackford. The Goddess has brought back the eternal flowers in our town square. She used them to warn me of a threat to one of our wolves."

She stepped away from her throng, the women at her feet moving away from her. She turned her head up towards the glittering ceiling. The look of longing on her face made my heart ache. I stepped towards her, walking between the sharp toothed nymphs. The satyrs moved, hands going to the swords at their hips, and I froze. Aoife held out her hand to stop them without breaking her gaze. My hands sought her cheeks, turning her face down so I could see into her eyes. Her skin felt like marble beneath mine, cold and unmovable.

The flush of warmth spread from me to her. We could both hear the feminine laughter that followed. She was with us. Suddenly, I threw my hands up to the ceiling. I felt the energy run up my arms, channeled and aimed. It was as if a whirlwind of petals spun around me, the magic brushing at my skin.

Diana...

The ceiling lit up with true light. The moon filtered in between the roots of the trees. Their little lights sparkling like stars, the sky rolling with gray and lavender clouds over midnight blue. Aoife and I laughed as we reveled in her power. The darkness cleared from the windows of the cathedral dirt walls. Glass filled their place, stained with gem colors and depicting towering trees, flowers, animals. I could hear the sounds of the forest, the chirping of birds, rustling of branches, and the distant trickle of a stream. The goddess had used me as a conduit to fill this Court with her power.

Aoife's fingers tightened around my arm.

Faintly, I could hear the howls of dogs again. Their call sounded like hounds in a raccoon hunt. It had found its mark. Something else had happened when I had channeled all of that power. It had been coming for me, that I knew. The howls and bays of hounds had called out to me before, but now they had found me. I was their mark. What did that mean for me?

"You will stay," Aoife told me, her voice low. Turning her attention to Darren, she raised her voice and said: "Leave this one with me and I will give you the support that you ask for."

Behind me, I heard Darren and Jason move. Their growls were low but audible. The satyrs disappeared from my range of vision. Behind me I could hear the whisper of their blades being drawn and I let out a growl, trying to pull my arm from her grip. They would attack Darren and I was bound to defend him. Together, the Goddess and I had give Aoife a fix of the drug she hadn't tasted in centuries.

"Take your hands off of my Guard, Queen Aoife. I sacrifice no wolf."

Her head snapped up, the smile on her lips slightly crazed. Her smile was just a little too tight, her eyes just a little too wide. She gestured towards the beauty of the ceiling, of the windows. Her gaze finally stopped at her free hand, watching her fingers wriggle as if they had new life.

"Why would I let the bringer of my power leave the Court? This one is so much more than a wolf. She is wolf and hound, touched by our ancient Goddess and chosen by our father God."

I looked back at the two men. Darren's eyes were dark and angry, his body vibrating with anger. The satyrs formed a wall between us. Jason suddenly grabbed the wrist of one, jerking him forward and pulling him off balance. The satyr fell to the floor and the other one jumped into action. Slicing through the air, his short blade just barely missed Darren's cheek.

Aoife glanced down at the nymphs that crowded the base of her throne. She must have conveyed some silent command because they began to slither forward. They crawled seductively towards Jason, their arms outstretched as their magic spilled out around them. The glamour washed around them like heat off of the pavement in the summer. It pushed around Jason and clouded his eyes. His movements slowed until all he could see were they nymphs.

"Save us," they cried. Their fingers moved to point at Darren. "Save us from the beast!"

Without question, Jason turned away from the satyrs and towards his Alpha. They had him wrapped around their fingers, body and mind.

I tried to wrestle my wrist away from Aoife, but her grip was like stone. This meeting was not going as planned. We had come here to ask for their help and all we had succeeded in doing was igniting a squabble. I turned my face up to the moonlight that filtered in through the tree roots. The goddess had blessed Aoife with a gift, didn't that mean that she deserved it?

Thoughts of the Clan came to mind. I truly believed that they were monsters, yet the Goddess had chosen to give us back long forgotten magic. Only if we help Darren could win. We would surely burn ourselves to the ground if Jonathan were to take over. The heat of sunlight returned, hotter than ever, and I had a moment to think that if we deserved a chance, so did they.

"The Goddess graced you with a gift and you choose to cage it for your own greed?" I asked.

The Goddess still filled every inch of my body. She felt too large to fit into such a small vessel, pushing at me from the inside out until my blood thundered in my ears. But this time, it wasn't the Goddess speaking and Aoife seemed to listen. Her grip softened while her lips slowly parted. She might have been Queen, but she had a higher power to answer to.

"If you act like a spoiled child when someone tries to give you a gift, what makes you any better than us? What makes you a Queen?" I was being bold, but with her grip still on me, it was the only choice that I had.

She sighed and let my arm go. "I let the rush of power not felt for centuries go to my head. You are an exceptional Faoladh, girl, and I can see that our Goddess has big plans for you."

I didn't know what to say to that, but behind me I could hear Darren's cry. The fighting was still going on. The nymphs cowered behind Jason as he moved against the man he called Alpha.

"Give me time to create order among my court again then I will show you my support in your endeavors. Be brave, wolves, for none shall escape the Horned God and his Wild Hunt."

Aoife turned her attention to her court to call back her forces. Some of the nymphs drew back, suddenly docile. Other drew back their lips and hissed in response. I saw Aoife's eyes narrow. There was a reason that she was Queen and I was sure that those nymphs would later learn that. Without the glamour, Jason dropped to the floor, his body trembling with spent energy. He looked to Darren, his eyes filled with an unnecessary apology.

Apparently happy with how things had gone down, I felt the Goddess's magic pulled away, leaving my skin feeling old and my head pounding. My knees quaked, but someone rushed to grab me. Darren and Jason were both by my side despite their wounds. They hoisted me up so that I could find my own footing and allowed me to put my weight on them as we left.

"None shall escape the Horned God and His Wild Hunt."

The satyrs repeated it over and over as we passed them, their voices becoming a hum that rattled inside my skull.

None shall escape the Horned God and his Wild Hunt.

As we walked back down the hallway, I could hear the roars of Aoife turn into sobs. She may not have been able to keep what she wanted to, but she had been given a greater gift. Perhaps she had deserved it in the end. She had only been too afraid to lose it again.

As we stumbled down the confusing corridor, our pace slowed. A touch of magic still rode me. I could feel it pulsing beneath my skin, needing direction. Darren's hand cupped my arm, gently pulling me along. His brow was knit together in anger and a touch of fear, his eyes more brown than green. As I studied his face, I noticed there was a deep cut across his cheek. I ran my thumb across it, an intimate gesture. The warmth that I still held flowed into him, smooth skin appearing beneath my touch. I sucked in my breath at what I had just done. I turned to Jason, whose shirt hung in tatters. He had started the tussle and bore the most damage. I didn't remember him getting socked in the eye, but it was puffed and slightly purple. The warmth flowed like water as I ran my hand over the slice marks across his chest and laid my fingertips to the swollen eye.

Jason watched me warily, his fingers touching his own cheekbone. Howls began to echo through the corridor. One after another, the howls continued. I could hear the pounding of their feet against earth as if another Clan were hunting us down.

"Maybe we should be leaving," Darren suggested.

He grabbed my shoulder and pushed me forward. We fumbled for the exit as the sounds of howling and pounding footsteps grew louder and louder behind us. It made my heart race. We were being chased down.

No. I'd heard these howls before. I was being chased down. I was their mark.

We burst through the door, thinking that we had escaped our invisible pursuant as the heavy door shut behind us. Like an invisible force, it blew past the door and slammed into me. I felt the impact of each hound. Their short fur brushed my skin and my wolf stirred. These were her creatures, kin and subjects. She threw her head back in a howl that filled my head. Dozens of hounds huddled around her, now occupying more space within me. They didn't have the presence of mind that my troublesome wolf did, but their magic stirred inside of me.

Suddenly, I let out the breath that I had been holding and fell to the ground. The sky above us was dark and dusky, the limbs of naked trees creating dark lines that snaked into my view. I couldn't think about what had just happened, let alone say anything just yet. I laid there, letting the magic settle into my bones. Hundreds of imaginary dogs writhed around me. Hounds, wolves, coyotes all surrounded me. They all bayed, barked, and howled for my love.

"What the hell just happened?" Jason nearly shrieked.

What the hell is happening?

Both Darren and I turned to stare at him. Before we knew it, we were both dying of laughter. Jason glared at us, crossing his arms over his chest. There was a high of wild magic still riding me, but I knew once the laughter was gone I would be in for one hell of an emotional fallout. Too much had happened all at once and my human brain refused to process it. And I didn't have to anytime soon because Darren's phone began to buzz.

Wiping away tears of laughter, he put the phone to his ear. I watched the last of the laughter fade from his face. I could hear Henry's pained voice on the other end.

"You guys need to get back to the Manor. There's a problem."

"What kind of problem?"

"The Manor is on fire, that kind of a problem."

Darren's lips fell into a grim line as his face turned ashen. Frantically, he began to wave us back to Jason's truck.

"What's going on?" I asked. My own panic was rising. Our feet pounded the earth as we ran. I jerked open the door to the Chevelle and threw myself inside. The older car gunned it out of there, Jason's truck hot on my heels.

CHAPTER TWENTY-THREE

The heat pressed against my face, making it hard to breathe. Or was that the fear? I didn't know what it was. All I knew was that there was a blazing fire where the Manor should have been. I thought of sitting at the breakfast bar with Henry or my Grandmother. I thought of the office that I'd been in not too long ago.

Where was my Grandmother? My mind went into overdrive. Was she still in there? Was the fire closing in on her while we stood around? I didn't realize that I was running toward the blaze until someone grabbed me. My feet left the earth. I beat at the arms wrapped around my waist. I needed to get inside. I needed to find her. I'd already lost too much family. My tears were lost among the heat of the fire.

"Diana!" a voice shouted. "Calm down. What is wrong with you?"

No words could come out. All I could do was scream. My wolf rose. The fire scared her. She wanted to run. I slammed my fist on my captor's arm. I was done running. We were not prey. We were not weak, I told her. We help our family. She growled back at me in response. Good, I thought. Grow a backbone. We're going to need it. But first, I needed to get inside. I needed to help my Grandmother.

Then I saw a figure. She was outlined by the light of the fire, only a black shape of a woman. But it was undeniably her. I saw the line of her jacket and neat skirt, but her feet were placed apart in a fighter's stance. My Grandmother. I stopped fighting, going limp in my captor's arms. I glanced behind me to see Darren's eyes wide with worry. I took a deep breath to let him know that I was okay. I wasn't ready for words. Maybe I'd thank him later for saving my life.

Maybe.

After a long moment of searching my eyes, he set me back down. I bolted for my Grandmother and threw my arms around her, welcoming the smell of her. But she only wrapped a loose arm around my shoulder. Her eyes were fixated on the fire. It was very slowly dying down, but we could already see that there was nothing left of the Manor but bones and stones. Had anyone been locked inside? Had anyone been in there when those cowards set it ablaze? It had to have been Jonathan and his lackeys. A growl trickled up my throat. Fear tactics. That's all they knew. Brutality and fear tactics. They were no better than the wolves I'd met across the country, the ones that tried to keep me as their own. That was no way to run a Clan.

"I had Jason call 911 again. The fire department should be here soon." Darren said. There was a note of reprimand in his voice that I didn't understand.

"Why are you mad at me?" I challenged. "I wasn't the one who set the fire."

"No, but I could have called the authorities earlier if you hadn't lost your goddess damned mind and rushed towards the inferno. Faoladh or not, that would have killed you, but you just rushed toward it like you were invincible. What was so important in there that you could risk your own life for?"

I had the grace to feel a little ashamed of myself, but my eyes moved to the woman I was still clinging to. I'd panicked, thinking that she was still in there. Jonathan was systematically destroying my family, or at least trying to. He'd brutally murdered my father and I was almost certain he'd killed my Grandfather, lest not forget Henry's wife. Now he took the very center of our Clan, her home. But she stood with her back straight and eyes defiant. He was not going to take this woman away from me, too.

"Fine," Darren said, apparently seeing my reason for panic.

"Did he think that this would frighten us?" my Grandmother asked. "Hand me some marshmallows."

Her words were humorous, but her voice was steel. She was done with his bullying shit. Maybe she'd moved past the regret that she

151

hadn't taken Jonathan's life, leaving him to raise his boys. Maybe, like me, all she saw was blood. The fire truck careened up the long driveway, sirens blaring. I should have heard them miles away, but I'd been so distracted by the fire and my own fear. What else had I missed, I wondered as I watched men and women jump from the truck and gather up the hose.

"All of the Clan financial and personal files were in there," Jason said, finally joining us.

My Grandmother shrugged. "That's just paper. And a house is just wood, stone, and a bit of metal. We are flesh and family. There's nothing he can do to break that and if he can't understand that then we cannot allow him to take Alpha from Darren. Power is all he understands and I plan on seeing it ripped out from underneath him."

"Where is he now?" my voice was nearly a whisper.

Darren's eyes locked on mine, both of us wondering the same thing. The fire was just a distraction. Nearly the whole clan was now gathered outside the fire. The authorities, some of them our own, clustering to push us all back. All eyes were here in the middle of nowhere.

A thought burst to the surface and before I knew it, my feet were running towards the Chevelle. Jason was right behind me, following my lead. Darren would be safe with my Grandmother. Someone else was left unguarded and we couldn't afford to waste time. As I punched the car into gear and backed it up, the authorities moved to stop us. My wolf growled in my head. Their heads turned as the frame of the house collapsed under the weight of the water. I sped down the driveway while a column of embers leapt into the air. We had to make it to Balefire in time.

In the rearview mirror of the Chevelle, the Manor's fire had lit the sky with an eerie blood red color. It almost didn't look natural.

Hurry. A now familiar voice spoke in my head and I knew that I'd been right.

"Where are we going?" Jason asked now. He'd trusted me enough to blindly follow, but he needed to be prepared. I'd only known him a few weeks, but I made a mental note to thank Darren for bringing him into the Clan.

"Balefire."

"Shit," his voice breathy.

Magda was only human, my Grandmother's daughter or not. She couldn't heal like we could, she couldn't take as much pain as we could. Killing her might be the last brick in my Grandmother's madness. She spent too much time on four legs these days, having lost half of her family already. Taking her last immediate family member, her own child, would tip her over the edge into her animal. We'd lose not only her tactical mind, but her strength.

We'd lose Magda.

Darkness was now thick outside the window, the sun gone and moon hiding its face. My hands shook as I put them one over the other to spin the wheel. I jammed it into park outside the restaurant's entrance and nearly fell out the door. I lunged for the door, only to find it locked. The massive wooden doors wouldn't budge, even for my inhuman strength. My heart hammered in my ears. I couldn't hear anything but the pounding of blood. I shot down the alley between the restaurant and a shop I couldn't name. Even if it was locked, I planned on breaking down the flimsy door to the kitchen. Nothing would stop me.

A scream split the air. No. No. No. I couldn't afford to be late. The same panic that had ridden me earlier pushed forward. Adrenaline filled me. It rushed from my head to toes. I grabbed the kitchen door handle and yanked, the locking mechanism snapping with a satisfying sound. My wolf growled. I no longer needed hands, she told me.

Claws. Teeth. Fight.

I smiled and knew that it must have been a disconcerting look to Jason. But the change rippled over me as I tore my shirt and pants off. It was smooth, flowing from skin to fur without any of the usual popping sounds of rearranging bones. I came up to Jason's stomach in my wolf form, my own black reflection staring back at me in the stainless steel. I turned and ripped off my underwear with my teeth.

Another scream cut through the air, melting into sobs. I shot forward. The smell of Magda and grease was all over the place. She touched everything here, worked here everyday. That was no surprise, but a stronger scent reached my nose. Blood. I growled, but followed it anyway. It led me past broken glass and ceramic shards. The human in me imagined her chucking plates and glasses at him as she backed away. A cast iron frying pan was on the floor. The smell of blood radiated from it, but it wasn't Magda's. She had drawn blood. I would have smiled, but it wasn't Jonathan's.

I reached the swinging wood door that stood between the kitchen and the dining room. The whimpering I'd heard grew louder.

"She smells like the bitch we met in Texas," a voice said. It was one of the wolves that had tried ambushing me in the cemetery.

I pranced nervously as Jason nudged the door open. Magda was on her back on the bar top. The tall wolf held her down with one hand to her chest, a kitchen knife in his other hand. There was a glaze of red on the metal. Even from here I could see the whites of her eyes as she watched the blade move.

"But she's not a wolf, it makes her smell kind of hollow. This isn't going to be as fun as if it were the bitch," the tall one said.

"Don't you have an imagination? They look enough alike, must be family."

"What happened?" the tall one asked Magda. "Did you miss the party when your family was handing out the werewolf gene? Someone made us. Someone cut us to the bone, pushed us to the brink of death until our wolves came out. What would happen to you if we did the same? Would you still miss out?"

Almost simultaneously, Jason shoved the door open and I lunged. My claws sought purchase on the bar top as I jumped again, jaws wide. But the tall wolf's reflexes were faster. He slid aside and brought the knife up.

"You thought that we didn't hear you bust the door down back there? Thought we couldn't smell you?"

The knife came down across my flank. I felt a warm burst across the muscle, but I was too angry for pain. I landed on the floor, sliding back. The tall wolf faced me, but Jason was right behind him. So I turned my attention to the short wolf.

"How's your shoulder?" he asked with a smirk. "Must have hurt like a son of a bitch. Had you been human you never would have been able to use it again," he kept talking as he moved. "Magda here might not be so lucky."

Angry, I jumped. I made a mistake. I hadn't watched him close enough. He brought up clawed hands and caught me. Together we tumbled to the floor. His claws fought their way past my thick fur, tiny pinpricks just breaking the surface. I snapped at him, trying to break free of his grip. Twice now, I'd bested him. Third time would not be his charm. It couldn't be. I kicked with my back feet, feeling the fabric of his shirt giving away. The back claws weren't worn away like a normal wolf's, but fresh and sharp from the change. Another kick and I felt flesh tear. But his grip grew tighter. His claws sunk deeper before he wrenched me away from his body. My body was weightless.

I slammed into tables and chairs. My body twisted around the metal. That would leave a bruise even after I shifted. Fumbling, my paws caught metal legs. I struggled to stand as he approached. A growl rumbled through me. He'd hunted me across the country. It was the only way that he could have fallen in with Jonathan's band of merry psychopaths. He'd hurt not only me, but someone that I loved. I made the decision that the world would be better without him.

I pretended to whimper as I crouched low A smile lit his face. It even reached into his eyes. This was how he liked them, afraid. If that's what it took, I could play the part. I whimpered for real as he touched the gash in my leg. He lowered his face to mine.

"Realize that you can't win?" he whispered.

Not exactly.

I lunged forward, jaws open. I couldn't reach his neck, so I went for his face. My teeth met his temples and I bit down as hard as I could. His claws fought against me, scratching and pushing. I bit down harder and shook. His neck made a snapping sound that seemed to echo through my ears. His body fell limp, dragging me to the ground with him. Blood pounded in my ears. For a moment, I sat prone. Was he really dead? Was it over?

"Diana?" Jason asked.

I rolled my eyes up, the other wolf's head still in my jaws. There was blood dripping down Jason's forearm and a smear across his forehead. On the bar, Magda had gone completely white. She raised her hand, staring at it in shock. It took a long moment for me to wind down enough to think, to realize what I was seeing. The hand she led up was missing two fingers. The change rippled over me, the smell of summer wavering around me. I thanked the Goddess and rushed to my aunt's side. Her hand started shaking, completely losing control. She was going to pass out.

Jason reappeared with my jeans and hoodie in his hand. I tugged them back on as he scooped Magda up in his arms. The Short wolf's body was still lying on the floor. I prayed that the authorities were still busy putting out the fire at the manor.

Outside, I opened the passenger door so that Jason could slide in, still cradling Magda in his arms. Taking deep breaths, I went around to the other side. The engine turned over and I reached for my phone. I called Darren and told him what had happened, putting him on speaker phone because I needed two hands to steady the shaking. There was so much death and destruction around me lately. I glanced over at Jason and Magda in the seat beside me, sending a silent prayer to the Goddess to stay with my aunt as we rushed to the hospital.

CHAPTER TWENTY-FOUR

Jason pushed through the door of Magda's farmhouse, his skin still ashy. Sometimes it was easy to forget that he had been human. There had been a time in his life when all of this was just a figment of someone's twisted imagination. He had been a human child with human dreams. Now, it was very much real and very much dangerous.

It hadn't been the fight with the satyr or the fact that the other clan-less wolf had gotten away that really hurt Jason. It had been the nymphs' glamour, a bit of magic that slipped into his mind and tried to make him betray us. He was a soldier. He had fought beside fellow soldiers before and nothing would have made him do what he did earlier today. I couldn't say I blamed him when I saw him wrench open the doors to the liquor cabinet. It was a short term solution, but I followed suit.

I felt like a balloon that had been blown too large and then deflated. The Goddess had been inside of me, overfilling my body and taking over what was mine. Now that she had receded, I could still feel her presence in the corners of my mind. She would always be there, watching my every move. My wolf was able to push forward to fill the empty space. When she did, she was surrounded by hounds and coyotes. Her growls were loud over their bays and barks and it all shook my skull. But behind all of that chaos was the fact that I had killed again today. It wasn't my first time and it was never fun, but it seemed to drain away a piece of my sanity each time.

Now was not the time for her, her new friends, or even shame. This was my body, my life. Mine alone. Jason poured himself a shot of vodka and before he could set the bottle down, I took it from him. I took a swig from the almost full bottle before taking it into the kitchen with me.

"Don't think you're hogging all of that to yourself," Jason shouted after me.

"What is wrong with the two of you?" Darren asked as I passed him.

I skidded to a halt. The heat of anger burned across my skin.

"How can you think about drinking when all of this is happening around you?" He motioned around himself, referencing the hell that we were living in. The manor was gone. Aunt Magda's fingers were gone.

I spun around and pushed into Darren's space. Glaring up at him, I said: "This is exactly why I want to drink right now. Do you think that being a pawn and a puppet is what I wanted out of my life. We went out there today to help you win this stupid fight and we are the ones who got fucked up for it. If it hadn't been for a Goddess that took residence in my freaking head, we wouldn't have gotten out of the fucking fae court. If it hadn't been for Jason and me acting fast we would have lost more than just Magda's fingers. You don't have to thank us right now."

I spun away and stormed into the kitchen. Distantly, I heard Darren say only that he would check in with my Grandmother. He didn't say a word about my sudden explosion. After a moment, Jason and I followed him.

The Manor office was gone. There was no way we were getting it back any time soon so we set up an impromptu meeting in the farmhouse's living room. Riding the short term buzz that the alcohol had given me, I pulled my feet underneath me and reached for a slice of the pizza sitting on the coffee table. The label on the box was Balefire's familiar script. I didn't know who ordered it, but it was obviously from much earlier in the day. Yet, after a day like this we deserved it. Even if it was cold pizza, it was better than no pizza.

"Thaddeus said that while he may be the strongest of the vampires in this area, he has little control over their associations," Darren said, sounding very much like my Grandmother.

I eyed her, wondering what she was trying to instill in our new Alpha. Did she have this kind of influence over my Grandfather? Most likely, I concluded after giving it some thought. She has control over everything.

She nodded. "Then what of your appeal to the Fae Court?"

"The Fae currently have their heads up their asses," I said before anyone could speak.

My Grandmother shot me a dirty look, but I shrugged it off. What I said was true. I thought back to the broken look in Aoife's eyes and how she needed to be reminded of her duties to her court, her people. Aoife needed time to get her act together and we didn't have time. My Grandmother knew that. Darren knew it, too.

"What do we do now?" I asked since no one else would.

Darren sucked in a deep breath, forcing the gears in his brain to work. We were alone in our fight, pushed into a corner at every turn. Sure, we had a Goddess on our side, but her help had been pretty limited so far. We couldn't put all our faith in her to make things right. Now was the time for Darren to prove that he was meant to be our Alpha.

"We can't draw this out any longer. I think that it is high time that we make a formal challenge."

"May the best man win," Jason muttered.

"Um, yeah," I said. "It's not like we can just walk up to him on the streets and initiate a challenge. Besides, no one has seen him outside of his house in a while."

"We bring it to the town hall," Darren offered. "From there I can initiate the formal challenge and declare it take place under the next full moon. That's within my rights since the clan has no official leader. Hopefully he still pretends to be sane in public."

"Again, how are we supposed to get him there?"

I imagined capturing one of Jonathan's men, Todd perhaps. He could be the message the same way that he planned on making a message out of me. No, I stopped myself. That was playing by Jonathan's rules.

My Grandmother rolled her shoulders back. "It's simple. You send a messenger."

"Petra," Darren begged. "I know what you're thinking and the answer is no."

She leveled a hard stare at him. She had decades of experience on him. She'd done things that he would never understand. I would know as I was practically following in her footsteps. I didn't like what I thought she had planned, but there was no stopping her. I had seen her face when she looked at the burning ruin of her home. She'd been filled with steel and rage. Thinking of how we often found her on four legs, running away as much as I had been, I reached out and placed a hand on Darren's arm. My look said to give in. She needed this, as dangerous as it was. I glanced back at her. I didn't know if she even wanted to live through it. I didn't like this either, but she was a capable woman.

There was now a bottle of rum between us, only a quarter of it left. I sat back in my chair, putting my bare feet on the table. My stretchy shorts rode up on my bare thighs. Jason's jaw began to slip as his eyes roamed my thighs. I felt my face begin to burn.

"How did you get those scars?" he pointed with one finger, the rest of his hand wrapped around his glass, at my leg. "That's more than just the one knife wound from earlier."

I covered the scars with my hand, looking away from him.

"Don't you close up now," I heard the legs of his chair hit the floor as he leaned forward. When I looked up, he was rolling the sleeve of his flannel shirt up. The raised lines of skin criss-crossed over his forearm, barely hidden by his ink. "There are more where that came from. They're decades old now, but won't fade."

I pulled up the sleeve of my t-shirt to show him the puncture marks on my upper arm from being held by half shifted hands. Jason reached out, running a thick finger over the pink scar tissue. When he lined his fingers up with the scars, I jerked my arm away from him.

"I was a lone female werewolf," I explained. "Other Clan-less wolves hunted me down out of instinct. Some of them wanted to own me and I didn't agree with that."

Jason grimaced. "These scars were more than one attack?"

I nodded. "Five on my arm, four big ones on my thigh, three on my hip, my shoulder now and..." my fingers reached to the back of my skull to the line hidden in my thick hair. "You were attacked by a Clan-less wolf and ...infected?"

"Yeah, not a fun time either," he threw back the rest of his drink. He looked away from me, at the two wolves playing in the living room. "I was just a kid when it happened. I was just a stupid kid that thought he was invincible because he joined the army.."

The scars ran across his chest and down his stomach. I wondered how much of him had been pulled apart. It must have taken a long time for the werewolf gene to kick in, felt even longer while he lay outside in the cold. I couldn't imagine that kind of pain that young, not even close. We spent a good hour and a half trading horror stories and neither of us could decide which was worse. Neither of us wanted to dig deeper than the scars and that was alright.

The farmhouse was dark and quiet around us as we filled the kitchen table with empty liquor bottles. It moved through our bodies, working fast as it rode our quickened metabolism. I had lost count of how many drinks I had.

Soft footsteps grew heavier, approaching the kitchen. Jason's eyes left my scars and moved to the kitchen archway. I let my head fall back and saw an inverted Darren frozen in the doorway. His eyes were wide, the whites showing around his hazel irises.

"What is going on here?" his words were clipped short.

"Just having a drink, boss." Jason raised his glass in salute.

"We were comparing battle stories," I said with a giggle.

"You are wasted," Darren stepped forward.

"What do you care? We aren't on sentry duty tonight." I leaned a bit too far towards him and found the floor rushing towards me.

Darren lunged forward, but something else caught me. Jason's arm on my shoulders pulled me and my chair upright again. He straightened my wayward hair and my shirt before sitting back down.

"Why didn't you tell me that you were engaged?" I pointed an accusing finger at Darren.

His face twisted in an expression of pain. I couldn't understand why he was the one hurting right then. He was the one who had lied to me, seduced me.

I shot back up out of my chair, hot words on my lips, and the world swam for a moment. I had to drop back down into the chair to keep from falling to the floor.

"I don't think that she drinks too often," Jason laughed, a hand brushing my bangs from my forehead.

Behind me, Darren sighed. It ended in a low grumble and Jason's hand disappeared. My eyelids began to droop. I spread my arms over the table, creating a nest that I fully intended to sleep on.

"No, you can't sleep on the table the night before Thanksgiving," Jason tenderly touched my shoulder and pulled me back.

I stuck my tongue out at him, eyes still closed. Behind me, Darren chuckled. I could hear him moving closer. My wolf was quiet, the alcohol making her almost non-existent. She didn't prance at how close he was to us or beg for his touch on our skin. No, he was just Darren tonight.

"I'm going to take her upstairs. She needs to sleep this off."

His thick arms wedged themselves beneath me and suddenly, I was lifted into the air. My stomach rolled, but settled once we began our ascent of the stairs. At the top of the stairs, his grip on me tightened, holding my body close to his chest. His chin nuzzled my head lovingly.

My eyes drifted shut again and the next thing I knew, he was lowering me onto the mattress. He pulled the sheets over my still clothed body, his fingers tracing my cheek. He must have thought that I was fully asleep, because he began to talk.

"You beautiful rebellious creature," He said, his voice tender and quiet. "You have made me angry, scared, and frustrated every day since you have been home. You also have made me incredibly proud. I only wish that I had the strength that you have. I also wish that you didn't have to earn that strength the hard way.

"You make me crazy inside. My wolf loves you with every inch of his being. Sometimes..." He paused his voice trailing off. "I love Fionna more than anything, but you make me wonder if I've made a mistake. You make me wonder if you could be my mate."

I couldn't. Determined as he was to protect everyone, frightened Fionna needed him more than me. The Clan needed him more than he needed me.

Don't forget what comes first, I thought before slipping into a dreamless sleep.

There was still a buzz in my head from the night before. I wasn't used to drinking at all, let alone as much as we did and I was sure that I couldn't have gotten more than a couple hours of sleep. Bruised and broken Magda and my Grandmother were in the dining room of the farmhouse, trying to make room for half the Clan to have Thanksgiving dinner. Magda's hand was bandaged, but she fumbled with kitchen utensils all morning until Sabrina kicked her out of the kitchen with an order to rest. It hadn't stopped her, the Warren in her thrusting her defiance at being the victim into everything she did today. I set my back against a counter, eyes closed as I listened to the noise of family with a cup of orange juice in my hand. Sabrina was at the kitchen island with a ball of bread dough in her hands and a cloud of flour around her.

"I'm sorry about what Christopher did at the funeral reception," Sabrina hung her head as she leaned against the kitchen island. "I'm sorry about the way I treated you."

I shrugged, grimacing when it made my head start pounding all over again. She didn't have to apologize for someone else's actions.

"Hey, I'm trying to be nice to you," Sabrina snapped.

My head shot up to find an angry pregnant woman with flour up to her elbows staring me down. I was surprised to find a tingle of fear shoot down my spine.

"I'm sorry," I mumbled in response.

She sighed, deciding to simply stick her tongue out at me. I laughed. Then we were both laughing. Aunt Magda walked in, seeing the flour coated Sabrina laughing with me. She raised an eyebrow before backing out of the room. That only made us laugh harder.

We kept talking while she worked. She spoke about a side of Christopher that I hadn't known existed. She was excited about her pregnancy, but scared for her future husband's safety. I couldn't blame her. We were all afraid right now. She told me that Aunt Magda had offered to let her move into the farmhouse while all of this was going down, but that she refused. She couldn't let it be known that she chose sides; she knew the risks that it might cause.

Sabrina was smarter than she let on or she had heard the speech from her step-father enough times that she had smartened up. She knew that there was always one of our wolves watching over her, usually Frank.

Eventually the conversation left the heavy topic of the civil war and we began to talk about more mundane topics. She showed me her latest tattoo and I told her that my mother had worked as a tattoo artist for a short time. I showed her a few pictures of her tattoos from my phone. Who knew that I would be good at girl bonding? I looked up at the woman with round cheeks and reddish brown ringlets, ink sprawling across every inch of exposed skin. It took a different kind of girl to bond with me, I decided. Sabrina was as headstrong and loving as I wished I could be. Well, maybe I had the headstrong part down.

"Oomph," She jerked upright, grabbing at her stomach.

"What's wrong?" I remembered my mother going into labor for the little ones. I didn't want to be around when Sabrina went into labor. The idea was frightening.

"Just a kick. She is a feisty little thing," Sabrina smiled.

I reached a hand out, but paused mid-air. Glancing up as if to ask for permission, I waited.

"Go ahead," she laughed at me. "But, only because you waited for my say so."

My hand laid flat over the soft cotton and latex blend that covered her stomach.

"You would be surprised at the number of people who just think that a pregnant woman's stomach is suddenly public property," her laugh became choked.

Something hit my hand. It was hard and sharp. I felt the glow of sunlight creep over my skin. My hair even rustled as if there were a summer breeze moving through the Manor's kitchen. Turning my gold eyes up, they connected with Sabrina's. It was as if we both knew it at the same time.

Sabrina was carrying a werewolf. Her baby was going to be a little girl wolf.

Her eyes widened, suddenly dancing with tears. She threw her arms around me in a crushing grip. Part of me wondered what she did at Balefire to get that kind of strength while the rest of me marveled over what had just happened.

"That was the Goddess," I whispered.

The throb began slow and subtle in the back of my head again. The Goddess herself had just been present, but she couldn't get rid of my hangover? Was that a bit selfish of me? Probably.

"I'm going to have a wolf girl," Sabrina marveled, her hands hugging her stomach. "It feels a little strange being a complete human about to give birth to something so much more than human."

"For all accounts, she will be pretty normal until puberty swings by."

"I've seen the lady wolves around here and there is nothing normal about any of you," she paused. "I don't mean that as a bad thing. I hope Olivia is as strong as you and your family."

"Thank you," I didn't think that I was all that special, but her words made even my hangover bearable.

CHAPTER TWENTY-FIVE

Thanksgiving was about to happen in the farmhouse. The sounds and smells in the kitchen were almost overwhelming as everyone jostled around me. Aunt Magda was in her prime, barking orders like an executive chef. Kitchen duty had become unbiased towards gender, Aunt Magda's holiday army included Christian, Sabrina, Henry, and myself. Henry was tending to two turkeys that were being cooked outside in the grill he had driven over. Sabrina had bread and dessert covered while Christian and I became mere grunts and gophers once I confessed that my hangover had subsided.

I chopped, mashed, and tasted my way through the kitchen. Christian did more gopher tasks, running to fetch fresh herbs and setting out mise en place. I could smell poultry and wine, pumpkin and cinnamon, garlic and chives. Dinner was going to be amazing.

Without a doubt it was going to blow away all of the cheesy meals that I had shared with my mom over the years. One year, we had turkey TV dinners. Another, we shared a rotisserie chicken from the local grocer's deli. When those Thanksgivings began to include the two little ones and my step-father, they became hectic and messy. My step-father's family tried to visit from time to time, but they only made me feel like an outcast in my own home.

I ached for my mother as I mashed boiled potatoes. I missed waking up to find her asleep on the couch with a sketchbook in her lap or paint in her hair. I missed her cries of triumph as she finished a painting or as she threatened an elementary teacher at a parent teacher conference. I missed my mother while surrounded by a cacophony of motion and noise. She burned with a wild passion for everything, but like the center of a storm there was something calm about her as well. I missed the sanctuary that I could find in her.

Wiping away a stray tear with the back of my hand, I tried to focus on the task at hand. She was in California with the kids, probably thinking about me just the same. A familiar smell entered the whirling scents of the kitchen. Warm and male. I looked up to see Darren leaning against the kitchen's door frame, hands in his jeans' pockets. His brown waves were messy from sleeping on the couch and he wore "Man of Steel" t-shirt.

He looked warm and comfortable, as if he would have a soft layer over hard muscle if I snuggled up to him. Perhaps later, after the food had long disappeared, I would find myself beside him on the couch, packed tight because of the number of wolves filling the house.

But that wasn't what I would normally have thought. My wolf had hi-jacked my thought processing, throwing memories of the night before at me. It might have been a confession of love, but I couldn't act upon it no matter how much my wolf complained. I frowned and gave her a firm push to the back of my mind. That spot belonged to Fionna now. It isn't our place to take it from her.

Go away, Darren Blackford, I looked back down at my project and heard his footsteps lead away. I didn't ever want to talk about last night. It needed to be brushed under the rug with a lot of other things.

"Why don't you two just fuck already?" Christian suddenly asked.

I shot him and angry glare. Sabrina laughed as she picked apart and nibbled on a dinner roll.

"Everyone can see the tension!" He said as if to say it was an innocent question.

"He's engaged!" Sabrina exclaimed.

"We already did," I whispered.

"You two already had sex and the tension is still this strong?" Sabrina whistled. Then her face went somber. "But he's with Fionna."

"But seriously, we can see how much you two want to be together. Fionna isn't Faoladh." Christian added as if it were legitimate premises for breaking up a marriage.

"I don't want to be with Darren," I said too defensively.

He gave me that 'you're kidding yourself' look. I shrugged, throwing the chopped herbs into the mixing bowl that Sabrina presented to me.

"I joined the Guard so that I could help and Darren couldn't try to get involved with me. I messed up once with him, it isn't happening again."

Christian's look softened as he watched me. It became a mixture of pity and confusion that I couldn't stand. I wouldn't be a homewrecker. That wasn't me.

"Darren is such a great guy. I hope that he knows what he's doing," Sabrina said, her voice low as if she were talking to herself.

Because the only reason he is such a great guy, as you say, is because he is trying to make up for the awful guy that he had been. I didn't say it aloud. Almost no one knew what had really happened that day. If I had asked, the majority of people in the Manor at this moment wouldn't know what I was talking about. The day that my father died was just that to these wolves. The story hung between Darren and me, a gap that wouldn't be crossed.

I left the conversation hanging by grabbing my coat and going outside to visit with Henry and his grill. He had a long necked bottle in his hand and his leather jacket was slung over the back of a wicker porch chair. I spared a moment to think that it was kind of dangerous to have wicker so close to the grill, let alone be drinking while grilling, but pulled up a chair and sat down anyway.

Henry threw me a look over the rim of his aviator sunglasses. I shook my head; legs sprawled out before me as if I had thrown myself down. He passed me a beer and I popped the lid but didn't drink any. I could smell the yeasty beer, wet earth, and smoky poultry. I didn't feel as caged as I had inside. Henry and I shared the silence, a perfect understanding coming between us.

Suddenly, three wolves broke from the wood line. They ran across the lawn, nipping at each other's heels. I didn't recognize two of the wolves, but the third was immediately familiar. The golden brown pelt with white paws was unmistakably my grandmother. She headed the three wolves, feet pounding the lawn as she raced ahead of the other two. They struggled to keep up with her.

I turned to Henry, jaw dropped. He chuckled.

"Does that happen often?" I asked. "Just...playing like that?"

"From time to time," he swigged his beer. "Keeps them feeling alive, I guess."

I threw my legs over the arm of the chair, nose over the back of it to watch the wolves play in the yard. They tumbled across the lawn, tearing up tufts of grass and yipping loudly. It was a chaotic mess of fun, I thought. Was this what it was like to grow up with the Clan? To play with one another like this and to look like a family? I had forgotten in the years that I was gone. I had experienced my first shift alone and scared, not with the solace of a Clan.

I was tucked between Christian and Jason as we watched old Batman films. Darren laughed at the pun filled jokes of Mr. Freeze and Jason nodded off beside me, his head leaning against my shoulder. Half of the Clan was wandering around the farmhouse. Many of them were sprawled out in chairs or on the floor of the living room, watching the movies as well. Food and wine had relaxed us all into catlike states of immobility, occasionally tossing a funny remark or a pillow at one another. Darren was snuggled on the floor with his fiance, Fionna. She had arrived late to the party, but was here none the less.

Funny, how I was finding it hard to breathe. My legs twitched and jerked. I had to pull myself from the tight spot between the all of the men. Jason jerked upright, awake and alert suddenly. He mumbled something about me leaving, but I didn't stay to listen. I thought that I could feel the gazes of other wolves, but maybe I was imagining it.

It had been too comfortable, even with Fionna there, and once more I tore away from any semblance of comfort that I found within the Clan. On my way to the kitchen, I cursed myself for my own behavior. These were wolves that I could trust. They put their trust in me and we were supposed to be a family. Why did I keep pulling away?

I grabbed myself a clean plate, making my way towards what was left of the pumpkin pie that sat on the counter. With the butter knife hovering over the pie, I angled it to make a bigger slice than I had originally portioned. Cinnamon graham cracker crust, honey and spice cheesecake, and pumpkin pie were layered beautifully. I leaned against the kitchen counter as I ate my more than generous slice of pie.

Moments later, as if there were a magnetic pull between us, Darren appeared. He reached for the spoon standing in the stainless steel bowl on the counter and plopped a dollop of whipped cream onto my slice of pie.

"Go away," I said around a mouthful of pie.

He laughed and leaned on the other side of the island counter. We sat like that in silence for a while. With sugar in my stomach and a solid object between us, I could handle it. I liked it almost.

"I can't get rid of you, can I?"

"You try pretty hard, I will give you that."

I laughed.

"Do you put that much effort into everything that you do?"

I shrugged as I grabbed the rest of the pie and turned towards the fridge. "Depends on how badly I want something."

The mood became somber once more. I closed the fridge and when I turned around Darren had come around the kitchen island. The wall between us was suddenly gone again. Something beat in the air around us. I wasn't sure if it was my pulse reverberating through the air. I glanced to the doorway, catching a glimpse of platinum hair. Fionna wasn't too far away.

Did I want him to close the distance between us? My body and my wolf did and that scared me. Together, they begged for him to come closer. The wolf thought that he was a wonderful mate, strong and dominant. I felt her leap and I stumbled forward. Confused, Darren reached out to catch me.

Stupid conniving wolf, I thought. Can't you just leave things alone? He's taken. You cannot steal what isn't yours.

"Are you okay?" He asked, hands on my arms.

"Yes, it's just..." I let my words trail off, not sure how to explain what had happened to me.

Was it bad to say that I still didn't fully understand my own species? I had been away from those like me when she really came to the surface. When puberty hit, it was like I developed a split personality on top of the ability to shape-shift. Inside, we fought and quarreled. Was it like that for others like me? I never had the chance to ask. I assumed that what had happened before my first shift had made me crazy. The first time that I had changed had been after my father had died. Not being able to come out of that first change had split me in two.

She had her voice, her own will, and I had mine. She raised her head, trying to move me closer to Darren as my body moved with her. I began to tremble. I wouldn't be a homewrecker, there was no room for gray area when the Clan was involved. I wouldn't destroy his relationship to appease my wolf. He was my Alpha and I had a job to do. I couldn't put the burden of my issues on him when he had the Clan to think about, himself to think about.

"You're not okay," His hands moved to my elbows as he directed me to sit on a stool. "What is going on?"

My shaking hand reached out to touch his face as he sat beside me. She wanted me to press my cheek against his, to nip his neck. She had claimed him already and that was frightening as hell. I had no choice as my own body worked against me.

"I don't have any control," I whispered.

Darren's brows knitted together, his hand covering mine. Patiently, he waited for me to explain.

"She pushes me to you. She says that you're already hers. I don't get to say no because if I do then she fights back," I whispered it all to the floor.

"I've always been yours, Diana. I've never had a say in it, I just never fought it. But you left and I had to move on."

Darren stood up, letting my hand fall away. Unable to look up, I listened to his footsteps walk away before I started to cry. I slipped from the stool and collapsed to the floor. I cried with my back pressed against the cabinetry of the kitchen island, my arms around my knees.

Chapter Twenty-Six

Jason and I had been patrolling that morning. The sun was just peeking over the horizon and the world had a pink cast to it that seemed fragile. We reached a path that cut through the woods, leading back to the Manor, intent on returning home for our shift change, when we caught a smell in the air. Blood and magnolia. A growl vibrated my muzzle. I tapped Jason with my tail before easing forward. I could hear the shuffle of feet in the dirt just before a loud thud. My heart raced. I knew what was ahead of me. I just didn't want to believe it.

Hair falling around her shoulders and clothing tattered, my Grandmother had fallen to the hard ground. Her breath hung in the air as she struggled. The smell of blood grew stronger as I approached her. I whimpered. This was my hero, my role model. My Grandmother thought that she had everything together. She thought that she could play everyone like a pawn, even the enemy.

Her message had been simple. Meet at the town hall in two nights. Jonathan chose to send his own message, a much louder and messier one.

Before I knew it, the change had rippled over me. It happened in the blink of an eye and felt like a bone rattling cold chill. Never minding that I was buck naked in front of Jason, I bent over to help my Grandmother. She blinked up at me through blood soaked bangs. A dried trickle of blood caked the side of her face. I expected to find pain and fear in her eyes.

There was only steel. I smiled, it was small but it was all she needed. She put her hand on my shoulder and together we got her back on her feet. She cradled her other arm close to her chest and put a good amount of her weight on me.

Jason circled us before running back to make sure that she hadn't been followed. I wouldn't have put it past Marcus to follow her, watch her stumbling and bleeding. A few moments later he returned, staying on four feet while we made our slow way back to the manor. I would have called ahead, told Darren to send out more wolves, but no clothes meant no pockets.

It felt like forever before we reached the farmhouse. Darren rushed out to us, wolves on four feet flowing out from behind him and running into the woods to take up their positions. Jonathan had tried and failed to hurt me, so he chose to move down the ladder. Hurting the ones I loved only made me angrier. It was hard to be afraid when you were angry.

My Grandmother fell into a table chair that had been pulled from the dining room and into the kitchen. Darren appeared with a duffle bag and tore open the zipper to reveal first aid supplies. Feeling useless now, I grabbed my clothes from the nearby laundry room and set about making hot cocoa. The heft of the metal pot in my hand felt good. It felt like a weapon as I set it on the burner. I cranked up the heat and poured in whole milk.

"Tell me what happened," Darren said as he wound a bandage around her arm.

She shook her head. "All you need to know is that he got your message. He'll be there tomorrow night."

My laugh was empty. I found the tin of chocolate mix, breathing in the smell of chocolate and cinnamon as I popped the lid. Of course she wouldn't talk about the details. She had done her job and, for better or for worse, she had made it home. I whisked in the chocolate mixture, not bothering to measure. I wanted it dark and smooth.

When I was done, I found three mugs and filled them each. I was bringing the first mug over to my Grandmother when I noticed what she had been hiding. Darren had peeled away her shirt and was tending to what lay beneath it. My eyes took a moment to process what it was that I saw. Her chest was a mess of cuts and slashes up close, but from where I stood I saw what it really was.

A name. Someone had carved their own name into my grandmother's skin.

Marcus.

Was that all?

The idea ran through my mind before I could shut it out. She looked up and our eyes met for a brief moment. She knew what I had seen and smiled as if she knew what I had thought. Scars could be healed. The fist she laid on the table was a mess of bruises and cuts, the tip of one missing, as if they'd tried to take her fingers the way they'd taken Magda's. Petra Warren had fought back. But my mind kept working. I looked at the missing finger tip and wondered if they had tried to cut her fingers one knuckle at a time.

Was that what they'd done to Magda while the Manor burned down? Had she not told us of the excruciating pain they'd put her through? I shuddered at the thought and felt a small flame of rage rising inside of me. I forced it down with a hard gulp and forced myself back into motion.

I walked around Darren to place her mug on the counter beside her good hand.

"A bit out of practice?" I teased.

"Diana!" Darren's voice became shrill in a way that I'd never thought it could be.

My Grandmother and I both laughed. He looked between us like we were crazy. Maybe we were. As the only two female wolves right now, we both had worked our way into the thick of danger whenever possible. She knew what she had been getting into. Hell, she must have faced it before when she was doing my job. The only difference was a few years of inactivity.

And it had cost her a fingertip and a whole lot of pain, I reminded myself. Still, she reached out for the cocoa and took a swig. I followed suit, thinking that it needed a shot of rum. Still, it was dark and it released hormones inside of me that calmed my wolf. Chocolate was good for everything.

"You two are insane," Darren grumbled.

"Don't we know," I said.

He looked up at my Grandmother, just now noticing what the mess of cuts read.

"I never should have let you go."

She gave him those steel eyes. "What would have happened to the person you sent in my place? Had you sent Jason or Christian, they wouldn't have come back. Not alive at least."

She hadn't mentioned my name. Had she made her point just using the boys as a reference or had she purposefully left my name out? Did she think that I could stand up against Jonathan and whoever stood with him? Was she insane? I narrowed my eyes at her and she just smiled. It was weak, but it was her signature smile nonetheless.

She thought that I was stronger than the boys.

I felt a surge of pride and fear all at once. I spun around, needing to put my hands to work, to occupy my mind. I couldn't think about possibly standing up against Jonathan. He had nearly killed me years ago and he'd had several chances to do so since I'd been back.

I yanked open the fridge door, pulling out ingredients to make sandwiches. My stomach grumbled with need and I could only imagine my Grandmother's. Each sandwich was piled high with meat and thick sliced cheese. This wasn't an occasion for vegetables, I thought as I reached for the fatty mayonnaise.

"Maybe you should go rest when we're through," Darren suggested as he cleaned her hand.

"Actually, I'm thinking of stealing my granddaughter's lunch."

I could hear Darren's growl of frustration from behind me. He was trying so hard to care for her, but she didn't want to be the person he was treating her as. She didn't want to be the old woman. She wanted to be the warrior again. But was she still the warrior she used to be? I thought of the pain I still felt from time to time in my shoulder. What else did they do to her that we can't see?

"Don't worry," I said. "Two of these are for you."

"You're keeping three for yourself?" she asked, pouting playfully.

She was in such a good mood for having her ass practically handed to her. What were Jonathan's men looking like right about now? Had the fight revived something inside of her that had been dead? Or was the thrill of adrenaline and pain her new high?

"No," I said. "One of the sandwiches is for Darren. I'm not that selfish."

"I only get one?"

I nodded. "You're not missing any fingers or spent the last eight hours on four feet."

"What about me?" Jason appeared and grabbed a bar stool close to my Grandmother. He set a hand on her shoulder. She reached up to hold it, but quickly jerked back when she realized it was her right hand. A shadow passed through her eyes before the steel rose again.

"You can have mine," Darren said as he stood.

"I was just joking," Jason tried to take it back, but Darren shook his head.

Darren looked tired. All of this was weighing on him. It didn't help that he was the kind of man that put everything on his own shoulders to begin with. This had been my Grandmother's choice, but he was bearing the guilt for her disfigurement. I thought about wrapping my arms around him for a moment, but reminded myself that I needed to keep a distance from him. Instead, I said something I never thought I'd say.

"Go home. Go home to Fionna and take some time for yourself. We have things covered here."

He hung his head for a moment before nodding. His eyes found my Grandmother, filling with pain and shame.

"Leave," she demanded. Jason nodded, agreeing with the both of us.

This had to end soon, I thought. It was slowly killing all of us, figuratively and not so figuratively.

CHAPTER TWENTY-SEVEN

There was always a plan hatching in my Grandmother's head. With her hair pulled high upon her head and a dress straight off of a forties femme fatale, she turned away and left us standing outside of the town hall. She hadn't looked this good in days. She must have shifted a few times between yesterday and tonight because many of her wounds had healed, leaving shiny pink scars all over her body. Sure, her clothes were always immaculate, but now there was an air of control about her again.

It was nighttime, the moon riding high in the sky, shining brightly as it showed us half of its face. I brought my attention back down to earth and the wolves that were crawling the glowing streets. In the distance, I could make out the forms of Todd and Marcus, a pair of slim shoulders butting up against broader ones. The wind brought their scent down to me, only confirming what I already knew. Chills ran down my spine and I stepped closer to my new Clan mates as I remembered my last run ins with those two.

That was only two of the wolves out tonight. My Grandmother had successfully called a meeting of the Clan at the town hall. We were all hoping that the ground was neutral enough that we could pull this off. The divide had gone on long enough and something had to be done about it. We couldn't stand another moment of sneak attacks and pointless deaths.

Darren appeared at my side and I turned a weak smile up to him. When I saw his attention shift and his whole body stiffen, I thought I knew what was coming.

I was surprised when I looked up to see Fionna coming our way. She opened her arms wide to wrap them around his neck, forcing me to step aside. She kissed him lightly.

Darren's arm snaked around her shoulder, pulling her thin frame closer to him. She kept her eyes cast downward, her so-blond-they're-almost white bangs falling over her face. She was meek and looked like prey. Maybe he saw her as delicate, as protectable.

I felt a twang of sorrow when I looked at her, knowing what she must be going through. Yet, I wondered how she got tangled up with us in the first place. A cream colored slip hugged her body beneath a lace sheath dress. It gave her even more of a dainty look. A woman like this didn't belong amongst monsters like us.

She looked up through her bangs and gave us a meek smile.

"I didn't know if you would be able to make it tonight," Darren said, his eyes taking on a funny look.

My eyes widened. We were using the town courthouse as a neutral meeting place. Darren wanted to put an end to Jonathan's sneak attacks by announcing a formal challenge. What place did Fionna have at a meeting like this was beyond me. Sure, she had helped us get an invitation into the Court, but being here tonight could get her killed. She turned to me with a soft smile and held out her dainty and unusually long hand in greeting, but I let it hang in the air. Alarms were going off in my head. They were loud and impossible to ignore now. She was wrong in every way.

I tried to catch Darren's eyes, to see what he knew. A funny feeling crawled up my arms, like static. It was familiar and made my stomach roll.

"Good evening, Diana," Jonathan crooned. "I see you have met my future daughter-in-law."

The woman perked up, her blonde bangs falling away from her eyes to show that light in them. She gave Jonathan a sweet smile that Darren didn't catch.

A growl tickled up my throat.

"I do hope that we can get to know each other more during your stay," Fionna said to me. "I've been looking forward to it, really."

A genuine smile split her glossed lips and the look in her eyes said that she meant it. It just creeped me out even more.

Slightly irked that my skin was crawling, I grabbed Darren's arm and pulled him away.

"What is it that you aren't telling me about her?"

"Are you jealous?"

"Of course not. You tell me why she is here tonight or I am done. I am done helping you with whatever plans you have."

I glanced back over my shoulder at Fionna who was chatting away with Jonathan. Her hand gently touched his arm when she laughed at his comment. Her behavior was nothing less than flirtatious and it made me sick.

She must have caught me watching because she waggled her long fingers in my direction. I frowned and turned back to Darren. Our eyes met and the best that he could do was shrug. Fionna was a strange contrast to Jonathan, but I thought that they might be two kindred souls.

I wondered if Darren knew.

Father and son had agreed to meet. So many of us had been hurt during this civil war without actually getting anywhere. The Clan was still divided after the wolf bit my shoulder, after my aunt lost her fingers and my grandmother had a name carved into her chest. This would go on forever if we let it.

The two opposing groups filed into the largest room of the building. Darren's group kept to themselves, huddling close around the low stage that sat at the front of the room. Jonathan's henchmen, because that's all I could think to call them, leaned against the far wall with smug smiles. Their egos were so over inflated from all of the bullying that they had been doing around town. In the folding chairs sat a few, ashen faced Faoladh that stared either straight ahead or at the floor. The frightened herd. But that was Jonathan's vision. He imagined us stronger through more violent ways.

Marcus stood beside Todd, glaring at me with empty eyes that flicked from me to my grandmother every so often. He wanted my blood, but this was a peace meeting. The pact had been made and no harm could befall anyone while they were here or even after the formal challenge. My skin crawled when I pulled my attention away from him. He would be watching me the whole time, waiting for me to leave so that he could break that pact.

But he wasn't the only monster in the room.

"Next full moon, we put this to rest," Darren said, not in front of the two crowds, but standing in the small space between them.

Murmurs began to roll around the room. Everyone had an opinion of their own, but just became a dull roar. I moved closer to where Darren and Jonathan were talking at the head of the assembly room.

Jonathan nodded, no smile on his face, but with his eyes alight. "On the next full moon, we will cast a challenge before the Clan. The wolf who leaves the circle will be the next Alpha."

My eyes fell on Darren. His spine was straight and his chin held high, even though his father pressed into his space. Jonathan was here using fear and death to try to win control. If we had any say in who led us, then why were we arguing over the matter? We had the ability to simply choose to follow Darren, to choose something good. But nearly half of the Clan chose to follow fear and death. It broke my heart. It saddened me to think that Jonathan could rope in all of the most submissive, those most vulnerable, and keep them wrangled in with the most vile wolves that this Clan had borne.

Didn't they know that if he won, they would die? Or were they so convinced that those flowers blooming outside were his doing? That the Goddess wouldn't return for the Warren family or their supporters?

I had found a feeling of safety, pressed between my Aunt and Grandmother. That was how Clan should feel and that was lost for so many wolves. It would be lost forever if Jonathan could kill his son. It was then that I could smell the everlasting flowers, carried in by a stray breeze. It was followed by a gentle heat, like basking in the sun on a summer day, but it was November.

Here we go again, I thought.

It filled me up, the light. I could feel it burning through every inch of my body. My back arched and my mouth opened, but I refused to scream. I would not scream. She was inside me. We were one in the same, the Goddess and I. And never before had I felt her so powerful. I lifted my head up to face the Clan, smiling despite the power that still burned inside of me. I felt as if I should fall to ashes right then and there, but then she rose and spoke through me.

"I came back to you," she said through my voice. "I thought that I would give my creations another chance at love and magic. Yet, you continue to destroy one another, wrestling for power. That is not what Clan means."

Clan means family and protection.

Among the crowd, people turned to one another, not quite sure what was going on. Whispers circled around the room, debates on who was really speaking. She turned my body towards those that stood behind me. As I passed my Aunt and Grandmother, my arm reached out to caress their cheeks. They could feel the burn of the light as a little of it touched them. Darren fell to his knees as I came closer. She loved him, the Goddess. She loved him dearly, knowing that everything good she had made of her children lay in him. She loved him just as much as she loved me. She only wished that it was in her power to change the ills we had faced in life.

But if she could, then we would not be the people she loved.

She dropped me to my knees before him, gripping his face in our hands. His jaw dropped as the power bled into him. We leaned in, taking his lower lip between our teeth. His lips closed around ours and we fell into a kiss. I pulled us back, afraid that the Goddess would devour him in her love.

She let out a heavy laugh from my body, one that rumbled from my belly up. Full of happiness and love, she turned to the last two people standing on the stage. Jonathan's face was blank, only a slight furrowing of his brows gave away his anger. This was the man that bore the male wolf she loved so dearly, the man that killed my father.

Then there was the scowling fae woman. Fionna's lips were twisted into a frown while her eyes sized me up. Despite having just kissed her fiancée, I watched Fionna's lips curl upwards. The Goddess looked upon her and cringed. She knew something that she could not share with me yet. Fionna was no one's puppet, no one's lover. It made my stomach roll.

"Will you continue to destroy my creations? My dreams?" She asked Jonathan through me as she stood. "My gift was first given because of the need to protect. Why would you make a monstrosity out of my children, turn them from a shield to a blade?"

"I don't know what you are talking about, Diana."

She laughed again. "The girl does bear my namesake, but you are not talking to her at this moment and you know that. Answer me: Will you continue to destroy?"

His lips twisted into a sour frown. He stood silent. I wasn't sure if he was afraid or defiant. She took that as an answer before I could decipher it.

"So be it then," she said. I felt the light rush out of me. The burn traveled up my spine and was followed by a wave of ice. Yet, a warmth continued to burn within my chest.

This wolf has chosen his fate. I have left a gift with you, a legacy, that you will need.

My knees gave and I crumpled. The floor welcomed my cheek with a cold slap and the room began to swim. The edges of my vision turned black, but I focused on the small ball of warmth that was burning in my chest. It burned where my heart should be. I pulled my arms up, bracing myself against the floor. My vision began to focus as I picked myself up.

I looked up at my family, Darren, and Jonathan. Petra smiled while Magda's face was still a look of pure bliss. Darren began to cross the room to help me. I warned him off with one hand. I could stand on my own.

As soon as I could, I shuffled across the stage towards Jonathan. The warmth in my chest burned out through my eyes in rage.

"She is going to leave us because of murderers like you," I growled at him.

183

He leaned in close, thin lips touching my ear and said : "I'm not the only killer standing on this stage."

Ice washed over me. What did he know?

I glanced over at Darren. The Goddess thought that she could save us, but I could feel everything crumbling around me. Jonathan was destroying us in body and spirit. What gift could the Goddess have given me to bring this to an end? I thought of an end, but it only made me feel colder.

Retreating back to my family, I saw that Fionna's eyes had a dark glare to them that was aimed directly at me. Her cheeks were flushed and the smile looked forced, showing too much teeth. She reached out to lay her hand on my arm and I instinctively jerked back as I felt a touch of static. The Goddess had labeled her suspect just as I had. I wanted nothing to do with her.

When her bangs finally fell away from her eyes, I took a step back. They narrowed at me, full of malice and coldness. Something else fluttered through those eyes as I watched and her face changed. It was no less soft than before, but it held a touch of strength that hadn't been there before. Paired with the smile, she looked just as dangerous as Jonathan. The dark shades of blue and green that swirled in her eyes seemed as inhuman as my own gold eyes. Deep dark blue surrounded spikes of emerald green. Here was a wolf in sheep's clothing, I thought to myself as I backed away from her.

CHAPTER TWENTY-EIGHT

"When did Darren get engaged to that woman?" I asked Aunt Magda from over my mug. Hot steam rose up from the cocoa and caressed my face. I needed it after last night.

She stopped what she was doing and stared in space as she thought. Her eyes found mine. "I'm not really sure now that you ask."

"You mean there was no big engagement party, not even a rampant rumor?" I set my mug down, intrigued now. "A lot of the wolf wives like to gossip at the Balefire. You of all people would have to have known."

She sighed, almost drowned out by the knick-knick of her knife against the plastic cutting board. Strawberries became sloppy red cubes as she learned to use her hand once more. I reached across the counter if the kitchen island to grab the bowl of leftover butter-cream frosting. I scooped up a few of Magda's strawberries with one spoon and topped it off with vanilla butter-cream with another spoon. It was smooth and sweet across my tongue.

Aunt Magda slammed her knife down on the counter. "I don't even remember him introducing her to any of the Clan."

My frosting spoon hung in mid air. Magda looked at me, her head cocked. I could see the muscles in her jaw working.

"Why don't I remember her? I mean, they're engaged and none of us have met her?"

"Because she doesn't belong." I stated.

Aunt Magda's lips twisted into a scowl. "Are you sure you aren't suspicious of her just because you're jealous?"

A pang of hot anger shot through me, but I took a deep breath and forced it back down. I didn't want to talk about it right now.

Taking the frosting bowl in one hand and my tea in the other, I climbed the stairs to the Farmhouse's makeshift office, a sloppy spare bedroom. I bumped the door with my hip to open it and found Darren inside, sitting behind a desk and a stack of papers. He was probably working on making new records of the Clan finances so I went about my own business without a word. Setting my tea on the floor and my frosting in my lap, I leaned my back against the desk.

"So how did you and Fionna meet?"

I could feel him grow still behind me. This was the first time that we had spoken of her. I didn't think he expected me to approach the subject at all.

"It's okay," I lied. "We can talk about her."

A long moment passed before he spoke. "We met at a farmer's market."

"A farmer's market?" I laughed. It takes a special kind of man to go to a farmer's market. That kind of man is stereotypically gay, a hipster, or already married. I didn't know if Darren had suddenly become a hipster, because I knew the other two didn't apply, yet.

"Solstice Winery and the Trudeau's Farm each have stands at the market. I've been visiting to network with them."

"You've had your eyes on being Alpha for a while," I realized. "Haven't you?"

"After you and your mom left town, I started spending a lot of time with your grandparents. I knew it wasn't safe being home. It turned my life right-side up to have someone other than my father in my life for once. Arthur was a good man."

I remembered my Grandmother making a statement by saying that he had practically raised Darren. I didn't know that it had left this much of a mark on Darren. But we had also gotten off topic.

I could hear his chair against the floor as he pushed it back. "What does that matter right now? The goal is to keep Dad from assuming control of the Clan, not to investigate my fiancée."

I went back to pouting. He was right, this was about Jonathan. I'd worry about his love life later.

"So the plan is, we don't really have a plan?" I asked, spinning around to face him. "Last night, we announced that there will be a formal challenge on the next full moon. We didn't pull anything out of our asses that wasn't already up there."

Darren just gave me a look. After a few moments he finally spoke. "It's the best route that I can take. There is an end to this, I just don't know if there's light at the end of this tunnel. If I win, then I have unquestionable control for at the very least the next year."

"And that's if you win." I said what we were both thinking. "What if you don't win the challenge? We both know Jonathan for the monster that he is; we know what he is capable of."

His shoulders started to fall, but he pulled them back up. There was fear in his eyes. I set my bowl aside and pushed myself up onto my knees. Crawling over to the side of his chair, I held his face between my hands. It was too intimate a gesture, but I could remember the love that the Goddess had felt for him. It burned with a steady heat, one filled with pride and faith. She only worried that he didn't have what it took to kill. No, that was a gift she had given that to another wolf.

"What will you do if he kills me?" Darren suddenly asked, his hand moving to cover mine.

I was thrown for a loop. My emotions surged like a tidal wave and crashed through me. I stumbled over my words, unable to tell him anything that I was feeling. My wolf howled for him, fearing the loss of the one she craved.

I pulled back, letting myself fall to sit on the floor. Looking out the window behind him, all I could hear was her frightened howling. What could I do if he lost? I couldn't leave now. There was too much that I held dear now. There were people I loved, people that needed my protection. Jonathan had been right. He hadn't been the only killer there last night.

"You know," I said, changing the subject. "I don't blame you for my father's death. I don't blame you for anything that happened that day. Not anymore."

He sucked in a deep breath as if he could breathe for the first time. Maybe I had taken some imaginary weight off of his shoulders.

His back straightened and there was a new sheen in his eyes, the beginning of tears.

Grabbing the Bianca's journal and the bowl of frosting, I decided to leave the conversation here. He could revel in all of the emotions that he was feeling, but I wanted to ignore my own. I wanted to bury them deep and move on. It was what I did best.

Downstairs, I grabbed a fresh mug of tea and pulled the journal onto my lap. I wasn't sure that I would find anything, but I had to look. Jonathan couldn't have killed his sister just for the thrill of it. If that was all it was about then she would have been dead years ago. I flipped through the pages, scanning for script that looked panicked or...just different. There, in a margin, someone had written: beware the glamour. I furrowed my brows in confusion as I glared at the paper. I willed it to tell me it's hidden story, knowing that there had to be more to that.

The scrambling of claws against hardwood floors caught my attention and my head snapped up from the file. In the hall between the kitchen and living room were two wolves. They tugged and tugged, a rope toy hanging taught between them. I cocked my head and watched from my seat on the couch. My brain registered that these were werewolves, but here they were playing with dog toys. It was almost beyond imaginable.

I pulled my knees up, letting the warmth from the mug in my hands flow into me. The sound of werewolves playfully growling and nipping at each other was relaxing in a way. I studied the patterns of fur on the two playing wolves, trying to memorize who was who in wolf form.

The one wolf had gray and brown fur with a brown line running up the center of its muzzle to blossom across its head. The other was more black than gray, but the tips of his ears and feet were tinged with gray. We shared so little in common with our canine cousins that it was questionable if we even came from wolves. The shape was nearly the same, but with tighter, stronger muscle and a human voice hiding in the canine skull.

I suspected that the two wolves playing on the floor were probably Christian and another young wolf, being still kind of stupid. I just couldn't tell which was which. The black wolf victoriously pulled the toy from the jaws of the gray and brown wolf, prancing away happily. Not knowing what to do, the gray and brown wolf stood still as it took in the room. His eyes found me and it was suddenly bounding over to me with a goofy smile. The wolf's tongue lolled out of the side of his mouth once he came to a halt before me. He nipped at my pant leg and nudged my toes with his cold nose.

"I don't want to play," I whined.

He barked at me and grabbed at my pant leg. He tugged my leg from the couch, my heel falling with a thump. I pulled back my lip in a mock snarl as I returned my leg to its former position. Once more, the wolf grabbed my leg and pulled. I held fast until I hear the familiar tearing sound.

"You ripped my pants!"

Goofy smile back, the wolf took off in the direction the black one had gone. Stupid animal, I thought. I heard a mess of claws scraping against the hardwood floors as they tried to get traction. What were they up to? Setting my mug aside, I decided to investigate what the two wolves were up to.

Scattered across the hardwood floor were the contents of my travel bag. An electric blue lace bra hung from the muzzle of the black and gray wolf. I dove for the piece of fabric, but he darted away. My socked feet slid across the floor as I stumbled after him.

The wolves all came to a sliding stop as a figure stepped into the narrow hallway. Darren loomed over the black and grey wolf. The bra slipped from his muzzle and he whined as he lowered his body to the floor.

"What the hell were you two doing?" Darren boomed. He bent to pick up my bra from the floor. "Go circle the Manor a few times, make sure there's no one else out there."

I opened my mouth to claim the bra, but nothing came out. Our eyes met as the wolves scrambled out of the hallway. My face burned, probably as red as it was warm.

"I believe that this belongs to you," Darren held it out by a finger through the bra strap, making it look even naughtier to me.

I stood awkwardly for a moment and a smirk turned up the corners of his mouth. Narrowing my eyes at him, I snatched the bra away and spun around. All over the floor were t-shirts and underwear. My cropped Batman t-shirt, my Five Finger Death Punch shirt, ivory lace panties, and black boy-shorts were scattered about like a fabric explosion.

Darren knelt down beside me, helping to corral my clothing. I snatched the articles away from him. A wolfish grin spread over his face as I pulled my clothes close to my chest. He held up something that I hadn't seen.

Dangling from his fingertips was a very small pair of sheer electric blue bikini panties.

"Why did you pack these?" He teased. "You came home for a funeral."

"I don't know," I lunged for the piece of blue fabric.

Darren jerked back, almost losing his balance. I swept my foot out, hooking it behind his so that he fell back with a thump. I lunged over him, reaching for my captured panties. His arm snaked around my waist as I hovered over him. I cried out just as he pulled me down to his body. He smothered my growl with his mouth, teeth grabbing at my lower lip. I couldn't help but moan as a jolt ran through me.

He took that as an invitation, rolling over so that his weight pressed me into the floor. His fingers intertwined with mine, the panties pressed between our hands. His hips ground into mine as his other hand cupped my face.

Not again. My wolf leapt for joy. I could feel her fur brushing the inside of me, only adding to the sensations that were flooding me. Darren was hers.

Always. Mine.

"Darren," I was able to say between kisses. "We need to stop."

He pulled back, breathing heavy. My lips throbbed with the urgency of his kiss.

"Don't do this," I wanted to, but I couldn't. My hands fought against my will. They wanted to feel his firm stomach beneath his shirt, feel the curve of his ass, feel the length of him that was brushing my thigh.

I poured all of my control into my body and wriggled out from beneath him. I grabbed my clothing before running upstairs.

My back slid down the closed door behind me. As much as I disliked Fionna, it didn't mean that I could sneak in and steal Darren away from her. It felt like such a horrible thing to do, even if his body felt so right pressed against mine. What if I was wrong? What if Fionna was truly his mate? It was as if all thoughts of her left his mind when she wasn't around. It hurt every time this happened.

In the meantime, he had one purpose to focus on. He had to become our Alpha. He had promised himself to another woman and he had to hold that promise. I had to help him do both. The moon was growing full and I had to try to fix myself, pull the pieces of me together, in the meantime.

CHAPTER TWENTY-NINE

It was finally the night of the Challenge. Tension and excitement sparked through the Manor like a live wire. Darren clutched my hand, hiding his fear in the tight grip. Any other time and I would have pulled away. Not now. This was the night that would decide everything.

This was the night that he could die.

My grandmother wore white jeans that tucked into light gray boots. Her crest sat atop the buttons of her button down shirt. Mine felt heavy against my breastbone, hidden behind my charcoal v-neck shirt. I wanted it against my skin tonight. From the Manor's window, I could see the glow of light coming from the town square. It made me cold with fear. Yet, I rolled my shoulders back with determination.

We heard the last car pull into the driveway and we all knew that it was time to move. Aunt Magda sat in her green Ford, waiting for my Grandmother to join her. Darren had asked Aunt Magda to stay, but she hadn't listened to a word of it. Darren had two female wolves on his side and one very determined human woman. I knew that Jonathan was afraid of me, but I wasn't sure why. Was it because he knew that I was willing to go that extra step that his son wasn't? That must have excited and terrified Jonathan to his core. I cringed, thinking what this terror might make him do next.

Christian, Jason, and Henry got into Jason's big truck while the older Guards climbed into a beat up Jeep. Our makeshift convoy began its trek from the Manor to the town square. The Challenge would begin at the Goddess's altar, making it a beacon for the winner. Magic of the full moon would surround us, cloak us against the prying eyes of humans. The fight would eventually spill out into the woods that bordered the town.

Tonight, we would pit father against son in hopes that a true Alpha would come out on top. I had no doubt that Darren's dominance would blow away his father's. It was Jonathan's dirty tactics that worried me. Jonathan wanted control at all costs; not a thing stopped a man who felt nothing. I hoped that he truly would feel terror by the end of this night.

Inside the car, where no one else could see us, Darren reached for my hand again. He brought it to his lips, kissing the back of it. I couldn't bring myself to argue with it tonight. I prayed there would be plenty of time later for me to yell at him.

"Stay safe tonight," he whispered in the darkness. The glow of the dashboard illuminated his tired face.

"I'm not the one you need to worry about," I said. I think I had come to terms with my fate.

"But I do anyway." His eyes met mine for a second and probably saw what I'd been thinking, saw the resolve on my face.

I pulled my hand away and shook my head. He wasn't going to talk me down from my own fate. I'd outrun it for too long now, anyway.

"I accepted you as my Guardian only so that you would have a reason to stay, Diana. Now that I look back, it seems such a foolish idea. I can't focus thinking that you are out on your own while all of this is going on. How many times have you cheated death since you have been home?"

"I refuse to be your liability," I made sure of that. "You can't do the job we need you to do if you are worrying about me all the time."

He glanced at me, a short gaze that seemed to take in so much. "Don't you realize that I love you? I can't fucking help it."

I took in a deep breath, but came up with nothing.

"I have since we were stupid kids."

"Shut up, Darren. You can't love me."

"Don't tell me that I can't!"

"No," I snapped. "You can't be involved with you Guard. Causes conflict of interests. Not to mention you're getting married to another woman soon."

You're marrying the bad guy, I thought.

I turned to stare out my window, refusing to even look at him. He could probably hear my heart beating away in my chest. He could probably smell my wolf rise to his invitation. She craved his wolf, the beast with black and gray fur. Did he understand why I asked to be a part of his guard?

Darren needed to stay at a distance. I couldn't return the feelings that he was offering. Yes, of course attraction was alive and well between us, but that didn't indicate that I was capable of anything more. I didn't want anything else, I lied to myself as I gazed out at the silhouettes of pine trees.

Overhead, the moon was full, round and glowing bright. My wolf brushed against my skin. She wanted to run free. With everything that had been going on, I hadn't trusted her to let me come back so I had put off changing for too long. Trust me, I tried to tell her, I can take care of us, too.

Being in the car made me nervous. There was no exact reason why, but a heavy weight sat on my shoulders anyway. Something bad was going to happen. Behind us drove Aunt Magda, my Grandmother and Christian. Jason's truck brought up the rear. The night was cold and absolutely clear, stars sparkling above us and the moon showing half of her glowing face. I wished I could say that it was reassuring, but the unsettling feeling was still gnawing at me.

We were almost there; we had almost won. It wasn't a race by any means, but the challenge had been made. Our supporters were waiting for us at the altar, where all ceremonies were conducted and where each run began. I wore my best boots, made of supple beige leather that rode up to my knee with a single buckle at the ankle, for the occasion.

Darren slammed on the brakes. My arms shot out to brace myself against the dashboard. I came face to face with the band stickers on his dashboard, slowly raising my head. I pulled my gaze up from Rise Against to peer outside the windshield. Dark shapes blocked the road. Road flares ignited in their hands and I could see the shape of a truck with a workman's compartment on the back as well as two other sedans blockading the road. Several people piled out of the cars, others moving around them from where they lit the flares.

"What the fuck?" I muttered.

"What the fuck indeed," Darren agreed. He pulled his phone from the cup holder and texted those behind us. "Stay here."

Darren shoved his door open and got out into the night. Like hell will I stay behind, I thought. I jumped out of the other side of his car, earning a glare from him. I spun around at the sound of muffled yells. Men had flanked the sides of the cars behind us, holding their doors shut by any means. A trickle of cold fear rushed through me. I quickly covered it up with the heat of anger. It was better to be angry than afraid, I thought.

Too many Clan wolves stood out on the streets tonight. They held guns and knives, keeping other wolves in their cars. It was just Darren and I now, the rest of our help locked in their cars by their own Clan. Side by side, we marched forward. I could smell the lingering scent of Jonathan. My eyes sought out the tallest figure in the darkness.

At least I was willing to fight for my life. I always had been. Jonathan had taught me that. Why hadn't these wolves learned it as well? Where was the need to protect? Did they need to watch someone they loved die, like Henry did? Part of me worried that tonight they would have to watch someone die. Tonight they thought that they would be watching Darren die and I couldn't let that happen.

"Bitch, those eyes are creepy," an unfamiliar voice said.

I turned in the direction of the voice and snarled. My eyes must have caught the reflection of the moonlight or the flares, glowing like a wild animal's. Marcus and a group of guards stepped forward. They cradled guns in their arms. Who brought guns to a wolf fight? That was just plain unfair. I silently prayed that none of them knew how to properly shoot. Maybe then we would have a fighting chance.

"You won't be making it to the Altar tonight, son."

I placed myself in front of Darren while scanning the scene. I counted three guards and Jonathan ahead of us. I had no clue how many of them were behind us, holding our friends hostage.

"Turn around, go home," Jonathan continued. "Even if you issued the Challenge right here, right now these fine boys here would shoot down your shiny new family. So, why don't you declare me the victor and we can put all of this behind us?"

"You're fucking insane," Darren growled from behind me.

"Pish posh, I think you're all insane for trying to hide what you are. We are merely animals, son. Why not embrace that fact? Everyone here wants to embrace it, right?"

There was a chorus of roaring approval from at least half of his entourage.

"You're not an animal," I spat at him. He quickly closed the space between us. "You're a horrible fucking monster of a human being. You're a cold hearted, murdering son of a bitch."

His smile was wide, teeth white and flat. I smiled in return, a wolfish smile of sharp teeth.

"This is coming from the bitch that is more wolf than human," he cupped my chin in his long fingers.

I tried to jerk out of his grip, but he held on tight. Darren reached out, pulling at my arm, but someone appeared to my right. Well, shit. The long and cold barrel of a rifle was level with my skull. A bullet to the brain, silver or not, would kill any of us.

"Don't do this," Darren roared. There was nothing he could do, nothing that he would let himself do with the barrel of a rifle aimed in my direction. Would I be stupid enough to try something? I glanced to the man at my side, the one who held the gun. Todd. He wouldn't hesitate. He would enjoy the kill. I fell slack in Jonathan's grip.

"Turn around," Jonathan said. "Name me Alpha, go home, and you will find her on your doorstep in the morning."

Dead. Sure, he would find me on the doorstep, nothing but a corpse. Yet, there was nothing we could do. Our people were barricaded in their cars and Darren stood alone amongst the monsters. Beyond Jonathan, I could see a slim figure in the dark. A soft wind pushed my hair back and brought a scent to my nose. It was familiar, yet different. I had smelled a version of that before, but this time it was paired with pine and silver. My mind attached a name to the figure, even though I couldn't see her face. Fionna stood just out of my sight's range. It had to be her.

"Tell me she will be alive and well when you bring her back," Darren bargained.

"I will return Diana Warren to you in the very state that I have taken her in."

I looked to Darren, our eyes meeting. We both knew the lie for what it was, but we had no other options. I gave him a slight nod, what I could manage with Jonathan's grip still on me. I could handle myself, I hoped. We would find another way to win this yet.

"I surrender my bid to Alpha," Darren said through clenched teeth. "You are the one and only Alpha of this Clan."

Jonathan smiled wide, reaching out with his empty hand to clamp it onto his son's shoulder. "That is all I wanted to hear you say."

Darren said nothing, only jerked his shoulder out from beneath Jonathan's grip. There was a pain in the depths of his eyes. I couldn't tell if it was from having to leave me here or if he mourned for the father figure that Jonathan could have been.

Gripping his hair in his hands like a man gone mad, Darren growled and turned back to his car. He slammed his fist on the roof, turning to look at us one more time. This time, no one was here to save me at the last minute. No Helen. No mother. Not even Darren.

Holding me back, keeping me away from the fight had been Darren's way of helping me all those years ago. Had I gotten away from them and run to my father sooner, I probably wouldn't be standing here now. I wouldn't be in Jonathan's arms with a rifle held to me. It was okay this time; I had learned how to take care of myself. I refused to die needlessly. I only hoped that Darren had some sort of a backup plan, something for when the shit really hit the fan. Because, let's face it, when it came to Jonathan, it was only a matter of time before it did.

When Darren finally got back into his car, they scooped me up. With the gun still pressed against my temple, Marcus pushed forward to throw me over his shoulder. A hand gripped my hair, jerking my head up. I found myself face to face with one of the Clan-less wolves. I ground my teeth together and silently bore it.

"Don't count on seeing the sun rise, pup. Even if she needs you for her spell," he said. "None of your little Clan will survive, especially not your so called leader. It's the age of the Hunter, now."

I heard the scrape of metal on metal just before Marcus hoisted me into the workman's truck. Pain seared across my scalp where the Clan-less wolf had ripped my hair out. A dull throb began in my back, making me wonder if I'd landed on someone's wrench.

I heard the lock slide into place, a sense of finality settling in. What were my choices?

My heart was thundering in my chest, the beat rising into my ears. I struggled to get myself under control. My wolf paced inside me, snarling with rage. While we were locked up, Jonathan planned on destroying my family. I had just reconnected with them, learned what they meant to me, how they could help me fix the broken creature that I had become. I couldn't let Jonathan take them away from me again.

CHAPTER THIRTY

I could hear the low laughter of men in the cab of the truck. Suddenly, the truck halted and I flew forward into the wall of the enclosure. My head swam after crashing off the steel. They were going to be brake happy pricks, I thought as I steadied myself. The laughter got louder on the other side of the wall that I hit. Todd and Marcus were on the other side, my ears told me.

They were broken inside, disturbed. I remembered how Marcus would bring dead animals back to the grade school classrooms. He had caught them with human hands, strangling squirrels and rats before moving on to housecats. He had seen nothing wrong with shoving them in his desk, with sharing his triumph. Wasn't that the first sign of a budding serial killer? I remembered Todd's cold eyes as he stared down the barrel of the rifle at me. I wasn't afraid of him. Every time I had run into him, he had someone else there to hurt me. No, it was Marcus that truly scared me.

I shivered. Panic was rising and my wolf wanted out. She couldn't defend herself locked inside the body of a girl. She clawed at me and for the first time in a while, I felt the physical pain. It tore at me from the inside out. Normally, I would have argued with her, but this time I needed her help.

Hurried, I pried off my new boots. I felt a pang of regret as I threw them to the side, but if I survived this, I would buy myself three new pairs of boots. Black leather and soft brown leather, with buckles and zippers. I fell forward, palms braced against the rusted steel of the truck bed. The change ran through me like a pleasant shudder. She would protect us. She would fight.

I wriggled out of the rest of my clothing, using my back feet to kick them to the corner of the truck bed. I would be ready for them when they opened that door. I lowered my body, steadying myself for the stop and go that tossed me around.

"Wakey wakey, Bitch. We are almost there!" Marcus slammed on the back of his cab.

My growl in response was low and nearly silent.

"She's too quiet back there," Todd said.

"Pull over and I'll go back there to wake her up."

"Fionna won't like you messing around with her. She won't arrive in one piece."

Did he just say what I think he said? I had been expecting Jonathan's name so much that I had to pause and sort out what I had just heard. But they weren't answering to Jonathan. It was Fionna that held all of their leashes. What did she want with me? I remembered the look that had been on her face the other night and a realization came over me. In that moment, after my display, she had made a decision.

Beware the glamour.

"Pull over," Marcus growled. "I don't care what she wants."

I faintly heard Todd sigh. He jerked the truck over and slammed on the brakes. I rolled to the side, disoriented and tangled in bra straps. My heart hammered while I listened to the truck door slam and waited. The lock on my enclosure groaned as he pulled it open. I struggled free of my clothes. Backing into the far corner of the enclosure, I readied myself.

Fight. Survive. We always will.

Crazy eyes sparkled behind the black curls that fell over Marcus's eyes. He searched the darkness for me, his crazy grin fading. It turned to a scowl when he found a wolf staring back at him. I leapt at him, snapping at his throat. Instinctively, he tossed me aside. I rolled down the bank of the ditch. My paws splashed in dank rainwater.

I was free of the truck! Collecting myself, I ran. I took off in any direction, as long as it was away from those two. I could hear Marcus's howl of frustration behind me. I was free.

A boom filled the air and I could smell gunpowder on the wind. A hole in the earth exploded beside me. This was not good. I zigzagged across the open field, but it was still an open field. I was exposed. Even though my fur was dark, I was in their sights.

Another shot was followed by a howl. There was a rifle and a sociopath werewolf after me. I leaned away as the grass to my left exploded. My heart raced. I wasn't going to be able to escape this. I wasn't going to live after tonight.

Darren's face came to mind, his soft eyes watching me with worry and pride. I remembered the press of our human bodies together in a night that I had thought had been a mistake. I wanted to feel that again. I wanted to wake up in his arms and feel safe. I couldn't believe that I was admitting this, but I wanted it more than anything as gunshots rang out. I needed Darren.

There was a pounding beat coming up fast behind me, four feet hitting the earth, not two. Marcus had caught up, but I wasn't going to go down without a fight. I had battled bigger than him like this before. I had won, no matter how bittersweet that victory had been. I would keep winning. I had something to live for. Someone to live for, I reminded myself.

I stopped and my momentum spun me around. My back feet dug into the ground as I launched myself at him. I was smaller than him and he didn't expect the turnaround. My teeth caught his left flank as he tried to swerve away. He slid in the wet field and I quickly rebounded.

Go for the jugular, I thought. Go for the jugular. He snapped for me, but I danced out of his reach. He chased me around this way for a while, growing more and more frustrated by the sound of his growls. Adrenaline was still pumping through me. I darted forward, but he recovered quickly. His teeth snapped at my flank, grazing flesh. I stumbled, a hot pain racing up my leg, but I kept going. I couldn't stop. He was right behind me, snapping and biting. Another bite sank into my flesh. I fell, rolling on the ground. While the pain burned through my leg I forced myself to my feet. I stayed steady on my feet.

He snapped again, but I danced away. My body slammed into a tree. Pain jolted up my leg. Tree at my back, Marcus circled me. He snapped at me over and over. His teeth never touched me, but I pressed myself tighter and tighter to the tree. I had to make a dash for it.

But how? Anywhere I looked, Marcus was there. He was a massive wolf. The smell of Todd and gunpowder became stronger and stronger by the moment. They were going to try to corral me back into the truck.

Fuck that.

I feinted to the left. Marcus vaulted himself at me head on. I dropped my body to the ground and he flew over me. He crashed into another tree behind me, body dropping into the mud. I took the chance and leapt on him. Pain filled my leg as I hung in the air. This was the chance. If he moved, It was all over for me. I prayed that I was faster than him as I fell.

Finally my teeth clamped onto his throat. They slid past fur and flesh until warmth burst in my mouth. Shaking my head back and forth, I tore the flesh open. He struggled beneath me, making me jump back. I took flesh and fur with me. He staggered as he tried to stand, but he was bleeding out too fast. The wound was too big and his heart was beating too fast from the chase. I danced away from him and he continued to snap and lunge at me. His movements grew sluggish despite his body trying to repair itself. It couldn't make blood out of thin air. In a few moments, it was all over.

The giant wolf's body collapsed onto the ground. There was gore and blood surrounding us. I turned tail and ran before I could watch it begin to change back into human form. I didn't want to see the person I had just killed, no matter who it was.

A gunshot rang out in the air. The tree beside me exploded with splinters. My brain spared a moment to think damn, his eyes are good in the dark. My wolf took over and darted into the woods, ducking between trees.

My body ached. Pain jolted up through the pads of my paws as I ran. I was pushing myself too hard. There was no way I could stop. I lifted my nose to the rushing air, scenting the world around me. I had to find my way back to the Manor. I needed to get back to Darren. Back to Aunt Magda and the Clan.

Protect them.

CHAPTER THIRTY-ONE

Naked and exhausted, I climbed the steps of the farmhouse's porch. Suddenly, people were rushing out of the door to crowd me. Cries of joy and surprise were met with moans and groans on my part. Aunt Magda threw a blanket over my shoulders and rushed me through the doorway and into the kitchen. She set me down with a cup of coffee and poked her head out of the doorway to chase away the onlookers. The shift had helped to heal my thigh, light pink scars running across the skin. But my feet were another thing.

"I never thought that I would see you again!" She said.

"It's Fionna," I mumbled. "It was her all along."

"What are you talking about?" Aunt Magda gently laid her hand on my chin, tilting my face up so that she could look at me.

I grabbed her wrist. "Fionna was there. I could smell her."

"So, Jonathan kidnapped her, too?"

"No," I shook my head so strongly that it throbbed. "She smelled different. She smelled like something wild and metallic. While I was in the truck, I overheard Todd say that she wouldn't be happy if they roughed me up, something about her spell. She wants me. What the hell could she want me for?"

"Well, fuck," she said as she fell into a chair.

The chocolate laden coffee slipped down my throat, blossoming with warmth across my chest. I tipped it back until there was nothing left in the cup. Chemicals in the chocolate were speeding up my healing, my feet beginning to itch from the process. I thought that it could chase away the numb feeling, but it only masked it. The chill of death was sitting inside of me.

"If only we could find Darren to tell him," she muttered.

All memory of warmth washed out of me. I was completely cold right down to my core.

"Where is he?"

She opened her mouth to speak, but no words came out. She struggled for a moment before simply shrugging.

I knew how his mind worked. He had nothing to prove, nothing to make up to me anymore. Yet, he went out there again to rescue me. No matter how much I said that I forgave him, he would still feel the weight of debt because Jonathan was his father. He wanted to be my hero again.

My jaw clenched and Magda's eyes met mine. She knew what I was thinking. That was the only thing that made sense. Shit, this was going to get us into trouble.

Aunt Magda shot up from her seat, disappeared, and reappeared to throw a pile of clothing at me. Unabashedly, I dressed in the kitchen. She had thrown me black skinny jeans and a dark purple tank top with black underwear. Did she expect me to immediately run out on a search and rescue? I guess I had to admit that the idea had already crossed my mind, tugging at me so strongly.

"What the hell are we supposed to do?" I ran my fingers through my hair, giving it a sharp tug. The pain brought me back down to earth. My wolf sat back on her haunches, a low growl rumbling from her. Someone is out there hurting Darren, she didn't like that in the least.

Both she and I had already accepted Darren as our Alpha, but I knew that it ran deeper than that. He was the mate to my wolf and somewhere inside of me was the capability to love him. If we were to survive this war, then I would gladly follow him to the ends of the earth as his Guardian. I tried not to think of anything else.

"We know what he's doing, but where did he go?" my body was physically exhausted. I shoved myself from the chair, unable to sit still as my mind wandered and my wolf growled, and began to rummage through the fridge.

"I'm not sure," Aunt Magda said.

"He went to the altar," Jason appeared in the kitchen's doorway.

I emerged from the fridge, bowl of leftover meatballs in my hand. I pried them from the cold tomato sauce and bit into them like apples. My Alpha had walked himself into the den of wolves in search of me. I was eating because it was the only thing to do besides break something and I would need the energy for when I went out to break Jonathan's ass.

Did I really just think that? Yes, I had. The fear vanished when I knew he was hurting someone I wanted to love, when he threatened my Clan. Jonathan was no longer the boogey man. He became a living and breathing creature that could die. I would deal with Fionna when the time came to it.

"Why didn't you go with him?" Aunt Magda spun in her seat to glare at Jason.

"You can't sacrifice yourself properly if you bring muscle," I said, my grip on the bowl tightening. They wanted me. I was the Warren wolf, the girl who had killed one of their men, the one that had escaped Jonathan. The one that Fionna needed, apparently. Jonathan didn't want to kill one of his own sons, only cow them into submission using their greatest fears against them. And he was the muscle that Fionna was using to break the Clan. He was her tool. Just like Danny must have been.

I turned to Jason and said: "Men are stupid."

Men are stupid and women are conniving.

I threw the empty bowl into the sink and ran upstairs for my boots and a coat. I had no idea what I was doing, but I couldn't sit around and wait. I had to keep busy while my mind worked. I couldn't free Darren on my own; they would only use me to control Darren in the end. They would always use us against each other and it was my fault. I had denied it for so long that there was a gap between us, communication and trust falling through.

Black leather boots rose to my ankles, easier to kick off in an emergency. Black leather cloaked my arms and shoulders, a dark grey seam running from shoulder to wrist. In the mirror, I looked battle ready. I paused, lifting my shirt to examine the flowers that were painted brightly inside my skin. How had I gone from being a scared little rabbit to a wolf ready to dive into battle alone, ready to die for my Clan?

I touched the Warren crest that still sat between my breasts, glad that I hadn't lost it. It was heavy, absorbing my body heat, and reassuring as it laid there. I felt my dominance trickle over my skin. It jumped like electricity, a feeling that it never held before.

The smell of grass and mud and apples wafted into the room. I turned to see that Jason had followed me upstairs. His eyes burned as he watched me, fingers gripping the door frame.

"Don't you dare think of running off on us," he growled.

I could feel my wolf standing in challenge, her spine straight and her head high.

"Don't run away from the Clan again," his voice softened.

The change in his voice threw my wolf for a loop. She wanted to brush her cheek against his, to comfort and reassure the other wolf. I closed the space between us, my dominance still riding the air around me. I felt strong and unconquerable. It pressed around Jason, his eyes widening. It closed around him bearing none of the brute force it usually held. This was like a gentle hug, my wolf against his. His eyes closed and his face turned as if he could feel the fur of my wolf against his skin.

"I'm never running away again," I told him. "This is my Clan now. I vowed to protect it, didn't I?"

Eyes half open, he nodded.

"Is this what it feels like to be Clan?" he whispered.

Honestly, I couldn't tell him. It had been so long since I had been so close to wolves. His hands reached out to settle on my hips, warm and gentle. Behind him, I could see the other members of the Guard climbing the staircase. They could feel the pull of my embrace. Christian and another young Guard crawled the last few steps, their cheeks rubbing against the rough denim of my jeans. I barely knew the one wolf, yet he rubbed his face against my leg and let it ride over my hip. The older Guard members fell to one knee, bowing their heads to me. My dominance mingled with a newfound magic that exploded and filled the room with power that sparked with life and sunshine.

What was happening?

CHAPTER THIRTY-TWO

Finally, Aunt Magda appeared between the two older members of the Guard, Frank and Henry. She seemed regal standing between two kneeling wolves. I could feel the warmth of all the wolves around me, I could feel my dominance brushing against them, holding them gently as they showed submission.

"You are a Clan Queen, Diana." Aunt Magda knelt on both knees, lowering her body, but turning her eyes up to mine. "The Goddess chooses the Clan Queen and it is the Clan Queen that chooses the Clan's Alpha, challenge or not. Her word rules."

Aunt Magda wasn't a werewolf, but she had just acted as if she were. While she was wholly human, Clan was her family, too.

"Let's get your Alpha," Aunt Magda broke the silence that had fallen over us.

She and the old Guard members stood, they nodded to me in reverence then went back downstairs. They still seemed dazed, like they couldn't shake the touch of my dominance. I had to tell the younger ones holding on to me that it was time to let go, to stand up. Kicking them off, I backed away. I had to give them back themselves and that scared me.

What had I become?

Jason pressed forward, his body too close to my own. His fingers reached around my skull, knotting in my hair. He pulled and my body arched into his as my head fell back.

"No, Jason. No," I growled. I put my hands on his chest and shoved. He stumbled back and I walked past him without another glance.

I had no idea that returning to Wolf's Head would make me into something new, something that felt dangerous. I felt strong. I felt safe.

Hunt. Survive. Thrive.

All of us.

As I walked through the house, I was painfully aware of every wolf around me. Inside my head, new channels had been opened. There were gold threads that stretched from me to every wolf in the Clan, humming with their life. If I closed my eyes and followed the lines, I could feel the Faoladh on either side of this war. I could feel Danny wallowing away in the confines of the basement cell. I could feel my Grandmother running the woods in her wolf form.

I knew where Darren was. Through this new bond to the Clan, I could reach out and feel him. It was the strongest, brightest tie. He was hurt and had given in. I closed my eyes and touched him. I could visualize him slowly picking his head up as if I were there. I felt the surge of joy in him when we connected. I felt a warm surge as I remembered my desire for him when I thought I would die. I didn't want to let go of it.

They were at the altar, shielded from sight by tonight's strong magic. What they planned to do from there was a mystery to me, but whatever it was, it couldn't have been good. Jonathan wanted the Clan to himself. He wanted that control by any means. Darren stood between him and that control. The best way to ensure his victory would be to remove Darren from the equation.

I couldn't imagine what it would bring Jonathan by killing his youngest son. Yet, there was a woman pulling Jonathan's strings and we haven't figured out what her motives were. Not only that, but I had no clue what she even was. She wanted the Clan through Jonathan, through Darren, even me, but what did that gain this woman? Would the spill of her fiance's blood bring about something I couldn't fathom? Or were they just using my Alpha as a pawn?

I couldn't imagine Darren's blood spilt across the altar. He was my Alpha. He was mine. I let the hot well of anger warm my body. It was better than the numbness of shock. She had tricked him into loving her. She had used her magic over him and created the illusion of a love so strong that he had proposed. Had I broken that spell?

I will reach you. I will retrieve you. The wolf and I agreed for once in our lives. We would rescue Darren. He was our true Alpha.

I rode ahead, Magda in the passenger seat to make a quick escape if she needed to. I was sure that I wouldn't be leaving in the Chevelle tonight. To Jonathan, it would seem like I was coming in half cocked and without back-up. While I did have back-up, they were a few minutes away. I had to play it safe until then.

My wolf eyes could cut through the dark to see Darren's solid form kneeling in the dirt. A half circle of people surrounded him. This could not be good. Trying to pull on the power that I had found back at Aunt Magda's farmhouse, I steeled myself to enter the town square. It settled around me like a cloak. The others could feel it, their heads rising in curiosity.

They will bow to us. My wolf reveled in the current that touched all of the wolves. I could feel those that stood in the circle of the altar. I could feel the wolves in the forest that watched over me. I could feel those that cowered in the shadows. They were Clan, my wolves, and they were all out tonight under Her moon.

I continued forward, watching wolves break away from the semicircle that stood around my Darren. Two of Jonathan's Guards watched me with angry and defiant eyes, yet still dropped before me. I could feel Christopher's apprehension and fear as he dropped to the ground. The man next to him burned with a crazed fire all of his own, one that separated him from my Clan. Jonathan.

The power that flowed through me ebbed and I had to struggle to keep a hold of it as my heart pounded in my chest. Darren fell forward, his cheek slapping the cold earth. There was blood trickling down his temple, his hair matted with it. Fear and anger began to mingle, making my stomach churn. The connection to the Clan snapped with an electrical spark and died.

I crouched in the dirt, unwilling to go to my knees in front of Jonathan and his wolves. Tenderly, I touched the side of Darren's neck for a pulse. My hands shook. I could feel Jonathan's stare as it prickled on the back of my neck. My confidence from earlier had dissipated and now he stared at me like prey. My trembling hands couldn't find a pulse and my heart sank. What could be won without my Alpha?

Suddenly, Darren stirred at my touch. His eyes drifted open and settled on me. He mumbled something, more of a breath than a word. My heart leapt in joy. He had held onto life with an iron grip. I grasped his hand and held it close to my body.

I felt that electrical jolt fire through me. My eyes widened as the pain burnt to my toes. I could feel everything. I could feel the animals scurrying around in the brush; I could feel Jonathan's terror as he watched us. This is what it meant to be a werewolf. We were meant to be in tune with nature and the moon, running as a family and Clan.

The Clan bonds opened at my will, flaring to life again with invisible ties to every werewolf in the area. The strongest connection was the one between Darren and me. I pulled on the others of our Clan, drawing energy into the man that I called my Alpha. He must have felt it because he sat up straighter, taking in a deep breath with sudden ease. His eyes opened a bit wider, taking me in. Behind me, a wolf dropped to his knees, gasping. I dropped the line, jerking back like I had touched a flame.

"Diana," he mumbled.

"Yeah, it's me. I know I'm not the best rescue team," I said, half joking to avoid panic.

"I..." He paused, struggling to take another breath. "I choose Diana to take my place..."

212

CHAPTER THIRTY-THREE

I sucked in a sharp breath. Fuck. A week ago, this would have been the last place I would have wanted to be. My hands clenched into fists, and I turned my gaze towards Jonathan. He had his own son tied up and beaten. He had sent his sick wolves after me time and time again.

While I knew that he wasn't at the reigns of this operation, I couldn't think of anything but him. I wanted him dead more than I ever wanted anything. It was Jonathan that destroyed everything he touched, tearing it to bloody pieces for fun and greed. It was about time that the world was rid of him.

The feeling of sunlight cascaded over my skin despite the darkness around us. The wind moved through the trees around us. The Goddess was with me. She didn't make any move to possess me again and I thought, maybe I did have to strength to go through with this. I laid my hand on Darren's cheek, sharing some of the power that the goddess had given me with him. His eyes opened a little wider as he came to full consciousness.

The Goddess and I had chosen him as our Alpha. It was as simple as that. But it wasn't, at the same time. As long as Jonathan was alive, he was a threat. That was the truth of the matter, plain and simple.

Taking a deep breath, I stood up and faced Jonathan. Darren had called the fight and werewolves were starting to circle around us. Magic was in the air, binding me to Jonathan. The circle had been set and we couldn't leave until one of us had won. That meant either complete dominance or death. As I stepped forward, I thought that the only way I would be leaving this circle was over Jonathan's dead body.

It snapped in place as if it were something real and solid, the sound popping in my ears. I startled and a small smile lifted the corners of Jonathan's mouth. My skin crawled with the force of the magic, as if telling me that I was trapped. There was nowhere to run, nowhere to escape the monster that haunted my adolescent nightmares. My knees shook under me, but I widened my stance to steady myself.

I could do this. Couldn't I?

Jonathan let his dominance flood outward, pressing into every empty space in the circle. Cocky, he strode forward. His dominance was strong, maybe strong enough to lead a Clan, but it wasn't enough to make me want to cower. I was my father's daughter, a Warren Wolf. Jonathan stood before me as if his mere height would frighten me. Tenderly, he ran a finger across my jaw before snatching my chin into his hands. His fingers dug in painfully.

I stifled the urge to growl at him as I smiled. I let my dominance out, letting it spread. It felt like unfurling wings that had been cooped up in a cage for too long. It slapped at Jonathan. He jerked back, taking his hand off my face. His eyes were wide, but now he knew that I was a contender. I wouldn't go down without a fight and a fight was what I really wanted. My wolf trembled with the anticipation, craving blood and gore in the name of revenge. Jonathan's heart was hers. She pushed forward and we melded together, animal and human. Parts of me were shifting, fingers and teeth.

I hadn't taken Jonathan's anger into consideration, too distracted by my semi-shift. He sucker punched me so hard that I fell back. My head hit the frozen ground. The world swam for a moment. Before I could breathe, Jonathan leapt onto me. His hands wrapped around my throat. I couldn't catch a breath as he slammed my head into the ground. The edges of my vision were closing in with every slam. The ground was hard and unrelenting. Just before I passed out, his hands left my throat and I gasped for air. He could have killed me right then and there. A whimper escaped me and rolled onto my side. Once my vision cleared enough to focus, I saw Jonathan standing over me. His smile made me run cold.

He was going to play with me first.

His foot collided with my stomach. I barely had time to vomit before he kicked again. Desperately, I reached out and caught his leg. In the process, my claws raked down the back of his calf. He roared in anger. He swung down with his fist and my temple hit the ground.

"I will tear you limb from limb," He grabbed the arm that still wrapped around his leg.

I panicked, trying to jerk away. He stumbled forward and I lashed out with my other hand. Claws sliced across his face. This time he howled. I rolled away from him, struggling to breathe. There was vomit on my arm and side, but there was space between me and him now. That was all I cared about at the moment. I had bested Marcus by being smaller and faster than him. How could I defeat someone who was fast and smart?

"Fight me like a wolf," I growled.

He held his hand to his face. Blood trickled between his fingers. I tried to fumble to my feet, but my limbs wouldn't support me. Jonathan was going to smear the circle with me.

"What did you do?" Someone's panicked voice pushed past my spinning world.

Struggling to focus, I could see the form of Aunt Magda towering over Darren. She looked into the circle, her eyes wide with fear. Jason was helping Darren struggle to his feet. There was my family. I was doing this to protect them.

I gathered my shaking limbs together, pushing myself to all fours. My chest rumbled with a growl of anger. Adrenaline poured into me, laced with anger. Jonathan stalked forward as if he was going to kick me again, but I wasn't anyone's dog. I summoned what was left of my strength to roll away from him again. Struggling to get to my feet, I ran. I darted into the woods that were part of the challenge ring. Smelling of vomit and fear, I slipped out of my jacket and tossed it into the brush. I ran deeper, hiding myself amongst the trees and wildlife, biding my time and resting.

He chased after me, his anger driving him but clouding his senses. For a while, he stumbled around the woods, moving further and further away from me. In that time, he must have calmed down enough to sniff me out because I could hear him circling back. Hunkering down, I prayed that he found my jacket first.

What was I going to do? My body ached, rebelling against every small movement that I made. Jolts of pain rocketed up through my abdomen each time I moved. I needed to fight back, to survive. Darren needed this. If he didn't win the position of Alpha, then there would be no more Clan. The family that I had suddenly found would be torn apart. The thought of losing what I had just found sent me into a small panic. I squashed it down for the time being.

My feet hit the earth again. Boots tore through the frozen ground. I had to run. I had to escape. There was so much to live for. Aunt Magda. Sabrina. Darren.

Oh god, Darren. I'm so sorry that I got myself into this mess. I'm so sorry for blaming you.

Jonathan was hot on my tail. His low, maniacal laughter echoed through the bare trees behind me. I was running like a scared rabbit, but I was anything but that.

I was a Clan Queen. I had powers beyond a normal Faoladh. Yet, my body was so exhausted that simply running was draining me. I couldn't reach out to my Clan. I couldn't pull any energy from them or even call for their help. I couldn't count on the Goddess that seemed to pop in and out of my life. I was alone on this one.

Something heavy slammed into my back. My own momentum threw me forward, sliding face first into the cold earth. Air was forced from my lungs. Trying to pull myself together, I heard his footsteps slowly approaching. He grabbed a fistful of my hair and jerked my head up. I bit back a growl. His clawed hand traced lines across my throat. My heart pounded in my ears. One slip of his claw and I would bleed out in the town square while I gasped for breath. I wondered why he didn't just do it already. Was this how he had treated Helen? His sister?

Tonight, Jonathan was going to finish the job he started seven years ago. Just this morning I had been thinking about how I would make sure that Jonathan would die before this war was over. If I was going to die tonight then he was going down. My fingers, dug into the dirt, began to change. I could feel it flowing through me. It took all I had to keep my body from changing completely. The wolf thrashed inside of me, begging to be let out. She had saved us against Marcus. She could save us again.

Images of the general store and Bianca's house flashed through my mind. My fingers curled into fists. My claws bit into my palms. His foot pressed into my back, my spine popping beneath the tread.

"You think that you can change now and save yourself?" Jonathan laughed that crazy maniacal laugh again. I could hear the joy of victory in it already.

Helen Kapinski, the woman who had helped to save me so many years ago with a simple phone call. He had shredded the woman to bits that he scattered across her own store. I pulled my hands beneath my chest, pretending to whimper in fear. While his grip tightened in my hair until I thought he would pull it all out, I waited for my claws to grow long and sharp. Small knives sat at the ends of my fingers. All it took was a snap of my wrist and my claws circled his arm. They sliced through muscle and bone with some force.

Jonathan roared in pain and reared back. His grip on me was forgotten as he cradled his arm. I took the chance to roll away from him. I scrambled to my feet, crouched low like an animal ready to pounce. On the ground between us was his severed hand. His blood was still warm in my palm.

Wide eyes quickly narrowed at me. I was tired and aching down to my bones, but this was my moment. The growling Jonathan stood in front of the massive stone altar. I leapt at him. The change rippled over me mid-air, like stretching tired joints. My paws hit his chest and my teeth ripped through muscle. We fell back in a heap, Jonathan's head bouncing against the stone altar. I heard a loud crack and he fell limp.

I padded backwards, anger roiling through my mind. I wanted nothing more than to kill this man. Not because I blamed him for my life, I was to answer for the rift inside of myself. No, Jonathan had taken more lives that I had held dear. He enjoyed the bloodshed, the fear. He loved fear.

"Don't," a voice whispered. Darren's voice.

I stumbled back. The change rippled over me, the wolf finally willing to give me control. We had defeated her greatest fear. She felt safe, proud and safe.

I felt something snap in the air, like an electrical charge that suddenly dissipated. I looked down at the man out cold at my feet. The challenge was over and he was still breathing. Unconscious, but still breathing. I let my shaking knees drop me to the ground. It was over.

As if they had felt it too, I heard others running through the forest. They thundered towards me. I reached out with my tired senses and felt Jason running my way. Christian was back with Darren, acting as his new Alpha's crutch.

"Maybe you were right to have been afraid of me," I mumbled to Jonathan's unconscious body. The creature of my nightmares was still alive, but only because of the mercy of my Alpha. It left me with a feeling of cold hiding behind my triumph.

Jason knelt beside me, a comforting hand on my shoulder. I was cold through and through now. He pulled me to my feet and led me back to my discarded clothing before going back to help Christian drag Jonathan's body away from the altar. The change was slipping over me like water now. I wiped away dirt and vomit before I threw on my shirt, underwear, and shoes for modesty's sake. I turned and left the scene.

The crowd that waited had grown exponentially. My jaw fell open when I saw nearly every member of the Clan watching me. I turned my head away, heading towards Aunt Magda and Darren to escape their gazes. They felt accusing and afraid and I couldn't bear that just yet.

"You are officially the new Alpha of Wolf's Head," I told him.

He caught me before I could kneel before him. He pulled me into a tight hug, two battered wolves clutching each other for support.

CHAPTER THIRTY-FOUR

I paced my room, nervous energy pouring out of every movement. Jonathan was still alive. Inside my head, my wolf growled. We had vowed to kill him at the Challenge. His life should have ended there. But, Darren had pleaded for mercy.

Of course he had. Darren still hung onto some idea that there was a father figure still buried deep down inside Jonathan. That the man who ripped apart Helen and Bianca, ripped apart my father, could still somehow be a loving man. It was preposterous and I knew it.

Why didn't he?

I cursed Darren for being such a bleeding heart. It made him a gentle Alpha and a gentle Alpha needed someone willing to get their hands bloody. As if from a distance, I heard the baying of hounds. They rubbed shoulders with my wolf, somehow being where they couldn't. I closed my eyes and looked inward. I caught flashes of sleek, white bodies and russet red ears, my wolf standing at the head of them. Her own form was changing. Where she was once all black, the red began to bleed into the tips of her ears.

My eyes snapped open. There was a part of my brain that seemed to know what was going on. Everything was okay. In fact, this was great. But, it wouldn't let the rest of me in on what was happening. I just had to trust myself as I quietly moved down the stairs.

So many of our Clan were at Balefire, celebrating. That left a meager few working guard duty at the farmhouse. I crept past them, heading for the basement door. If I was lucky, they would brush off my scent as I'd been here all day. The whole house should smell like me.

The basement door softly creaked open. I cringed, but pressed forward, quickly shutting it behind me. Darkness washed over me. My eyes took a long moment to adjust, but while they did I heard a soft chuckle.

Jonathan.

My heart pounded with every step I took. The hounds inside of me raised their hackles with my wolf. They were all on alert. At the base of the stairs, my eyes adjusted enough to see a slumped form behind the thick bars of a specially made kennel. One arm held to his chest, he pushed forward onto his knees to crawl towards me. His eyes caught the dim light and flashed red, a soft laugh still escaping him.

Not thinking, just moving, I unlocked the kennel door. His eyes opened wider. It was more excitement than surprise. Did he really think that he was getting out of here alive? I reached in and grasped the arm he was holding close. His breath hissed.

"You're going to come with me," I said.

I pushed him ahead of me. That twisted smile never left his face the whole time we snuck out of the farmhouse. Yet, he did everything I asked. He wiped his scent on everything I touched, dripping blood from his arm onto the kennel as well as the door that led outside.

Thankfully, there had been no wolves prowling the grounds. It made me cringe, but it helped nonetheless. I shoved him through the woods until we came to the arching gate that I'd found when I first came home. The towering stone wolves watched as I marched him up to a grave marker.

Michael Warren, Beloved Father and Alpha

"Is this some sort of bittersweet revenge?" Jonathan crooned. His voice was too cocky.

"Something like that," I said. "Honestly, I just don't want to see a world with you in it anymore. How you created a man as good as your son is beyond me."

My fingers began elongating and curling, the power of the shift flowing through them. The hounds barked and bayed inside my head, all of them jostling one another as they leapt about. I looked up just in time to see Jonathan's good hand swing back.

He screamed in pain as blood blossomed on his sleeve. The fabric tore along with flesh, ripped by invisible teeth. The hounds were no longer leaping around my wolf. Jonathan stumbled back. He flinched as more blood began to flow. They went for his legs, his arms, anything they could reach. Flesh and blood filled the air as they tore and tore.

Jonathan fell to his knees, wide eyes staring up at me as if I were the monster. Perhaps I was. It didn't matter anymore. The light faded from his eyes, even as the invisible hounds continued to tear at his body. The world was rid of Jonathan Blackford.

CHAPTER THIRTY-FIVE

It was as awkward as awkward could get. A small round table and a bottle of local wine sat between me and Christopher. He didn't look like he was any happier to be here. His eyes kept darting to his fiancé working behind the counter. She and the baby were about ready to blow.

It was Christopher who had invited me to dinner this night. I had killed his father, the knowledge of that sitting inside me like a stone every time I looked at him. It hurt when Darren had cried over the man's death. It looked, to the coroner, as if a pack of dogs had killed him. None of the bite marks matched the muzzle of a Faoladh.

Even though Jonathan was gone and Darren declared Alpha, Jonathan's wolves had been creating havoc on his behalf. Last night, Jason and I had been called to visit Solstice Winery when some wolves were found trashing grape vines. By the time we got there, all we found was some crumpled vegetation. I was convinced that it was just Todd and some of the Clan-less wolves acting out.

It had been our own guards that had found Jonathan's body, what was left of it at least. They weren't sure how he escaped. They were even less sure of what killed him. The whole cemetery had smelled of wet dog when they searched the place.

All alone, I breathed a sigh of relief.

"You're safe right now," I reminded Christopher as I looked to Sabrina. "Both of you. The Clan-less wolves aren't anything to worry about. Just miscreants."

He nodded and reached for his wine glass. The bottle that sat between us was from the same winery just outside of town, owned by Kalvin Patterson of our Clan. This Clan and even the town operated from the livelihood of so many small businesses. We had taken on the roles of protectors and crafters by erecting inns and farms and wineries. Even Balefire was a sanctuary for the Clan, one that drew in tourists and traveling foodies from all over the country.

It broke my heart that Jonathan had wanted to destroy that. He wanted to create monsters, vicious creatures willing to hunt human flesh. He would have destroyed the winery, Balefire, and even the town.

"It's only a matter of time," Christopher said after a long drag of his wine. The end of the world seemed to always be on the horizon to Christopher. Unlike him, I recently chose to hold on to the bright spark of hope.

I glanced to my Aunt who was leaning behind the front counter. She stared out the window, not paying much attention to the detective that was trying so hard to talk to her. I knew that all of Aunt Magda's attention was on this conversation. I hated how much it hurt her personal life. The lady detective was finally trying to reach out and Aunt Magda couldn't take what she had wanted for so long.

I was done with this feud wreaking havoc on the lives of so many around me. Darren, the man with the gold heart, was an emotional wreck at times. Christopher had a pup on the way and feared for his fiancée's well being every moment now that his father's wolves were on the loose without a leader. There was still a bounty out for my head, dead or alive as cliché as it sounded. Even with Jonathan gone we were a mess, unraveling at every corner.

"I know," Christopher whispered into his wine glass.

I was about to ask what when his eyes met mine. There was a bit of relief in them as well as...gratitude.

I sighed and let my head fall to the table. My face just narrowly missed the bowl of dip, but everything else rattled upon impact.

"I won't tell your secret. You did what had to be done when no one else would."

"Fuck," I muttered to the table.

"Feel better?"

"Not one bit."

"Then what are we going to do?"

"Everyone wants to be celebrating our victory when it feels like there is something else looming ahead and it's killing us still. I don't know what she wants, but I bet she's still trying to get it."

Christopher froze. He didn't even blink. Did he know something that I didn't? I bet he knew a lot, standing just on the line between the two factions this entire time.

"Sabrina wants you to be the baby's godmother," he changed the subject.

I looked up at him through my bangs, so that he couldn't read the incredulous expression on my face. I had barely known the woman my first week here and now she wanted to name me her unborn child's godmother?

"I agree with her," Christopher said. "We are having a girl. I'd like to think that my daughter would grow up to be like you someday."

"You have to be joking," I grabbed the wine bottle and left.

I would not become an alcoholic. I would not become an alcoholic...I threw back a swig of wine straight from the bottle. White wine seared across my tasted buds, flashing with notes of passion fruit for a moment. I was a broken wolf, disjointed on the inside with two voices that constantly roared at each other and fought for power over the one body that I held. There had been a goddess and an entire Clan and an invisible pack of hounds inside my head for a while. The Clan and the hounds were still there. On top of that, I was a murderer, a couple times over now. It hadn't helped anything and now Christopher wanted his daughter to look up to me when I couldn't even handle the situations that life was dealing me? It was a piss poor decision in my opinion.

I set the bottle down on the counter for someone else to take. When I turned back to the table, I found Sabrina in my seat. She and Christopher were engaged in a heated conversation. She threw pitying glances in my direction and I couldn't take it anymore.

Turning away from them, I cut through the kitchen. Prep chefs chopped away, a knicking a steady rhythm against the wooden boards. Pans sizzled and smoked, spattering hot contents into the air. Chefs were hustling and bustling as waitresses pushed and shoved at the window. The air smelled hot and delicious. Eventually I fell onto a bench at the chef's table, silent as I watched people around me work.

My body ached from the past few days, painful reminders of what I had been through. My head felt tender and my shoulder still gave me shooting pains. There was a taste in my mouth that wouldn't go away. Part of me called it the taste of lives taken. I didn't regret taking Marcus's or Jonathan's lives, it had to be done. I didn't want to have to think about it every day, though. I wanted it to be done and over, like a simple task to be forgotten. Then again, I knew that taking any life would never feel that way. It shouldn't feel like that. Murdering them should be filled with regret and sympathy, simply for the fact that it was sad that they had been so broken.

I was now the Clan Queen. It was because of me that Darren had been brought into power. He was our Alpha and now we were working to pull this Clan back together. That fell on Darren and my Grandmother's shoulders. I would be no help, no matter how much I wanted to be. My job was now to figure the rest of this out, I told myself.

I had been hoping that Christopher would tell me what Fionna wanted. I wanted him to tell me that she was evil. I wanted him to tell me how to put an end to it, but he didn't and it made me wonder if I was wrong. I had seen her, smelled her when they had taken me. She had been there of her own accord, I was convinced. Had she pulled the wool, or the glamour, over Darren's eyes?

Or, was I jealous? Was I so jealous of her relationship with Darren that I convinced myself of her guilt?

She acted meek and terrified when Darren introduced her as a fae. But the Goddess had looked upon her and saw a darkness that she didn't approve of. She knew there was something else going on and I wanted to believe her. She had given me so much, given the Clan more. She couldn't be wrong.

"What are you thinking so hard about?" Aunt Magda sidled up beside me on the bench. A tall plastic glass of coffee and ice appeared before me. The wine bottle was plucked from my grasp. I laid my head on her shoulder, wishing the wine would fade from my system. It made me too hard and angry. The old and angry Diana had been left behind a while ago, or so I had hoped.

"Everything," I said in response.

"Understandable. Definitely understandable."

If Aunt Magda fell, would we tumble like dominoes? Who would be there to keep my Grandmother, the woman who taught Darren his new role, in one piece? Who would fill our stomachs when our hearts were empty? I wrapped my arms around my Aunt, holding her tight enough to crush ribs. This was who I wanted Sabrina's baby to look up to, not me.

We were all so valuable, so irreplaceable to this Clan. Each and every single one of us.

Had this rift been born when Jonathan had killed my father in search of me? Jonathan had taken away a vital piece of the Clan and created a tear in the Clan's structure. Mom and I had raced to far away cities, putting as much distance between us and Wolf's Head as we could. Jonathan's act of violence had removed three members of the Clan in an instant. Then my Grandfather died. The rift between my Grandmother and her wolf grew larger with her son and husband gone. There was a hole that Aunt Magda and I were trying so hard to fill. But, I had been a broken piece brought into the game.

After giving Aunt Magda's hand a squeeze, I took a long drag from the iced coffee and pushed myself from the bench. Going out alone wasn't a good idea right now, but then again a lot of the things I had done since I landed in Maine hadn't been great ideas.

"Don't tell Darren," I said over my shoulder as I headed towards the restaurant's back door.

Aunt Magda narrowed her eyes at me, her humanity giving her the ability to challenge me in the way that Darren never could. I got lucky when my phone vibrated. It was a text from Jason. The wolves struck again, setting fire to the general store. I swore under my breath.

"I'm sorry," I said. "He will tell me how stupid I am tomorrow anyway."

Ducking out the door, I quickly shut it behind me so that she couldn't say anything in return. The night air was crisp and cold. My breath hung in the air as it slipped between my lips. As I threw my eyes up towards the tree lined sky, I saw that the stars blazed like white pinpoints. They were always brighter on the coldest night, as if it were the Goddess's reminder that there was some sort of hope in the worst situations.

My feet hit the blacktop of the rear parking-lot, but I crossed it quickly and touched the path that cut through the wooded lands. The thin and naked trees surrounded me, filling the land between here and the General Store. I didn't consider shifting forms. My wolf was quietly curled up in the back of my mind. She was sated, knowing that we had finally defeated Jonathan.

I strolled on two feet with my hands in my pockets. My mind was so caught up in the unraveling lives of my family that I didn't catch the scent on the air until it was too late. Pine mingled with metallic silver, tickling my nose until it felt numb.

My body froze, the tingling feeling of numbness spreading across my limbs. I couldn't move. I couldn't even wriggle my toes. It felt like an out of body experience, scaring me that I couldn't reconnect with my body. Yet, it woke my wolf. She was lethargic, but angry. Her eyes were sleepy, feeling the taint of silver in the air. She growled, trying to pull her teeth back.

Looking out into the darkness, I saw her pale hair take form first. It fell past her waist, ethereally white. As she came closer, I could see the black holes of her eyes. The real Fionna had found me. Distantly, I heard the rustle of feet through leaves. I couldn't smell anymore, but I had a feeling that the bodies surrounding me weren't wolves.

"I have been waiting to get you all to myself for quite a while now," Fionna crooned. "You have everything that I need to help my sisters."

The bird-like women from the Court moved to flank Fionna. They glowed in the night, as if moonlight was falling from their skin. Only it was a dusting of silver that they were giving off. And it was going to kill me.

I woke up hazy with a persistent throbbing at the back of my skull. I tried to roll over, but my limbs refused to move. Panic set in and I thrashed. Restraints at my wrist and ankles set sharp pains through my muscles. I was trapped.

The room came into focus slowly. I was lying on a bare mattress, inches from the floor. Nothing struck me as familiar. A feeling of dread crept into my chest, making it heavy. Hot tears rolled down my cheek. Inside, I could feel my wolf, backing into a corner with a whimper. She didn't like this situation one bit. The fact that she wasn't fighting scared me. If I changed, the restraints were tight enough to cause serious problems. I could permanently disfigure myself if joints couldn't realign in the proper fashion. I was already disfigured enough. My wolf was trapped inside my body, unable to fight. It scared the crap out of her.

My stomach rolled, the silver sitting heavy in my system. I had just enough room to lurch to the side as the contents of my stomach came up. It burned in a way I'd never felt before. Tears trickled down my cheeks. The mess that sat before me glimmered.

Silver.

Forced to be strong for my wolf, I shut my eyes tight. My stomach still hurt, but it remained calm while I collected myself. Hot tears dripped down my cheeks. I took a deep breath through my nose, holding it while my mind processed information. I drew a few more quick breaths. Scenting the room was easy. It reeked of vomit and Jonathan.

The woman who stepped into the room was almost unrecognizable. I stared at her for a long moment before it dawned on me who it really was. The fabric of the long, shimmering dress clung to her body. It moved with unnatural weightlessness. The closer she came I realized that it was made from feathers, long and thin feathers that were tipped with shimmering silver. Her hair was pulled back and a crown of silver feathers and pearls topped her head. Fionna came into the room as if she owned it and from the position that I was in, she did own it.

A growl rumbled through my chest and I barely tried to hide it. She knelt beside my cot, her hands inching up my shirt and running her fingers over the lines of the flowers that decorated my skin. I could feel it burning from the silver that still coated her skin. Gone was the terrified fae and in her place was a predator on a mission.

"A Fae tradition has marked you as their own," she said as she moved so that we were face to face. I could feel something pushing at me, her power that caressed my skin like a lover. I pulled my dominance and held it close to me like a thick shield against her. "You brought my old home to life again, little pup. You brought the skies back to the Court, but it is still in her hands. It always belonged to me; Aoife should never had held the throne."

Her long fingers wrapped around my arm, nearly crushing as she jerked me forward. Our noses were barely inches away from one another. I looked her in the eye, unafraid and not intimidated. Her eyes narrowed and suddenly her lips were pressing against mine. They moved like the brush of wings against my skin.

"The original plan had been to acquire a Clan of werewolves to fight my battle, but you foiled that for me, stealing my Alpha and my Monster," she admitted.

I growled low. She had been the one to start this war. Fionna was the one to push Jonathan into this and she did it only to control innocent people. Then she had dug her claws into Darren, making him believe that he loved her so that she had a back-up plan. A world was falling apart, but for what? So that she could gain control over a Court?

"Don't you go and blame the deaths of your friends on my head, dear," she said defensively before I accused her. "My lover had a very deep seeded anger inside of him that is all his own doing. It was his decision to start this war, to kill those women, not mine."

"No, but you wouldn't think twice about throwing an entire Clan at a Fae Court. It would be a slaughter-fest."

She shrugged her shoulders. "I will do anything to reclaim my Court. It needs me. My sisters need protecting from those who would look down upon them."

"You're just as insane as Jonathan," I spat at her.

She grabbed a fistful of my shirt and shook me. My head rolled, but I heard the clink of metal falling to the the floor. With strength that her thin body shouldn't have possessed, she lifted me and the cot from the ground with one hand. She held me helpless, snarling in my face.

"You think that it is fun to live your life as nothing more than a piece of meat? You think that I wanted to cower under the gazes of others? The swan folk have always been looked down upon, considered weak and malleable. I've been pushed to within an inch of my life centuries ago. Now that I'm stronger, older, no one will treat me or mine like that again.Not when I have the weapon of the Goddess herself."

I didn't have anything to say. My youth had been idyll. I had no idea of the real dangers of the world until I was fourteen. Then I lived everyday in fear. I knew what loss was, what being hunted felt like. I had the scars to prove it. I had no idea what Fionna had gone through, who had hurt her. But there was part of me that felt her pain and fear. I had lived it.

"Where was my Goddess in those times? Why has she returned to you when my sisters and I were being destroyed?"

I had no answer for her. I wasn't sure what set me apart from her. We had both lived in fear at some point of our lives, fostering a well of rage inside of us. I didn't so much agree with how she channeled that rage, but I knew that the same potential was sleeping inside of me as well.

Only, I had love. I had what was left of the Clan she had tried to destroy. The strength of their love now and my mother's love when I was at my weakest fed me. I had the hope of seeing something through with Darren's love. I didn't live off of rage alone. Fionna had, though. Nothing had kept her from fostering the rage. Not even her sisters, it would seem.

"I have the vessel of our Goddess in my hands now," she said. "Through you, I will have her power. I will have the Wild Hunt."

CHAPTER THIRTY-SIX

My blood froze. I couldn't even feel the burn of her hands on my skin anymore. Memory of the baying hounds moved around my head again. I didn't know if I could summon them on command. I didn't even know what it would do if I did.

"Share your power with me, little pup," she said against my lips. "Make me a Queen again."

"And what if I do," I said, letting my sharp teeth graze her lip. They sliced through her tender skin and drew blood.

She jerked back, her lips blushing with her fresh blood.

Her blood trickled past my lips. It tasted of wine and made my head spin almost immediately. Her dark eyes stared me down. I didn't want to know what was working behind them. I was at her mercy and unable to escape as a new predator sized me up.

"Give me my Yuletide present," her fingers clutched my chin, sharp nails biting into my skin. "And if you do, then perhaps I will give you your present early and spare my new family."

I jerked upright. "What did you do?" I growled.

"They will die," she whispered to me. "Darren is dying right now, the same way that I killed your Grandfather. Silver dust kills your kind so slowly. What we spread over you was just enough to keep you immobilized, but the amount that my sisters are feeding your Darren will kill him so slowly. I'm sure that it will affect my *niece* as well. Poor Sabrina will give birth to a stillborn if you do not cooperate."

"How dare you!" My rage was hot and searing. I gnashed my teeth, wishing that I could get another bite of her flesh.

"You care so much for this family" she mused, leaning back on her legs. "Why do you care so much for the people that you left behind? For the people that betrayed you?"

Hot tears fell down my cheek. Forgiveness was something new that I had learned. It lessened a burden that I placed on myself. I thought of Darren, of him dying. A world without him was...

I couldn't finish the sentence. I couldn't bear the thought of it. I reached into the lines that connected me to the Clan and felt him so far away. He felt faint and flickering. The feeling of frost settled over me. I turned my head up to her, growling through clenched teeth. My body was vibrating with anger. I let the heat of it chase away the ice of fear that was seeping into me. She was no better than Jonathan. Worse, even.

"Take me to your Court," I growled, giving in. I didn't know what I would do, but I needed to get this over. Fast.

She smiled and clapped her hands together. Almost dancing with joy, she approached me. At first I jerked away from her touch.

"Tsk, tsk, Diana. We are traveling my way." Her hand fell down onto my shoulder. Slivers of pain shot through it. The world began to spin around us. Colors blurred together and began to reshape. Briefly, I could smell freshwater and feathers. The dark figures of the Court's throne room began to take shape around us, the glowing stained glass windows bright against the dark walls.

I wasn't sure how to get myself out of this one alive. A fight was about to go down and I was caught in the middle of it. I shut my eyes tight and prayed for the hand of the Goddess to show up. She had been with me nearly every step of the way so far. Even if she could just save Darren for me. That was all I needed. The Court could come down around Fionna and me just as long as Darren lived. He was the one golden light that we had left amongst this carnage.

"I am here to claim what should be mine, Aoife," Fionna announced. Her eyes sparkled as they roved over the cathedral like Court.

"You have no standing, swan folk. You have no challenge to bear." There wasn't a hint of apathy in Aoife's voice. When she saw me cowering on the floor, rubbing my newly free wrists, her brows knit together. I spared a moment to wonder if I was still under the protection of the Goddess in her eyes.

"I brought with me the vessel of our Goddess," Fiona declared."You should cower before her power."

Aoife laughed, the bells woven into her antlers making soft sounds as her head bobbed. "I sought to keep her for my own, as well. But the nearer I got to clarity, I realized that this wolf cannot *call* upon the powers that she possesses. She is no great treasure or devastating weapon."

I wasn't sure if I should have felt relieved or insulted. I opted to simply keep my mouth shut and inch backwards. The plan was thwarted when Fionna grabbed my by the back of my shirt and flung me forward. I rolled across the hard packed floor.

"Call upon your power, Diana," Fionna growled at me.

How in the hell did she propose I do that? My wolf paced around my head, itching to push forward. The hounds were nowhere in sight. My fingers curled into my palm as I fought to keep her held back. If I could control myself, then perhaps I could avoid having to fight at all. It was the very last thing that I wanted to do as I stood between a massive, antlered woman and the rage filled, silver dripping, swan woman. Was there anyway that I could make them forget about me?

"Are you and your sisters so weak that you can't fight your own fights?" I said from my position on the floor. It was a shot in the dark, but it was all that I could think of.

"What did you say?" Fionna's hands clenched at her sides.

"It's no wonder that you and your sisters are abused so often. You're weak and cowardly."

"We are not!" She roared. A cloud of silver dust erupted around her. "I am not weak."

"You can protest all you want. It doesn't change anything."

I thought that my plan had backfired when Fionna stormed towards me. Her thin lips were drawn back over her teeth and her cheeks were sunken and dark. Her hand lashed out and all I knew was hot and searing pain. Then my body hit a wall. The edges of my vision became black, but I struggled to stay conscious. This was no time to pass out, I told myself. With a shaking hand, I wiped the silver dust from my face and body.

I hung my head, tired and scared. I heard the bells chime as Aoife stood and moved forward. Fionna was all sound and rage, while Aoife's feet were silent. When I brought my head back up, I found Aoife's long fingers wrapped tightly around Fionna's throat. The lithe woman's feet dangled inches from the ground, kicking and swaying as she fought for air. Aoife was terrifying at her full height. She towered over everyone in the room, antlers notwithstanding. I stayed where I was on the floor, too afraid to move.

In a burst of moonlight, Fionna's body suddenly shrunk. In it's place were massive white wings. Her thin swan neck slipped from Aoife' grip and she fell to the floor in a cloud of silver dust. I quickly slapped my sleeve over my mouth. Breathing more of that in would be a slow and painful death. Her massive wings beat at the air as she struggled to get upright again.

Even with all of this fighting, another sound drew my attention away. Distant howling rung in my ears. I heard the scratching of claws in the dirt and a low whimper. Glancing over my shoulder, I saw a white hound standing beneath the corridor arch. The tips of his ears were deep red and his eyes were black. Somehow my wolf recognized it as one of her hounds. It was one of the hounds that had found me the last time I had visited the Court. I fumbled to my feet and ran to it. It spun around and raced down the corridor.

It was fast, but I had a reason to run. Darren needed me. Sabrina and her baby needed me. The Clan needed me. I focused on the tip of its white tail as it cut to the left and to the right, taking me down a twisted path of halls. I had no idea if it was taking me to the exit or not, only faith. There was still a veil of black in the corners of my visions, but I wanted to get out of here bad enough to push through it. I would pay for it later.

The Goddess had been absent the entire time. I hadn't heard her laughter or felt the sunshine warmth of her presence within me. All I had right now was my mysterious white and red hound. I prayed that she was by Darren's side. That is where I needed her most right now.

Finally, I saw the circle of forest up ahead.

CHAPTER THIRTY-SEVEN

I kept going, not truly sure of where I was headed, but certain that I should keep moving. As I passed through the circle, I realized that this wasn't the exit. The forest, with thick trunked trees and crimson leaves, was still inside the Court. The chill of the coming winter hung in the air as if this were a real forest. The cold kept the smells of the forest from the air, but I could smell the fur of Clan that had brushed the rough bark of the trees around me.

Eventually, the smell led me to a small clearing. It was a circle of trees with a low-lying stump in the center. On this broad altar, there were small jars with rolled up notes inside, bottled wishes. There were bottles of half emptied wine and inky black feathers with silver spines. In the very center was a massive, sun bleached stag's skull. This was obviously an altar of offerings to the gods, here in the depths of the faery Court. Trusting that I was safe inside this forest, I let myself fall to my knees before it in exhaustion. Turning my head up to the sky, I saw that it was a soft blue-gray and had stars fighting to twinkle. There would be more tonight, shining the brightest as the temperature dropped further and further.

What would you have me do, Goddess? You called my body and mind home from time to time. This time, I call you to me. Tell me what path is right?

Could I sleep at night, knowing that I had taken more lives since I'd been here? Was I worthy of the power bestowed on me when all of this blood was on my hands? I told myself that it had all been the right thing to do. I had to protect those I loved at any cost. I thought we should have been safe with Jonathan gone, but Fionna filled his place. I had no clue whether she sat upon a throne now or not. It hadn't occurred to me who might win the struggle when I left the two fae women fighting. I couldn't stand the idea of her ruling the Court closest to my new home.

My heart was beginning to heal finally, my confidence and strength returning to me. Letting her live when I knew what she was capable of would destroy that. It would destroy our Clan.

I looked down at the flowers that graced my skin. The longer that I stared at them, the more that I could see in my own skin. I could see the stars that spotted the sky, some brighter than others. A cloud passed beneath the stars and I could hear howls and caws. The thunder of hoofbeats pounded in rhythm with my heartbeat and I looked to the sky for the source.

The hoof beats came closer, slower. I brought my eyes up in time to see a dark skinned hand reach for the antler of the stag's skull. It was masculine, muscles bunching as it lifted the skull up to his face. Dark skinned and imposing, the antlers now reached for the sky, much taller than Aoife. Leather and furs covered him waist to mid thigh, a knife hanging from the leather and a quiver slung over his shoulder.

The god of the Wild Hunt stood before me. Had I summoned him to me?

I got to my feet and he cocked his head, watching me through the dark and empty sockets of the skull. After a long inspection, he finally removed his hand from the hilt of his knife. I felt like prey beneath his invisible stare. It scared me, made my muscles shake. He extended black tipped fingers to me, his palm an offering. Taking a deep breath, I poured my will into my body just to move. I felt my wolf rise and the fear began to bleed into the sweet taste of power.

Finally, I forced my hand to his. Beneath my fingers I felt soft fur, familiar and warm. I could smell wolf in the air suddenly. When I sought his eyes, the howls of a thousand wolves and hounds filled my head. I could hear them everywhere, filling me up and spilling out into the world. It felt like the rush of a drug. My back arched and my head fell back. Mouth falling open, a moan didn't come out. A howl burst into the forest.

I had been handpicked by the Goddess, but it was the God's turn to judge me. He was the god of the Wild Hunt, the hunter extraordinaire. I could feel his hand reach into me and caress my wolf. If she could purr, I thought she would right then. I was his Hound of the Wild Hunt, his wolf to call tonight.

Hunt. With claws. With teeth. We will hunt tonight.

He saw my kills. He saw my fears and my determination. He saw my need to protect that which I loved, the need that trumped all fears and doubts.

He nodded to me. I would lead the Hunt this time. The Gods had answered my questions. We would hunt Fionna.

The hounds tossed their heads back, howling into the night sky. The Hunt had begun.

As if there were a GPS tracker installed in my brain, I knew which direction to head in order to find Fionna. I had tasted her blood and it took me to her. As I ran, human feet slapping the ground inside my boots, my fingers extended and sharpened into claws. My teeth grew longer and pressed into my lips. Fresh blood bloomed inside my mouth, the iron taste only wetting my desire for Fionna's death.

Above us, blackbirds silently filled the air. They wove in and around each other as if weaving knots in the air. The sound of hoofbeats was a distant drumbeat, the herd of rider-less horses charging forward with us, beating the sound of war as we ran. We passed through Wolf's Head, a parade of ghastly apparitions and creatures letting everyone know we were there. I was their Clan Queen, the right hand of the Alpha, and the Hound of the Wild Hunt.

I leapt over fallen trees and shallow ravines until my feet hit pavement. Did she know that the Hunt was about to descend upon her? Could she feel it in her bones as the call for her death led us to her?

I had become a woman my father would have been proud of, of that I was sure. Surely, I couldn't be all that broken.

The wind of the wild hunt pushed my feet along, the tunnels of the faery court blurring past me. The hounds brushed my legs. They had been a part of me this whole time. They had been searching for me, waiting for me to see them I had meant for the hunt, I thought.

We swept back into the Court like a hurricane wind. It seemed to open up to the Hunt, the skies widening into a vast forest to hold each hound and bird. There was no stopping the Wild Hunt.

Fionna was perched daintily atop the golden throne. Behind her, Aoife had been nailed to the wall by her wrists, arms spread. Her antlers had been broken off and her eyes removed, gouged out by swan beaks no doubt. Fionna's eyes burned with power and madness. She was just as insane as Jonathan.

Fionna sat upon the tree throne. It seemed gray and lifeless beneath her. The golden vibrance that had once surrounded Aoife and her court was now gone. She stood, showing defiance in her stance even though there was fear in her eyes. She had won the battle and taken the Court on her own. Yet, the fauns and nymphs glared up at her with anger and malice. The court she'd fought to win hated her.

Corpses of fauns and nymphs that had defended Aoife lay on the floor. Their bodies looked as though they had been torn apart by one another. Perhaps they had. I remembered the power of the fae glamour the nymphs had cast. My eyes sought the swan sisters out and found them standing behind Fionna and her new throne. They smiled, their eyes dark and cocky.

They thought that this battle was theirs. They thought that they had won. All they had accomplished was destroying their own home, their own lives. Aoife had been a woman lost until she's seen the Goddess through my eyes. Given time, she might have been a great Queen once more. Fionna's rage would always keep her from truly caring for her court.

The swan fae pushed forward, trying to surround us, but with a thought I sent the hounds out. They spilled out from me like white fire. I felt them push out with their glamour. As if that would save them. It flowed over my hounds, words falling on deaf ears. The hounds teeth found purchase in the swan fae's flesh and pulled them down.

Fionna's sick smile faltered for a moment. I focused my gaze on her, but her eyes flicked to the figure standing just behind me. It was his power that I was riding and she knew it. It was him that she had to fear.

"Fionna O'Shea," I called out her full name.

She stood, regal and tall. With her head held high, she stared me down.

"Do you realize what stands before you?" I asked, feeling the goddess within my voice. We spoke together this time, our thoughts the same. "Are you so confident in your power that you could stand defiant before the Wild Hunt?"

"I have my throne," she growled at us. My wolves circled her, moving like a fluid stream of fur and snarls. Their claws clicked on the cold stone floor of the hall."I will protect those that you would not!"

I knew she was not talking of Diana the faoladh, but of the Goddess. Fionna claimed she would do what the Goddess could not. A surge of power flushed through me and I felt a smile cross my face. This was the good part, the part that the hounds and birds and other creatures had been waiting for. The true hunt.

"Then run," I whispered.

The wall behind Fionna opened up into a forest. Aoife's lifeless body hung from a tree with golden foliage like the Court had a defiant streak of its own and mourned its lost queen.

All around me, I could feel the rising excitement as the creatures shifted from foot to foot and licked their chops. I only had to think the word and they surged forward. The wind rushed around me, cool and full of energy like an oncoming storm.

A heavy weight fell upon my shoulder I glanced back to find the God's hand resting on my skin. A wordless command was sent through the dark gaze of his skeletal mask.

Stand down.

My feet rooted themselves to the ground. Fionna was not my fight, he might as well have said. Anger boiled through me. This should be my fight. Her blood should have been mine to spill. She was the reason that my grandfather was dead, the reason that the Manor had burned to the ground, the reason that good men turned their backs on their clan.

A growl trickled through me as I watched the God step past me. Each footstep he took sprouted life across the floor of the court. Green tendrils and shoots pushed through soft blankets of dark moss. The birds flew past him, their black bodies shrouding Fionna as they descended upon her. I heard her screams of pain and fear and felt a shiver run up my spine. Their unnaturally sharp beaks and claws tore at her from every direction. Her blood was dark and rich as it ran in rivulets down her pale skin. It soaked into the throne and the floor and I felt my stomach turn.

Fionna flew from her place at the throne, suddenly taken by fear. The looming body of her kill made her stumble to the side before she could lurch towards the dark forest. Black feathered birds dove at her, aiming for her eyes like she had done to Aoife. I watched her eyes widen with fear. She was powerless. It had to be her single greatest fear

She threw her arms over her head, running with her face to the ground and no sense of awareness. I could no longer tell which birds were spirits of the hunt or true animals. They surrounded her so that any where she turned to run, hounds nipping at her or birds slapping her with their wide wings.

The power of the hunt and the God seemed to seep away from me before I realized what was happening. My hounds disappeared, fading away from existence altogether. No longer was I a demi-god. I was just broken Diana. The God glanced over his shoulder at me and I heard the unsaid command.

Run.

Before I watched the scene play out my feet jerked into motion. I spun on my heel and raced towards the exit.

A feeling of deja vu came over me. Wasn't it not too long ago that I raced down this same corridor away from Fionna and her small army? This time, I knew if I didn't run fast enough that the Hunt would turn its sight on me. The tunnels bent around me, reshaping themselves. I could feel it like a heavy rock in my stomach.

I feared that they would trap me here. I feared that I would not be able to escape what I had just been a part of only moments ago. The echo of ghost hoof beats thundered through the tunnels. I did not want the God and his Hunt to chase me. But, I felt the chill of late autumn air and knew that I was close to reality once more.

The tunnel opened up into the forest and the smell of blood and decay filled my senses. Barely a yard away, Jonathan's body was starting to rot. I couldn't stop myself. I couldn't look down at the body by my feet. I just ran as fast as I could in any direction.

Outside of the forest, I tripped over my own feet and fell to the ground. My stomach turned and I vomited. With a moan, I sat back on my haunches. My stomach cramped and I doubled over, painfully empty. Hot tears were falling down my cheeks. I had killed the monster of my past and participated in the death of another monster. What did that make me? What did any of this make me other than a new monster?

My wolf pushed at me and for once, I gave in to her. She caressed me, consoling me with reassurances as she emerged. I let her protect me the way that she had all of those years ago. She only wanted safety and Clan. That's it. She never meant to hurt me in this way.

CHAPTER THIRTY-EIGHT

I looked down at the red, squished face and felt my heart begin to melt. I wanted to damn my female hormones, the maternal instincts that I couldn't deny. Yet, baby Olivia's little upturned nose and solemn twist of her lips was undeniably cute. From that face, I thought she was going to make a very fine female werewolf someday.

Somewhat reluctantly, I handed her back to her mother. Sabrina had the same flushed cheeks and her hair was a wild mess, but the look on her face was that of bliss and nothing more. Over her bed, Darren caught my eyes. I didn't know what he read on my own face, but there was a soft smile on his lips.

No, Darren. I know where your heart needs to be and it isn't with me. I turned away, needing to leave the room before I started to cry. In the hallway, I let myself fall to the ugly green upholstered chair. My wolf wanted Darren, screamed for him. I was his Clan Queen. My body ached for him and even my heart was beginning to ache for him as well, but it wouldn't work. His heart belonged to the Clan as a whole. Maybe a small part of it was with me, but I didn't think I'd ever have Darren the way that I wanted to. Not when I had to be his monster.

It just wouldn't work out. Not after I had killed his father and destroyed all dreams of rehabilitation. I told myself this over and over again, hoping that my heart would understand even if my wolf didn't. Later, maybe the hormones from today would make me fall into bed with him again, but I would walk away from it still belonging to no one.

Jason nudged my foot with the toe of his boot, tugging on the Clan bond that now thrummed between us. I shook my head, refusing to speak. I admired my Grandmother, her stoic appearance over the turmoil that she must have been feeling. Her husband was in the ground and her Clan, her family, had been through the biggest upheaval it had ever seen. Yet, she stood at the center as if she were the commander of an army. I wanted to share in her strength, to have a piece of that iron will that formed her core. I couldn't seem to find it. There was only confusion inside me.

Darren emerged from Sabrina's room. The magic of a newborn child had faded and there was a shadow living in the back of his eyes when he looked at me now. I knew why and I couldn't take the pressure of his gaze, the blame that it forced upon me and the blame that he carried himself. Physically, he'd recovered from Fionna's silver poisoning, but he hadn't recovered from the poisoning of his mind. It made me shoot up from my chair and race towards the exit. Behind me, I could hear Jason call out. It was too late, the heavy door swinging closed behind me.

Outside, I began my walk back towards the center of town again. My Grandmother had told me of the dreams she had of a charging troupe filled with wolves and wild horses. She and a few others of the Clan had seen Fionna's death in their dreams. Someone had said that some tourists recall seeing the ghastly ride storm through the center of town. They recalled it like visions of ghosts or nightmares.Since Fionna's death many of the other wolves had been taking wide paths around me and casting darker glares than usual at me. They might not know exactly what happened that night, but they had a pretty good idea.

Since I had touched down in Maine again, my life had been turned upside down. Not only had I chosen to say with the Clan, a Goddess had chosen me to be her vessel and spoke through me, I'd killed the creature of my nightmares, led the long forgotten Wild Hunt, and become a Clan Queen (whatever that meant, I hoped that I would have time to figure out). Just thinking it made everything seem so absurd. Could this be my life now?

My head felt almost empty now that there was only me and my wolf taking up residence. I found that I wanted desperately to fill that space. It felt unbalanced and skewed, the space between my wolf and me, and I didn't have any clue on how to mend it. I didn't know if I ever could. Would I live out my life broken and fighting? Or would I become the next big monster of Wolf's Head?

"Diana!"

Pounding footsteps sounded behind me and my body tensed against my will. It was only Darren, I told myself. I knew that voice a mile away.

"Hey," he said as he caught up to me.

"Hi," my voice was barely more than a whisper. My fingers reached for my hair as the awkward feeling edged its way between us. There was a couple of feet of space between us that neither of us would close no matter how much we wanted to. His pain and my secrets hung between us, claiming the space.

"Jason and I were going to head back to the farmhouse for a marathon of crappy movies and a bathtub's worth of alcohol," Darren announced, breaking the awkward silence. "Are you going to join us?"

"Only if I can eat my body weight in ice-cream."

"That doesn't mix well with alcohol. How does Magda's pumpkin rolls sound? A whole pan all to yourself," he said, teasing.

I sighed with relief and smiled. The thought of a Bruce Campbell marathon accompanied with pastries and liquor sounded like just what we all needed. I saw Jason coming up to us and realized just how much space Darren had closed between us. He smiled back at me.

Monsters didn't have movie nights, right?

SAMPLE CHAPTER

OF

Bound By Blood

Leah Chiasson

SAMPLE CHAPTER

OF

Bound By Blood

Leah Chiasson

Chapter One

I was woken by the buzzing of my phone on the nightstand. The sheets were tangled around my feet and a fine sheen of sweat covered my skin. My breath came in short, shallow gasps. Never have I ever been so happy to have my sleep interrupted by a late-night phone call.

Shaking off the remnants of my eerie dreams, I reached for the buzzing phone. Neil's number lit the screen. I should have known; that's the only kind of call that I would get at…I checked the screen again, the only call I'd get at 4:00 am.

I slid the lock key across the screen and put the phone to my ear before falling back into my pillows. Beside me, Jason mumbled in his sleep. A soft growling came from him and I resisted the urge to scratch behind his ear to quiet him. I didn't speak, but Neil spared no time and launched right in.

"I know that the guys aren't too fond of you showing up at every scene, but I think that this is one you need to see. It has your name written all over it, literally."

"What do you mean my name?" I shot back up again. The sheen of sweat turned cold.

"I mean exactly what I said. Get down here so that you can see it for yourself."

He rattled off an address as I fumbled for a scrap of paper. Eventually, I got it down and found myself staring at it. The address was for a new residential area that they were building, Fleetfoot Meadows. The land was raw and the houses cookie cutter pretty, if you liked that kind of thing.

"Fine, don't give me any details," I grumbled.

"Isn't that why you're the so-called psychic? Figure it out on your own." He hung up and I tossed my phone back onto the nightstand.

Behind me, Jason rolled over and his arm fell where my head would have been. I smiled, feeling warmth returning to me. It was a regular occurrence, us smacking each other around in our sleep, that I associated with having a normal life. It still surprised me that in two weeks' time we would be vowing to do this together for the rest of our lives. I would become his wife.

Reluctant to leave the comfort of Jason's warmth, I slid from the bed and made my way towards the clothes I had tossed on the floor earlier. I threw on a slim fitting, black t-shirt dress and skin tight leggings from the previous day, trying to rub the white deodorant stains from the dress. Finally, I gave in and decided that I'd cover it with my fleece lined leather jacket. Winter weather made dressing more convenient for someone like me. For instance, with knives strapped to the outside of each of my calves, I can easily cover them with leg warmers and pull my knee-high boots over them. Self-defense comes easier with smaller weapons and layers.

Never leave the house without at least a blade.

Mom's voice was always so sharp in my mind. It was strong and overbearing, but I knew it for the good advice that it was. Neil's words had left a crawling feeling on my skin that refused to go away. I had two blades tucked into my boots and I was throwing a sheer, dip dyed scarf around my neck as Jason began to stir. He sat up, propping his body on his elbow and staring me down with sad, puppy dog eyes. They were shadowed with fear and hurt, even if his lips were set in a firm line.

I shrugged, not knowing what to say. I had a job to do and it took me away at night sometimes. I hated it too, but I wasn't about to stop. It was better than letting myself become overwhelmed by the power stirring inside of me. That wasn't an option. Getting out of bed at 4am to meet the local detectives was a fun option in comparison. It allowed me to siphon off my power little by little so that it was no longer an oppressive force that threatened to take over my life.

Instead of arguing, I knelt on the bed and laid soft kisses over his face. A slight smile touched his lips as he reached up for my face. He cupped my chin like it was the last time he would see me. I wasn't a cop, but he knew better than they did what was truly out there.

The perks of being engaged to a Faoladh, a werewolf.

"I will be back before dawn," I lied. I liked to think of it as a promise, but with my luck it was one I wouldn't be able to keep

He nodded, the frown returning because he could see the lie for what it was. He gave no reply other than that before rolling away from me.

Fine. Be that way.

I gave the car a good ten minutes to warm up while I made coffee and the seats were still frigid. I blasted Dorothy as loud as I could possibly bear to help wake myself up as I backed out of the driveway. The Challenger slid on a patch of ice in the driveway, but quickly righted herself before I slipped it into drive. Every road was like that, covered in a thin sheet of iced that tossed my car from side to side.

I cursed the October cold snap, but was thankful it wasn't snowing and there weren't many other cars on the road at this time of the morning. The urge to speed to the music was nagging and persistent, but I preferred life over charred ruins. Besides, this 69 Dodge Challenger was my baby in all sense of the term save for literal. I'd dragged her out of a field when I was fourteen and spent the rest of my teen years learning to put her back together.

There were several police cars parked on the edge of the newly formed neighborhood. Their flashing lights danced in the naked trees off in the distance. They cast shadows that I wasn't entirely certain were shadows from the way that my skin prickled. I parked the Challenger behind the black sedan, careful not to slide into it.

The uniformed officer at the door watched me with wary, cop eyes. He was unfamiliar to me, which meant that I was unfamiliar to him. When I dressed for work, I paid careful attention to the art of covering my plethora of tattoos, but the ink on the back of my hands and the gauged holes in my ears set off warning bells for some uniformed cops. I tried my best to look professional when I was called to scenes, but I probably looked like a weirdo making her way across the frozen ground. The uniformed cop gave me that "what is your ass doing here?" look.

"I'm sorry ma'am, but you can't come this way," he tried saying nicely. "You don't want to see what's inside."

I looked at the house for the first time. While it had structure, there were no doors or windows on it yet. A bright glow spilled out from the inside that said that there were industrial lights set up, the kind that construction workers used. The light sprinkling of snow outside was pristine and sparkled in the harsh light. I cocked my head as I studied it. That meant that no one had physically walked anywhere other than the icy walkway to the door. Forensic techs hadn't even touched it.

"Ma'am," the uniformed officer said again as I stepped closer. "You should get back in your car and leave."

"Detective Neil Matteson called me in." I narrowed my eyes at him and pulled the flimsy, laminated paper badge that Neil had fought for me to get. He took it with a skeptical look on his face. It didn't change as he looked from the card to me and then back to the card.

"E.B. O' Dair? What does the E.B. stand for?"

"E is for Evangeline and you're about to find out what the B stands for if I have to call Detective Matheson over here."

His eyebrows shot up. This would have been so much easier if I could have a permanent ID. But no, I'd have to wait for Neil to beg his superiors for my assistance on the case before I could even get the temporary ID.

"So, you're *that* Evangeline."

I didn't say anything, but my expression must have said plenty.

"You will see when you get inside," he moved aside to let me through, not once daring to look into the house himself.

My coffee rolled around my stomach as I climbed the shoddy, makeshift 2x4 steps. The first smell that greeted me was metallic and sweet. Tones of charred meat and wood shavings came afterwards. The bright lights blinded me to the scene as I came in. As my eyes adjusted to the light, I could make out six, dark shapes burnt into the floor. Three shapes contained charred bodies that were reaching toward the far wall, but the other three were simply burns on the floor.

There were three missing bodies.

The charred smell that hung in the air was human flesh. My coffee rolled again, but I forced myself to stay where I was. I took a deep breath, ignoring the smell in the air, to steady myself as more came into focus. The three remaining bodies stretched their arms toward the far wall, pulling my gaze upward. The plywood walls were smeared red. The victims had painted shapes of words that dripped down to the floor. I didn't want to think about what the red paint was or where it had come from. All I thought about were the words.

Evangeline.

I am coming.

Evangeline. Evangeline. Evangeline. Evangeline.

I glanced sideways at Neil. He was watching the expression on my face closely. He thought that I had something to do with this. Why wouldn't he? My name was written all over it.

There was one thought spinning through my mind, but I shoved it to the side. It couldn't possibly be true. I turned my attention back to the charred shapes on the floor. Their black skin was crackling away from shrunken flesh and screaming lips had pulled away from their teeth. One lay on its stomach, trying to scratch and crawl its way to freedom. Neil was standing off to the side. When he saw me, he moved towards me but I held my hand out to stop him.

Another world existed, laying over our own, that no one knew about. It caught spirits and beings, holding them suspended between this world and the next. I was different in that I could see it like they were one world. It was a perk, if you could call it that, of the power that constantly thrummed through me. The bodies on the floor were charred and unrecognizable, but their souls had been trapped between the worlds.

Their screams were the shrill ringing in our ears. They were trapped, writhing between worlds as if they were still on fire. I pushed myself forward, trying not to look at the souls as I stepped between them. A woman saw me, reaching out for me as she screamed. Instinctually, I jerked away from her. Neil raised an eyebrow at me and I shook my head in response.

On the floor was a series of circles, lightly etched into the plywood. Reaching out to the floor, I had to catch myself. Instead, I turned to Neil and asked him to throw me a set of latex gloves. With the latex coating my hand, I traced the lines etched in the floor.

Someone had cast a powerful curse here. It had taken the lives of six innocents, I thought as I looked around me. Three were trapped here, screaming in pain. The other three were nowhere to be found, soul or body. What scared me was that I knew someone who was more than capable of doing something this foul.

Christmas was a few months to come, Dad. Why leave me presents now?

"What are your opinions on this?" Neil asked, tapping the end of his pen against his note pad. That little tic told me that he hadn't had his daily dose of bourbon before work.

"I can't say." I stood up. My eyes were drawn back to the circle etched into the floor. "There are souls here, but they're in no shape to talk. I can't say that I blame them after being burned alive. This place was ventilated enough that the smoke didn't kill them right away. If they were lucky, shock set in very quickly."

Neil swallowed hard. I wanted to say that this was the worst thing that I'd ever seen, but I lived with my mother for too many years. I'd seen Clan-less wolves tear each other apart. I'd seen the pieces of women come back to life to kill a cannibalistic monster.

"Shit." He jammed his notepad back into his pocket. "I was really hoping that you'd have something to tell me about this one. We have three bodies and what looks like three missing bodies."

I gave Neil a brief description of the souls that were trapped in the house. The Medical Examiner might be able to identify the bodies based on dental records, but that wasn't always a promise. People in this area didn't always go to the dentist or orthodontist. Health insurance was too damned pricey.

He gave me a helpless look. "That's only three descriptions, Evan. What about the other three?"

I shivered. I had a feeling that I'd come across them sooner or later.

Jason was waiting for me when I returned, a little past sunrise. I had gone back to the precinct to talk to a sketch artist. The poor man they pulled out of bed had looked as bleary as I felt, but we worked together until we came up with three accurate sketches.

Meanwhile, the forensic and medical teams had cleaned out the scene. All that was left were the three trapped souls, unable to more than wail in pain. Normally, with the souls left on scenes, I could send them off into the next life after they answered a few questions. These souls had resisted all my efforts to send them off. As I shut the door behind me, I met Jason's eyes.

"You look fucking awful." He didn't bother beating around the bush, but instead came and wrapped me in his arms. I stood, stick still. I didn't want to give in to his affection. A part of me said that I didn't deserve it until I laid those souls to rest. The guilt over what I assumed my father had done sat heavy inside of me.

In the end, I laid my head on Jason's chest. I think he understood. That, or he simply gave me only what I needed. He made it too easy to love him. Especially when he didn't call me out on my white lies.

Eventually, I pushed away from him and steadied myself.

"I have to do something tonight," I began.

"What exactly happened at that scene?" Jason asked as he turned back toward the kitchen. I followed him and fell into a kitchen chair. He claimed the sandwich on the counter before turning around and leaning back. "You're never this shaken. Usually, you come back a little more chipper than usual."

"Six bodies burnt alive, three bodies missing, and evidence of dark magic. Oh, and my name was written on the wall in blood," I said with bitter, false cheer. "I hope that they didn't write it in their own blood."

Jason bit into his sandwich and I could hear the crunch of bacon. This is what we did, evidence of the kind of lives we led before we came together. We ate while we talked about murder scenes. He saw me watching him eat and set about making another sandwich while I spoke.

"The walls not only had my name written on it about six times, but it said, 'I am coming.' I'm afraid that I know who that means and I really don't want to have to deal with him again. I've had enough with what he's given me. I don't want human lives on that list."

Jason's butter knife paused mid swipe. "Are you talking about who I think you're talking about?"

"Daddy Dearest. I mean, who else would attempt to sacrifice six souls in Northern Maine and write my fucking name on the walls? Only a narcissist of his scale would do such a thing, right?"

Jason didn't have an answer for me. Instead, he turned around with a BLT just for me. He'd cut it into two triangles and all. He'd been spending too much time at Balefire, but I couldn't complain. I bit into the sandwich, relishing the crunch of bacon and lettuce. He'd even slipped in slices of avocado and sriracha mayo while I hadn't been looking.

"I have to go back tonight," I said. "Those three souls need to be moved on one way or another. They don't deserve to become poltergeists. No one does."

"Then I'm coming with you."

My stomach dropped. "Like hell you are. My father is walking around between Wolf's Head and Watertown."

"All the more reason for me to go with you tonight. You're going to need someone to watch your back while you do your thing."

I wanted to argue that I was more than capable of taking care of myself, but I saw the look in his eye. My father wasn't going to hurt me. As far as I knew, he actually loved me in his own weird way. I didn't know if he would share the same sentiment about my fiancé.

"You are my lookout," I conceded. "The first hint that my father is there you let me know and then you run. It is not cowardice. It's probably the smartest thing to do in his presence."

I could hear a soft growl in his chest, but he was just going to have to live with it. I was not Clan. He couldn't use his psychic dominance to push me around. I gave him a level glare that said I would not be swayed on the subject. I couldn't afford to lose him. It wasn't going to happen.

"Fine," he grumbled.

I turned back to my sandwich, mentally cataloging everything I'd have to bring with me tonight. I would need more than just my own magic to go up against my father's workings. And I dreaded it like I'd dreaded nothing before.

***

Jason was silent beside me. His body weight translated into wolf weight and made for a massive beast. There was always the little rush of fear when I first see him after a change. He could kill me if he really wanted to. Maybe not easily, but in the end his size would crush me and that was just a little off putting.

My backpack was slung over my shoulder, heavy with awkwardly sized objects that were never meant to be stuffed into backpacks. My hair was tucked up inside my winter hat. It would be a bad idea to leave stray hairs at a crime scene. Maybe I could have brushed it off as having been to the scene the first night, but I didn't want to take the chances.

I climbed the wooden steps with trepidation. The ringing in my ears started and grew louder as my eyes adjusted. Their writhing forms all reached out to me. Their eyes were wide and mouths eternally screaming. It took me a most of the afternoon to figure out what he had done to them, but as I opened the darkness in myself up to the scene, I could feel what I had originally suspected.

Whoever had done this knew what they were doing. This wasn't some psycho playing at Satanist, believing the voices in his head. No, this was a master of the darkest arts, someone who could summon dark fiends and create monstrosities. I had a pretty good idea of who it might be and it most certainly was not the Easter Bunny.

Torture the last moment, burn the bodies alive, and trap the souls. Add a generous amount of that good old dark occult hoo-hah and you could create one of the foulest looking creatures: a ghoul. It was sickening to know that the missing twisted and blackened shapes on the floor would soon become ghouls.

I looked up at the specter of a screaming woman, her form flickering before me as the charred body summoned it back. Her eyes still pleaded for mercy, her fingers outstretched with trust. A few decades of being trapped here and her soul would begin to rot. Anger and pain would begin to consume her until she lashed out at anyone and everyone.

Had my own flesh and blood really done this?

She was a little soft around the middle and her hair had been cut short around her chin. Part of me wondered if she had been a mother in life. The man on the other side of her was even younger than me. He might have just started college and thought that he had the rest of his life ahead of him. It begged to question how these people had come to be here in this undeveloped neighborhood and who the other three people were.

Was my father the kind of person who could cut those lives so short?

I shook my head. My conscience had me drifting too far away from my purpose. Pulling the backpack into my lap, I fumbled for the smudge stick and long nose lighter. The soft glow of the lighter's flame tried to fill the room, but only left flickering shadows hiding in the far corners. As the bundle lighted, I dropped the lighter, too weary to stare into the shadows.

The three trapped souls would be an easy fix as I watched the smoke rise and tapped into the depths of my power. The bigger problem still loomed on the horizon. The other three souls were most likely in my father's possession, waiting to become ghouls.

GET **BOUND BY BLOOD**
MAY 13TH
ON AMAZON.COM

Acknowledgements

Largely, this book never would have happened without my husband, Seth Chiasson. He pushed me to keep working, to self-publish, and even paid for this wonderful cover art.

Speaking of, I owe a huge thank you to Bea Jackson of https://beagifted.com/. Without her, this book would not be as awesome on the outside as it is on the inside.

Finally, a shout out to my friends who dealt with me over this whole process, especially Carol Blake and Kayla Cox!

Thank you for reading!
If you've found this book at the library and liked it, you can help support a local author by purchasing a copy in paperback or digital, or even recommending it to a friend.

Where to Find Me

Facebook
https://www.facebook.com/Leahcorrinewrites/

Website
https://authorleahchiasson.wordpress.com/